A CROWN OF HOPES
AND SORROWS

NICOLE BAILEY

Edited by Milly Bellegris and Amy Vrana

Cover design by Stefanie Saw

Map design by Chaim Holtjer

www.authornicolebailey.com

❀ Created with Vellum

Content Warnings

Please note that these content warnings will contain some spoilers for the book.

A Crown of Hopes and Sorrows depicts issues including hunting, animal death (hunting related), misogyny, blood, death, and parental death.

The book also contains strong language and sexual content.

I hope readers will find that I've handled these topics with sensitivity. However, I wished to include a note for anyone who may find this content triggering.

Map

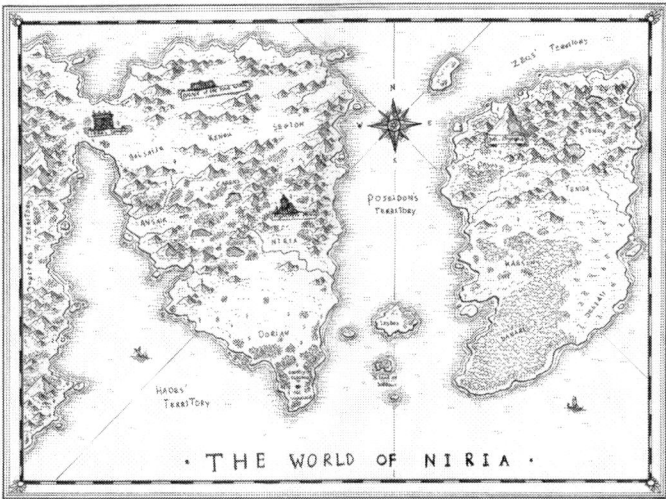

· THE WORLD OF NIRIA ·

Character Review

Apollo
Half-deity and prophesied god of the sun.

Temi (Artemis)
Huntress and Apollo's younger sister.

Hyacinth (Cyn)
Crowned prince of Niria.

Epiphany (Pip)
Princess of Niria and Hyacinth's younger sister.

Valerian (Val)
Master stableman at the palace in Niria and close friends with both Hyacinth and Epiphany.

Emrin
Prince of Niria and Hyacinth's younger brother.

Joden

Nirian high lord and political advisor.

Zephyrus

God of the west wind (spring).

Other wind gods include Boreas (north wind, winter), Notus (south wind, summer), and Euros (east wind, autumn.)

Galeson

High lord from the country of Segion and a suitor of Epiphany's.

Delon and Len

High lords from prominent Nirian families and friends of Hyacinth.

Zeus

Ruler over the deities of Mt. Olympus, god of the sky, and Apollo's father. One of the three major gods. (Married to Hera.)

Poseidon

God of the sea, Zeus' brother, and one of the three major gods.

Hades

God of the underworld, Zeus' brother, and one of the three major gods. (Married to Persephone.)

Ares

God of war, son of Zeus, and half-brother of Apollo.

Tartarus

The realm of monsters and torment that Zeus locks his enemies in.

Leto

Apollo and Temi's mother. High priestess of her village in Danari until her death during Temi's birth.

Kalliope

A high goddess who has a sexual history with Apollo.

Hierophant

Niria's high priest.

Jupiter

High deity of the gods from the west.

Review of Book 1

In **A Veil of Gods and Kings**, Apollo fought his destiny to become the high god of the sun. His father, Zeus, gave him an ultimatum: ascend immediately or spend the year mentoring under Prince Hyacinth.

To secure another year in the human world, Apollo traveled to the kingdom of Niria with his sister, Temi.

Prince Hyacinth had taken over leadership of the country in his father's absence. Apollo's presence—and the threat of the gods surrounding him—added to his burdens. Their relationship proved contentious as they grappled with their mutual dislike of each other.

Temi befriended Hyacinth's sister Epiphany. They practiced skills together, such as horseback riding and hunting. Struck by the needs of the people of Niria, Temi concocted a plan for them to sneak out of the palace and teach women their age how to hunt.

The hatred between Apollo and Hyacinth gave way as they spent more time together and fell in love.

Ares arrived with a warning from Zeus. Hyacinth's father also returned. Both reminded Apollo of the danger inherit to anyone connected to him. Apollo left Niria, hoping to spare Hyacinth.

Hyacinth went after Apollo and revealed to him that Niria had aligned with Jupiter and the other high gods of the west, intending to remove Zeus from power.

Apollo agreed to return with Hyacinth and help them. Apollo proposed a plan to travel together under the guise of increasing dedications to Zeus while secretly seeing what gods they can find to join their cause.

But Apollo learns there is already another half-god on their side. Temi was not a mortal, as she believed, but a half-deity like Apollo, veiled with powerful magic.

———

"If I had but two loaves of bread, I would sell one and buy hyacinths, for they would feed my soul." -Mohammad

———

Apollo

Who knew shoulders could be the most beautiful sight on earth?

Specifically bare shoulders, over an equally bare body, standing in a creamy sheen of morning light.

Hyacinth shifted his feet, muscles along his back and legs curving, his tan skin and short dark hair taking on a sparkle of gold from the sun.

He cocked his head to the side, feathering a finger over fabric hung in the dressing closet he stood before.

I blew out a breath and fell against the bed. "Seriously, Cyn, how hard is it to choose which robe to wear? They're all basically the same."

He clicked his tongue and looked over his shoulder at me, his hazel eyes growing honey-gold as they shifted into a ray of light. "Says the man who literally wears the same thing every day."

"It's practical."

He scoffed.

"Or"—I rolled back up, spreading out the wrinkled

comforter we'd wrecked the previous night—"you could wear nothing at all and stay here with me instead."

He turned towards me again, the long muscles along his torso shifting and wrapping around his form as he did so. "As much as I'd love to, there's a great deal to do today. And my father wishes to speak with you this morning."

Every salacious thought in my mind fizzled like a bucket of water dumped over them, all the images I'd conjured of my mouth trailing down his body, puffing away like smoke. "He wants to speak with me? About what?"

Hyacinth padded across the floor, shirt and pants in hand, and dropped onto the bed, making it bounce. He leaned in and pressed his lips to the hollow of my neck. I shivered and gripped my fingers into the firm flesh of his back. "If you come over here like this," I said, my voice growing deep, "you'd better intend to follow through."

He chuckled and pecked a kiss against my forehead. "I told you. We have things we must do this morning."

"What is your father wanting to talk about?"

"I think he just has more questions about your plan to seek other gods that may stand with us against Zeus."

"I explained my entire plan already."

Hyacinth shrugged the cream shirt on, his eyebrows drawing together, creating a v-shaped dimple there. "It was more of a statement. An idea of an idea."

"Well…" I thrust my hands out. "That's what you get from me. You're the man who decides things." I nodded towards the closet that sat open. "I like to work on impulse."

He tugged his pants up and stood, causing the mattress to bounce again. "Acting on impulse is not wise, especially with war and considering other's lives."

"As I said"—I jumped up and snagged my shorts and tunic, pulling them on—"that's where you come in."

Hyacinth chuckled and reached out towards the silk of his robes, his hands hovering between two of them. I stepped up behind him and wrapped my arms around his waist. "Wear the burgundy one."

"Oh, so you can decide."

I brushed my lips over the velvet of his ear. "I just admire looking at you. Burgundy brings out the color of your eyes." My voice turned into a hush of a sound, like a prayer. "You're beautiful, Cyn."

He leaned back against me and sighed. "I love you."

Those words felt like home to me after a lifetime of not having one. And despite the fear that still surged through me over everything we prepared to face, I would be nowhere else. I squeezed his waist before releasing him and he grabbed the robe, pulling it on, the embroidery on his lapels glimmering in glittering golds and greens.

"Also,"—I smirked—"I will one day have very important decisions to make."

"And what would those be?"

"When the high gods ascend..." I let that hang in the air for a moment. Hyacinth frowned, his brow furrowing again. We both knew being together would be impossible if that happened. I could visit, but earth sickness would impede me from coming frequently. It was inevitable, but I still avoided thinking about it. "You're going to give yourself wrinkles," I said, smoothing my fingers over the skin of his forehead. "As I was saying, if I ascend one day, I have to decide what I'm the god of."

Hyacinth closed the closet with a thunk. "I thought you'd be the god of the sun."

"Yes." I waved him off. "But high gods get to designate what other minor things they rule over as well."

Hyacinth gestured to his door, and I nabbed my knapsack before we strode out into the hallways with their rich carpeting and soaring ceilings draped with silk panels. "What might you choose, then?"

"Well, music, for one thing, because I'm fucking brilliant with the lyre."

Hyacinth chuckled. "I should disagree, just to bring you down a notch."

"But you know you'd be lying." I knocked my shoulder into his.

He rolled his eyes. "What else then?"

I tangled my fingers with his and stopped walking, grazing my thumb over his knuckles. "Maybe I'll choose poetry as well."

"I didn't realize you were such a lover of poetry."

"I'm not, but…" I smiled. "I love a man who is."

His shoulders eased, and he offered me a gentle expression. I relished it—having someone to love—and his reaction every time I said that word. He lifted our hands and kissed my fingers. "And what about archery?"

"What about it?"

"Wouldn't that also fit you, if anything Temi tells me about your skills are true?"

I chuckled. "Temi doesn't tend to stretch the truth. But if she is a goddess herself…" I paused, the ache of not knowing answers for her sake coursing through me. "She may want to choose that category. She can whip my ass in any competition involving weapons, I assure you."

"I'll have to see this someday."

I hummed a reply as we reached his father's office, and he knocked.

"Come in," King Magnes said.

We walked through the door, and I tucked my hands behind my back. Rich curtains adorned large windows that gave a view of the gardens that had eased their way into autumn, rust tones taking over once-vibrant greens. The king lifted his face and brushed his hand through his silver-streaked hair, the rings on his fingers sparkling. "Ah, yes. Good morning. Hyacinth?"

"Father?"

"Would you let Apollo and I speak alone for a moment?" My stomach sunk to my toes. Hyacinth froze, his lips parting as if to protest, but his father chuckled. "It's nothing malicious, Cyn."

A breath huffed out of Hyacinth's body and he shifted to me, a question in his eyes. I nodded, and he walked out, scanning over the two of us before pulling the door shut.

"Please have a seat," the king said.

I dropped into the chair I'd spent the previous summer working in. He sat as well and gestured to the bottles of spirits on his desk that splashed the wood with amber reflections. "Would you like a drink?"

It was still first thing in the morning.

Was this a test?

"No, thank you."

He nodded and worried his hands together. "How old are you, Apollo?"

I bit the inside of my cheek and leaned down against my knees. "I'm twenty, sir."

He released a breath. "Right. But how old are you in mortal years?"

Sunlight danced around, illuminating a shelf stacked with scrolls and folios. "Umm"—I cleared my throat—"twenty."

A frown pressed onto his face. "You've only been alive for two human decades?"

"Yes, sir."

"You're younger than Hyacinth?"

I nodded. "I am. Just by a year-and-a-half. I understand he was born near the Dionysus Festival?"

"He was, yes." The king hesitated, his forehead wrinkling. "I didn't know you were so young."

He must have thought I was some centuries old half-deity fucking his twenty-two-year-old son. My cheeks flamed. Thank Hades to Zeus we had done nothing in this office. Gods, I wouldn't be able to keep a straight face otherwise.

"Forgive me," he said. "I don't mean to come across" —he laughed and sank against this chair—"the way I'm clearly coming across. Hyacinth is my child. He's very dear to me. And, well…"

"Him being involved with a god is concerning," I whispered.

The thoughts I tried to avoid peppered back into my mind. I wasn't sure how long Hyacinth and I could be together. And I wondered if his father worried more about that or over the attention my connection could bring him. Magic hummed over my skin, and I swallowed the disgust that welled in me. How I wish I could be worthy of him.

The king studied me for a long moment, his brown eyes a darker shade than Hyacinth's but still holding the same streaking pattern. He tapped his thumb against his armrest. "Hyacinth tells me your mother has passed away."

"Yes, when I was very young."

"Epiphany was quite young when she lost her mother as well." He paused until I met his gaze. A concern lingered over his expression, his lips pinched. "I always worried for her—still do, if I'm honest. Every day I see for her—and Hyacinth and Emrin—what a burden it's been to lose someone who loved them so dearly."

I cleared my throat, unsure where this conversation was

heading. A prickling discomfort slipped down my spine. "It was many years ago when I lost my mother, Your Highness. She was a wonderful woman from what little I remember of her and what stories others told me before... we moved."

"I hope you and your sister can feel"—he pressed his fingers together—"like you have a home here, if the idea suits you."

I leaned back and chewed on the inside of my cheek. "That's a very kind offer. Of course, while we help with things involved with this upcoming war, we'll be very grateful to take you up on it."

"This isn't about the war." He cocked up an eyebrow. "We'll discuss those matters in the meeting later. I mean this personally, as the father of your partner. You have a home here."

I sucked in a breath. A home. That was the second time that morning I'd allowed myself to imagine that term, to feel like I had one and belonged to it. I wanted it so badly it hurt. "Thank you."

A few minutes later I strode alongside a frowning Hyacinth down a hallway lined with wide curved windows that let ivory light flood the carpets. "What did he say to you?" Hyacinth asked.

"Not much."

He side-eyed me. "My father doesn't waste time."

I shrugged and readjusted the straps of my knapsack. "He had some questions for me about our relationship, I guess."

Hyacinth stopped walking, his lips parting. "Did he interrogate you?"

"No, Cyn, it was nothing like that. Honestly. He was actually"—I shrugged again, my cheeks warming—"really welcoming in a way. The rest was fine."

Hyacinth's eyes narrowed, but he nodded. "All right."

I gripped his hand, relished how his fingers automatically draped around mine. "It's okay, seriously."

He blew out a breath and leaned in closer to me, his jasmine-smell sweetening the air. "After this meeting, there's something I want to discuss."

"What is it?"

"An idea I had. But let's go hear if the advisors have any better ones first."

I groaned. "Unlikely."

He chuckled and tugged my hand, pulling us both forward towards the conference room.

2

Artemis

I twisted the knife around my fingers, the metal of it reflecting the muted greens and crisp grays of the world. Silver grasses tangled together in the wind as horses in the distance bowed their heads, snatching bunches of weeds to eat, their long tails flicking away flies.

I always thought I knew who I was.

Artemis.

Sister of the half-god Apollo.

Friend to many.

Huntress.

Well known for my weaponry skills.

I flung the knife out, and it vibrated as it slammed into a target board.

Temi, the girl who sat trembling and scared as she'd watched her village burn down around her.

The same girl who swore she'd never be weak and afraid and helpless like that again.

I slipped another dagger from my belt and danced it between my fingers. But now I suspected that my skills, everything I defined myself by, were because I was—unbeknownst to myself—a goddess.

I slammed the second knife forward. It bit into the wood deeper.

I snatched a third blade.

Frustration pulsed through me. I didn't understand why my mother would have kept that a secret from me. She had to know and either didn't tell the women in our village who raised us or asked them to keep it from me. And why had I been hidden with a veil, anyway? After all, Apollo had always known of his divine origins, of his prophecy to become the sun god and the deep powers lingering within him. And whoever my bastard father was—whoever abandoned me and didn't step up and tell me about my life—I thrusted my hand forward a third time. The last knife sunk to its hilt.

The crunch of feet pattering through the meadow pulled me out of my thoughts. "You okay, Temi?"

I turned towards Epiphany, her long dark curls flowing out with the wind, a gentle expression flickering over the hazel of her eyes. "I don't know." My steps crushed masses of grass as I walked over and pulled my knives out of the board. "I think I'm still in shock. I can't believe everything in my life might be a lie."

Epiphany smoothed her hand across the wood, her fingers bumping over the dents and grooves. "Do you ever hit outside the center?"

"Rarely."

She smiled and trailed her elbow into mine. "Everything about your life isn't a lie."

"Isn't it though?"

"No. You're still exactly who you were last week."

I sighed and nodded towards the palace that peaked above the stables. We had a meeting to attend. "Maybe.

But, if everything about me is just because I have powers I didn't even know I was tapping into, what does that mean?"

Epiphany lifted her skirts as we continued through the pasture. "If that's the case, you were a goddess last week, too."

"Okay?"

She opened the gate but paused, cocking her head to the side. "The only thing that has changed is your perception of yourself."

I frowned. "That and of my father."

"You define who you are. Not your parents or anyone else."

I bit back a groan, but it was nice to have Epiphany there, dismantling my arguments. Something about her presence soothed me. "Yeah. All right, we don't want to be late for this meeting, do we?"

She shook her head, and we made our way across the lawn, through the gardens, and into the palace to a room with tall windows and several dozen men who frowned at us. Apollo, who stood at Hyacinth's side, shifted his eyes towards me, his lips pinching. I didn't like that—him worrying about me. I was supposed to be the one who worried about him.

Epiphany placed her hands together in her lap as I dropped into a seat beside her.

King Magnes sat and nodded. "Let's open today with discussing Apollo's strategy. Asher?"

A large man with thick, dark hair spoke. "After conferring with our various military leaders, Your Highness, we believe it may be a wise measure before we request alliances with other kingdoms."

The king bobbed his head. "Very good. Regarding

Artemis' idea about the widow's law for hunting"—he nodded at me—"any insight?"

Joden, who had a sharp nose and sour expression, lifted his chin. "How will this feel for hunters who pay taxes? I believe, Your Highness, it may encourage others to skirt paying their due and could cause unrest among those who continue."

King Magnes studied him and shifted towards a man with long, brown hair. "Do you have any insight, Roan?"

He sighed. "While I agree with Joden that some will grumble over the change, I doubt it will alter the number of people in the kingdom claiming their kills. And"—he laughed—"how many animals could a bunch of widows bring down, anyway?" A few of the other advisors chuckled.

I bit my tongue even though I wanted to assert that the women could clear their forests if they wished to. But that comment would only hinder the aim here. And I had a deep sense of respect that Hyacinth and his father took up the issue to begin with. I wouldn't thwart it.

The king nodded. "Very well; we'll pass it then and bring it back for further review at our next meeting. On the other topic regarding Artemis, have you had any insight, Hierophant?"

The priest shook his head, lifting his wrinkled face towards me. "I'm afraid not. However, we all know who may have information."

"Who?" I gasped the word out but then shifted in the king's direction and offered a half bow from my seat. He gave me a warm smile.

"Sappho of Lesbos."

Joden scoffed. "That witch trades in gossip and salaciousness."

"Which is precisely why," the priest said to him before

shifting back to me, "she is the best option for answers. She's very well connected with the gods, the western ones, and those from Mt. Olympus and regularly hosts them. Further…" He draped his fingers together "Yes, we all know she is a keeper of secrets of sorts. So, I believe she would be an excellent place to start a search for information."

The king's jaw jumped, but he nodded. "Sappho is an ally of Niria. We'd be wise, with the way things are changing, to touch in with that connection." Several of the advisors bobbed their heads.

"I'll visit her," I said. "Thank you."

Another advisor started discussing a different topic. Epiphany squirmed in her seat, her foot jostling beside me during the rest of the hour. When we made it out, she swept towards me. "Could I go with you?"

"Where?"

Her dark hair glimmered in sunlight that poured through the window in the hallway. "To Lesbos."

"Will you be able to?"

She winced, but straightened her posture. "If I am, would I be in the way if I came with you?"

I released a breath and squeezed her fingers. "I'd love to have you join me."

She smirked. "Then I'll figure out how I can go."

I chuckled, but if I knew anything about her, that was true. I looped my arm into hers, and we strode down the hallway together.

3

Hyacinth

I followed Father into his office. He left the door ajar and gestured to a seat, which I took. The ceramic birds on the desk gleamed alongside bottles of spirits. Tall windows silhouetted him as he opened his mouth to speak, but Epiphany appeared in the doorway, pressing her hands together. "Father, do you have a moment?"

He cleared his throat and waved her in. She drew in a deep breath, offering a glance at me before returning her attention to Father. "I'd like to ask your permission to travel with Temi on her trip."

Father sat up straighter in his chair and frowned. "Epiphany—"

"Hyacinth and Emrin," she interrupted, "both got to do a tour of the continent when they were my age. Why can't I do the same?"

Father stood and walked over to her. "Women don't go on tours."

She thrust her lip out. "Is that your stance then, Father?"

He released a breath and brushed his knuckles over her

cheek. "You have your mother's spirit. Gods help you." She raised her chin, her eyes shining as if she'd already won. Father sighed. "Sappho is... a complicated character."

He shifted towards me, and I nodded. "I didn't trust her in the least when we met her at the decade dedication." That had been five years before, though. I wondered if Apollo might have more recent insight. But he probably didn't know her well; he avoided gods and those around them.

Father tilted his head, his eyes growing distant. "Yes, but she has been a powerful ally of our kingdom for over a decade. I don't believe she'd harm your sister."

Epiphany bit her lip like she clamped back a smile. But I stood. "Can we trust her with Pip's life, though?"

Epiphany frowned at me. "You heard what Father said. She's an ally."

"A flaky one who it would not surprise me if she turned on us."

Father walked up to me, patting my shoulder. "That may very well be so, son, but your sister is right. She hasn't had the opportunities you and Emrin both have." I parted my lips to speak, but he shook his head. "And let's not act as though our city might not have its own dangers soon."

I clenched my teeth. "That's true."

"You may go." Father shifted back towards Epiphany. "On two conditions. First, guards join your party, and you stay with them." He emphasized the words. Pip fisted her hands together, her eyes sparkling, but he gave her a severe look. "I mean it, Epiphany Cressida Lysandra." Her expression stilled at him using her full name. "It could be dangerous. I want you to heed your guards if you travel."

"Yes, Father," she whispered, as though she worried he'd reverse his opinion. "And the second condition?"

"You remember you're a princess, representing Niria and our family."

She winced, but nodded. "I promise. I will."

He sighed. "We'll need to gather a traveling party, horses and someone to mind them."

"Valerian," I said. "Epiphany and Temi spent the summer under his tutelage with horseback riding." And gods knew what else, but I kept that thought to myself. "We have no other horseman who is as trustworthy, and they are already both at ease with him."

Epiphany's eyes had widened with this speech, but she remained quiet. Father grazed his fingers over his jaw. "Won't you want him for your own journey?"

"I'd feel more comfortable"—I inclined my head to Epiphany— "knowing that Pip was in reliable hands."

Father nodded. "All right."

Epiphany scrunched her fists into the lilac of her dress and then jumped towards us, giving hugs before exiting the room, pulling the door shut with her.

"Are you sure this is a good idea?" I asked.

Father squeezed my shoulder again. "Cyn, our world is about to change. It's going to be less safe for a while. And…" He released a breath and walked back behind the desk. "As Epiphany won't marry and move farther north where she might be safer, and I can't bear to force her to do so, she's probably in no more danger traveling to Lesbos than she would be at home. Perhaps having a member of our family touch in with Sappho may be wise. It could be good for Epiphany to have a more active role. And Valerian as well, actually." He frowned, deep lines forming around his lips. "I'd always hoped Lord Lucius would claim him." Father clicked his tongue. "But we can't manage others, can we?"

"It would make life a hell of a lot simpler if we could, though."

Father chuckled. "That may be so. But in the end, the only thing we actually have control over is ourselves."

"And if others betray us?" I gestured to the door Epiphany had just left through. "If Sappho hurts her?"

He blew out a breath. "If I truly believed that to be a possibility, I wouldn't allow her to go. But there are risks in everything. All these pacts we're making, there's a chance some may deceive us or not follow through once they've agreed."

"And you're okay with that?"

He smiled and clasped his fingers together across his stomach. "No, I'm not. Some countries we look to make alliances with have let us down in the past, even. But, as I said, we must do our best and move forward as we're able. Any relationship will have troubles. That's inevitable."

I crossed my arms. "I suppose."

"Now, I need to finish some work, but we'll discuss these two trips later?"

"Of course."

I bowed and strode out of the office, worry flooding my mind. I searched for Apollo, but didn't have to look far. The first place I checked—my bedroom—proved successful. He sat propped up on the bed, his lyre in hand, his fingers strumming a peaceful song, his eyes glued to the window. His veil had faded, and he shimmered in the light of his powers. His gold coloring shone through, highlighting his hair, adding a sun-kissed glow to his skin.

I hesitated, reluctant to interrupt. If I could capture a single moment to tuck aside and step back into, I might choose that one. Apollo at peace, his divine form relaxed, the beauty of his features at ease in a way no other got to see. It was a privilege to know him on that level, to be the one person he truly unveiled himself for. And it wasn't because he was a god. It was simply gratitude for getting to see him, the person, that rippled through me.

He shifted towards me. "Are you just going to stand there all day?"

I smirked and leaned against the doorjamb. "Maybe I like the view."

He chuckled, running his hand back through his curls before sliding the lyre into his knapsack.

"I have somewhere I want to show you."

He cocked an eyebrow but jumped up, bag in hand, and followed me. When we stepped into the atrium fifteen minutes later, Apollo crossed his arms, scanning over the emerald leaves and curving glass ceiling where a scarlet-feathered bird flew overhead.

"So? What do you think?" I asked.

"It's humid."

I clicked my tongue. "You're just choosing to complain about it."

He elbowed me. "You knew I'd do that coming in here, so you must find my complaining endearing."

He grinned, and his jaw softened with it, the long line of his neck meeting his tunic and dipping beneath it. My stomach warmed. "I suppose so," I said as I gestured to a bench.

We both sat, and I tucked my arm around Apollo's shoulder. He sank into me, and that warm feeling spread, drifting down my limbs. He leaned in and kissed me, his lips soft and yielding, unlike the sharp edges of his personality. "There's something I wanted to discuss with you, if you remember," I said.

He pulled back but allowed his fingers to linger, tickling along my neck. "What is it?"

"I've thought of an expedited way to find out which of

the minor gods may align with us."

"Did you?"

I unwrapped myself from him and leaned onto my knees. "We could seek the wind gods. They involve themselves with many of the lower deities and will know if there are any murmurings of dissent."

Apollo scoffed. "I can't stand the wind gods."

"You can't stand any gods."

"The wind gods hold a special level of hate for me." He smacked his mouth. "And how do you intend to get them to tell us what they know, anyway?"

A bird cried in the distance, and the limbs of a tree shivered as I smoothed out the silky edge of my robe, my voice dropping to a whisper. "You might not have been the first god I've been with."

Apollo snapped his head in my direction. "Are you serious? Wait…" His eyebrows jumped up. "One of the wind gods? Who?"

I fiddled the ring on my finger back and forth before straightening and meeting his piercing gaze. "Zephyrus."

"No," Apollo gasped. "Oh, gods, Cyn. Not him. He's the worst."

I rolled my eyes. "Haven't you been with other deities?"

"Well, yes."

"So, how is this any different?"

"It's entirely different. Zephyrus is…" He gave his head a shake.

"It's literally the same. Are you just jealous that you aren't my first god?"

He frowned, a seriousness draping over his features that made me wish I could snatch my words back. "Maybe, a bit," he whispered.

"Hey." I kissed him, letting my lips linger before resting

my forehead against his. "I've had sex with him once. You and me... it's a completely different thing."

Apollo's shoulders dropped, and he pulled in closer to me. "I'm sorry." He trailed his fingers along my arm like the gentle touch of rain. "This is new for me. I've never had someone who was mine before. It means"—he swallowed—"everything to me, Cyn."

"I am yours." I scraped my teeth over the corner of his jaw. "In every way. And this is new for me too. For one thing, I've never been serious enough with anyone to introduce them to my father before."

"Yeah, well, he'd terrify the fuck out of anyone, god or otherwise, I imagine."

"I knew you didn't tell me everything. What did he say?"

Apollo chuckled and lifted my fingers, kissing them before pulling back. "I love you. Whatever the cost, even a few questions from a worried parent"—I frowned, but he pressed forward—"is well worth it."

I groaned. "Anyway, if you need to hear it from me, our relationship means the world to me."

Apollo smiled, an expression so gentle it almost didn't suit him, spreading over his features. "I feel the same. Okay, enough coddling me. What was your idea?"

I leaned back against the bench. A fountain in the distance gurgled. "Perhaps it was a bad one, after all."

"Please tell me."

I sighed. "I thought we could go to the Palace of the Four Winds, and I could..." I rolled my hand out as if the air would offer words I couldn't find. "Talk with Zephyrus. See what he might know."

Apollo's lips pinched. "You mean flirt with Zephyrus?"

"As I said, maybe it's a bad idea."

Apollo groaned. "No, it's a good one. I just don't like it."

"Then I won't. Hurting you wouldn't be worth it to me."

"I didn't say you shouldn't do it." He draped his fingers on my thigh. My muscle jumped, the blood coursing under his hand warming. "I told you when I returned with you, I'm here with you and to help you with this war. So…" He let his head drift towards his shoulder. "If this is necessary, then so be it. I can see the point. He's bound to tell a lover things he wouldn't discuss with others."

"We're not lovers. We had one—disappointing, at that —night together."

A wicked grin slipped up on Apollo's face, and he leaned in against me, trailing his tongue up my neck. "Oh, that's too bad, Prince. Perhaps I could help you forget."

I hummed in response. "Maybe I'd like that."

"It's fairly private here."

"But also, one of my father's favorite places to visit unexpectedly."

He scoffed and pulled away from me. "Why don't you just throw a bucket of ice water on me?"

I laughed. "We've swum in cold water before; it did not help us keep our hands off each other."

"Yeah, which should be surprising on my part since you had just shoved me off a cliff."

"You jumped."

Apollo twisted his mouth up. "That's debatable." His smile faded, his gaze growing distant.

I bumped my shoulder into his. "What's wrong?"

"He has wings, Cyn."

"What?"

"Zephyrus. Seriously… how could you fuck a man with wings?"

I burst into a laugh and rolled my eyes. "The idea was intriguing."

"But, as you pointed out, disappointing."

"Yes, well, never judge a man's bedroom prowess by his wings."

Apollo snorted, but then his expression softened, and he traced his thumb over my jaw as gently as a breeze trickling through a garden of flowers. "That's not advice I'll ever need to take. The man I'm interested in, thankfully, lacks wings."

I smiled and bent into him, letting the tendrils of golden light that seemed to seep from him wrap us up together.

4

Epiphany

The letter in my hand weighed heavily against my palm as I ambled through the gardens where crisp oranges and auburns had eased their way through all the greens. I slipped my fingers under the seal and broke it. Gale's looping handwriting filled the page inside. *Dear Pip, (How strange it is to address you so informally in writing, but after the scolding you gave me in your last letter, I decided to acquiesce.)*

I grinned.

It has already started snowing here. I can't help but think that you would love it.

I sighed and folded the parchment up. Already my head ached as the letters bounced around on the page, my childhood struggles with reading echoing through my mind. I'd finish it later. As much as I liked Gale, he was a complication. An attractive complication who would probably make an excellent husband and whom my family and our kingdom would love to see me align with. But... my heart wanted other things.

I reached the stables where peachy light warmed the space, and the sweet smell of fresh hay mixed in with earthy animal scents. Horses huffed breaths and twitched their ears. I walked over to Meadow and scratched under her chin before ambling farther into the building.

Valerian stood beside a cart stacked with hay, sweat glistening his tan skin. He heaved a bundle onto his shoulder, climbed up a ladder, and tossed it with a chuff into a stack. My heart—the wicked, unsatisfied thing that it was —picked up its pace. Val's boots hit the ground with a thump, and he swiped the back of his arm over his forehead and grinned at me. "Hey, Pip."

I stepped onto the boards of an empty stall. "Can you get out of here today?"

He lugged another bundle of hay on his shoulder. "It's a damn shame, really, but they actually expect me to work." He winked before ascending up the ladder again.

I leaned back, so my gaze could follow him, my curls draping down along my dress. "I thought Hyacinth had given you permission to leave whenever Temi and I needed you."

"I didn't realize, with the king being home, that Cyn's whims still counted."

"Cyn doesn't have whims."

He dropped to the straw-littered floor again and smirked at me. "Pip, he's courting a god. He has whims."

I laughed. "So, is that a no?"

Valerian paused and leaned against a beam, pulling his gloves off. "I'm afraid I'd better stay on today." He nodded to the cart. "It's hay season. A lot of work needs to be done, and I don't want to shirk my part."

"I guess I'll have to tell you here, then. Unless..." I chewed the edge of my lip. "I'm bothering you."

His emerald eyes sparkled, the dark stubble along his jaw gleaming with highlights of auburn, and his voice took on a husky tenor. "You never bother me, Epiphany."

My stomach warmed, and I twisted my fingers together but pushed humor into my words. "Guess what?"

Valerian grabbed a tin mug from where it hung on a nail and dipped water from a drinking bucket into it before taking a swallow. "Ah, so it's going to be a guessing game. And you know I love them." He tapped his free thumb against his chin. "Let's see, it's nearly autumn, and you rushed in here. You and Temi have planned a hunting trip?"

"Okay, you're on the right track. But think bigger."

"Bigger? Hmm." He took another drink from his cup before discarding the mug. "You and Temi and the girls from the city"—he stretched the words out—"have planned a hunting trip."

I rolled my eyes. "No. What if I told you I could get you out of mucking stalls for a few more months?"

Valerian clicked his tongue. "Then I'd say you've become one of my favorite people. Which"—he smirked—"was already true. So, I guess it would actually change nothing."

I huffed a laugh. "What would you think of going on a trip with me and Temi?"

He pulled the gloves onto his hands, a tightness sweeping up around his eyes. "Is this like a sneak-out-of-the-kitchens trip?"

"No. In fact, Cyn was the one who suggested you could go to manage the horses on it. He knows Temi, and I feel comfortable with you."

"Ack." He jumped back into the cart, and it bounced. "Where are we going?"

"Have you ever heard of Lesbos?"

"The island?"

"Yes."

"A strange place to need horses, I suppose."

25

I shrugged. "We'll need them on the journey down the continent and someone to mind them as we cross the water."

He sucked in air over his teeth and skimmed his eyes over the various stalls. "Many of these horses have never been on a boat before. Some animals can be jumpy in that situation."

"And that's the perfect reason for you to come. You'll know which ones we should take."

He tossed me a smile that glittered through my nerves. "You act as though this is a choice for me."

"Well, it is."

"If Cyn wants me to accompany you, that's as good as an order. And, besides…" He smiled again, long lines pressing into his cheeks. "I would hate to miss the adventure. So, yes, I'll go. When do we leave?"

"Possibly in the next few days."

He bobbed his head. "Then I'd better help get as much of this done as I can before then." He shifted back to the cart and lifted another bundle of hay.

I froze for a moment. His rough work tunic clung to the muscles of his shoulders, the material draping and allowing peeks of the sweat shimmering over his skin. "All right," I said, my voice coming higher than I intended it. "I'll tell Temi."

He glanced over his shoulder, sending me a look that heated me all the way to my toes. "See you soon."

"Yeah," I breathed the words as I turned and walked out of the stable.

My stomach still fluttered as I meandered back through the gardens where the feather-like petals of Dahlia trembled in the breeze, tangling up alongside the fluorescently bright Celosia. I snapped a bloom of the latter and twirled it between my fingers where it tapped against Gale's letter.

Guilt gnawed at me, but this trip provided another opportunity as well. A chance to put off Galeson's talks of visiting that he kept bringing up in his letters. As soon as I spoke to Temi, I'd write to him and let him know about my plans.

Farther in the gardens near the edge of the wall where the mountains and lakes in the distance shimmered like magic draped in fog, Temi sat on a bench, her knife in hand, drawing the blade down a whetstone, her gaze distant. Her dark skin shimmered in the sunlight, her expression so noble it reminded me of how I used to think she had to be as divine as her brother. And it turned out that might actually be true.

"Hey." I dropped beside her.

She lifted her chin and returned to the scraping motion of sharpening the knife. "I'm glad you want to go with me."

I was happy to hear that. I wasn't certain if I had butted in on her trip. But Temi wasn't likely to falsely say she wanted me to join her. "Are you worried about it?"

"What part?"

"Sappho being known as a witch." If I were honest, it did concern me a bit. But not enough to keep me home.

She scoffed. "That? No. I've spent my entire life around gods. The legends of someone and their reality are two different things."

"So, you don't believe she's an actual witch?"

Temi pushed the knife into her belt and withdrew a second one. "It doesn't matter to me either way. I go for answers."

"Is that what worries you, then?"

Temi's lips pursed. "Yes. I'm anxious that I won't like what I find. But I think I'd rather know than not."

I nodded, an errant curl dancing along with the wind, and I brushed it behind my ear. "Maybe it will be good."

Temi winced. "Yeah, I guess we just have to go on this trip and hope nothing goes wrong."

"What are you worried about going wrong?"

"I wonder if I'll regret finding out. I've lived almost nineteen years without knowing. Might it be wiser to leave it alone?"

I shifted towards her, pulling my knees up. "Let me say this."

"All right?"

"If I asked you in reverse, do you think I should take a risk and tell Valerian how I feel, or should I just go on not knowing, wanting your honest opinion. What would you tell me?"

She rolled her eyes. "That's unfair. You already know my answer."

"Okay, then."

"You're a terrible friend."

"I'm an excellent friend."

She huffed a laugh but stretched her hand out, and I took it, curling my fingers alongside hers. Flowers fluttered in a breeze as the peaches of afternoon light whispered across the gardens. Temi sighed and rested her head on my shoulder.

"Come on," I said. "Let's go to the kitchen."

She raised her face. "Why?"

"Well, we're going to have an entire trip without cake. We should indulge now while we can."

"Does pre-indulging in comfort cake work?"

"No idea, but we're about to find out."

She smirked but hopped off the bench, and we ambled into the palace and to the kitchen together. The staff bustled about. The fire made the stone-walled room, even with its tall ceilings, hot. Flour dusted through the air alongside tangy garlic and bright citrus.

Valerian's mother strode up, her dark hair tucked beneath a scarf, her eyes wary as she bowed. "Your Highness. Are you in need of something?"

I bit my lip. "You don't have to call me 'Your Highness'."

She winced.

"I just mean, Valerian and I are friends and—" I stopped speaking as her expression seemed to teeter between mortification and worry.

Temi's gaze darted between the two of us. "We were hoping, if it's not too much trouble, for some cake."

Valerian's mother nodded at her. "Of course. We have some in the pantry." She bowed again and turned, her skirts whisking over the floor. She returned a moment later and handed a cloth-wrapped dish out. Her arms still held red scars from where she'd dropped boiling water over the summer, and my stomach twisted. Valerian worried about his mother but claimed she was too stubborn to step down from her position as head of the kitchen.

"Please let me know if you need anything more," she said as she cast her eyes down.

"Thank you," I whispered.

We strode together out into the hall, and I released a breath. "Gods, I'm an idiot, and she hates me."

Temi tucked her arm through mine. "Neither of those are true."

I fixed her with a look. "Oh, please. She absolutely does."

Servants walked by us, causing the candles along the hallway to flicker, and Temi remained quiet until they passed. "She's not a fan of the feelings you have for her son."

"She doesn't know."

Temi chuckled. "She does. She's not oblivious, Pip."

I groaned. "That does not make me feel better."

"Well"—Temi leaned her head against mine—"it's a good thing we have some comfort cake to split between the two of us, isn't it?"

I met her gaze and burst into a laugh.

5

Apollo

Temi and I bustled through the city surrounded by guards amid the clattering, swarming crowds of the morning markets. Hyacinth walked ahead of us, waving to people, grasping hands. They grinned at him, crying out, "My prince!" But then their gazes shifted to me, to the golden irises, the silver glowing, all the marks setting me apart as something different, foreign, dangerous.

They weren't wrong.

Temi elbowed me. "Stop glowering."

"I'm not."

She rolled her eyes but tucked her arm through mine. "People will see you as less terrifying if you—I don't know —look less terrifying."

"Gods are terrifying, regardless of how they look." She cringed, and my stomach twisted. "Temi, I didn't mean—"

"It's fine." We reached the temple steps and climbed up them. Banners with golden lightning bolts flitted about in the wind. We strode past the massive columns, the din of the crowd hushing as we stepped inside to the room where the smoky scent of incense laced heavily in the air.

"I'll join you in a minute," I said to Hyacinth. He hesitated for a moment, his eyebrows drawing together and forming that v-shaped dimple that made my heart patter, before nodding and continuing on into the temple with his guards. I turned to Temi. "How are you doing?"

She sighed. "It's been a lot. I'm not sure." She raised her hand, and silver bracelets on her wrist clattered, her ivory and gold dress rippling with the motion. "Who am I, Apollo?"

I chewed my lip. "I wish I had wise words to offer you. You know this is something I struggle with myself."

Her expression grew more uncertain. And I didn't like that. Her feeling anxious over my stupidity was one thing —that was basically a language between us. But her truly worrying disturbed me. It reminded me of her as a young child when Zeus had destroyed our village. Remnants of guilt still clung to me from that. I hated all the hurts Temi had experienced on my behalf. And now maybe she was a goddess as well. I couldn't help but feel that a hard future stood before her. And it made me miserable that I couldn't do a damn thing about it.

I cupped my hand over her cheek. "To start with, you are the best person I know."

"I may not be a person."

"The point stands."

She chuckled and curled her fingers around mine, squeezing them. "Thank you."

"Do you want me to go on this trip with you?"

A humming of sweet singing voices picked up from farther in the temple. They echoed off the ceilings, mournful and resonant, as they whispered their way to us. Temi cocked her head to the side. "I thought you and Hyacinth had your own journey you're taking?"

"We do but"—I snagged her fingers again, trailing my

thumb over the back of her knuckles—"if you need me to go with you... if you want me to go with you... I will."

Her lips pulled up into such a gentle expression she suddenly appeared as she had as a child, all smooth-cheeked and bright-eyed, no worries, no fears hanging over her. "That's sweet of you, Apollo. But you should go with Hyacinth. Besides, I'll have friends on my trip. Pip and Val are coming with me."

I considered her for a moment. "I'm glad to hear that."

"Maybe you could use your travels as a similar opportunity."

"For what?"

The voices grew in volume, a single deep one echoing off the walls as a dozen others hummed together in unison. She grinned. "Perhaps you can make some friends along the way."

"I have friends."

She cocked an eyebrow up. "Who?"

"You. You're my friend. And Hyacinth."

"We are your sister and your lover. I mean a friend. A person with whom you've never shared a bed with."

I scoffed. "Sounds annoying."

She chuckled. "Whatever. Come on." She nodded down the hall where the voices had grown into a crescendo, notes rippling around like a waterfall rushing towards us. "We're going to miss the ceremony."

I groaned, which made her smirk again, but she grabbed my arm, and we strode into the next room where choral singers stood before a statue of Zeus which was carved with noble eyes and a scepter decorated with light-ning bolts.

A sourness bloomed in my stomach.

Zeus.

My father.

Whom I would betray by joining Niria in aligning with Jupiter with the aim of bringing him down. He needed to fall, and I wouldn't regret it, but something panged through me anyway. After all, a war meant trouble for Hyacinth and his kingdom. And if Zeus caught wind of our schemes... A shiver skittered down my spine.

I swallowed as Temi and I turned sideways to weave past people until we reached Hyacinth's side. He lifted his face from the singers who had started into another song, and his hazel eyes met mine. Every worry I had washed away under the weight of his expression.

We're probably dooming ourselves, I'd said to him, *but as long as we're in this together*. I took a deep breath, shifting my gaze ahead towards the vocalists as they finished their second song. They bowed and walked out of the chamber, leaving a trio of priests who stepped forward. Hyacinth nodded in that direction, and we strode to the center of the room. A priest handed him a bottle of wine and murmured words of blessings over both of us. Hyacinth lifted the bottle, and the burgundy liquid splashed out, trickling over the altar, dripping down the notches in the stone, washing over the floor.

"May almighty Zeus hear our prayers," Hyacinth said, "and accept our offerings and reverence."

He handed the bottle to me, our fingers grazing and causing sparks to fly through me. The rich, dry smell of the wine filled the space, like it swam through us, as I splashed more on the altar. "Blessings on Zeus. May he honor his humble followers and guide us."

My voice came out resonant and strong. We needed Zeus to believe that the increased dedications for him was due to us campaigning for his sake, so he didn't look too closely at what we were actually doing.

"Blessings on Zeus," the group echoed.

As soon as the ceremony ended, we strode out of the temple and back into the fresh air and endless skies of the world. Temi bowed and slipped into the crowd of the city. "So," Hyacinth said as we continued alongside his guards. "Did you speak with your sister?"

"Yes. She wants me to go with you." I frowned. "I still wonder if it's the right call."

Hyacinth's hand twitched like he longed to reach out for me, but he pulled his arm back. We'd had a long conversation with his father, and they'd decided it was best if our relationship wasn't public knowledge yet with war on the horizon. Rumors of him being involved with a god were one thing. Confirmation of that was another matter. The image he had to maintain as a prince exhausted me for him.

"Could I be utterly selfish for a moment?" he said.

I turned towards him. The kingly sharp profile of his features shimmered in the afternoon light, his eyes turning to liquid amber. "Yes," I said, "of course."

"I want you to go with me."

A smile tripped up on my lips, and I ducked my face. "Even if we're going to pretend that we aren't together?"

"Only for the first part of the journey." He squeezed in closer to me, our shoulders brushing. "And trust me, that will feel like a punishment. On that note, I thought I might ask Delon and Len to join us."

"Why?"

He shrugged, but his voice grew heavy. "We're maybe six months out from being in a war. A trip with friends"— he leaned in so close it probably broke protocol—"and with my partner before it all breaks out sounds fun. Aren't you the one who told me I should do something solely for the joy of it?"

Warmth flooded through me, fizzling along my limbs, sinking down in my stomach. "Yes, it's a good idea."

"Come on, then. We should ask them, and we all need to have winter coats made."

"Oh, I will absolutely join you for that."

The crowds thinned as we grew closer to the palace. "You're excited to get fitted for a coat?"

"Not even remotely," I said. "But if you think I'm going to leave it up to you for what style you choose, you're dead wrong."

He clicked his tongue. "I have excellent taste in clothing."

"That's nice. I would like to choose a coat with terrible tastes, please."

He shook his head as we reached the palace gates and stepped inside, separating from his guards. "Maybe one day I'll rub off on you, golden boy."

"Maybe." We'd finally separated from the eyes of the city, and I leaned in and kissed his cheek. "Or, more likely," I whispered, "it will never happen."

He burst into a laugh, his breath warming my neck, and we peeled apart. "Is there anything else you need before we leave?"

I considered not answering. I'd spent my whole life keeping a distance, swallowing my thoughts and wishes and hopes back. But with Hyacinth, I could be something terrifying—vulnerable. Wind rattled leaves on the tree above us together, and I lifted my face to its spreading bough. "There's nothing I need, but there's something I'd like to have."

Hyacinth cocked his head to the side. "What would that be?"

I fiddled with the straps of my knapsack. "You know the folio I have, with poetry in it?"

He nodded, and his eyes sparkled with interest. He knew I carried that around because it reminded me of him.

"I wondered if you might... write a poem for me." I lifted my face to meet his gaze. "In it, I mean." I shook my head. "Only if you wanted to, though."

We'd soon face this trip where we had to pretend to not be together, where he'd interact with a past lover of his. A pinch of insecurity made me want to cling to him, to have some piece of him. And I knew I'd cherish something that he'd put his hand to, had poured out some piece of his heart into.

Hyacinth leaned in, his lips pulling up into a gentle smile. He kissed me before speaking. "Of course, I will... but you'll have to give me some time to think through it. I'm intimidated now."

I scoffed and started walking again. "Don't be. You could write anything, and I'd treasure it."

He smirked and looked out the side of his eyes at me. "It'll have to be something worthy if it's going to get a revered spot in your bag."

I laughed but slid my fingers between his as we headed back towards the palace.

6

Hyacinth

Temi's travel party gathered by the stables. Two dozen guards already sat on their horses. Emrin and Father walked over to Epiphany, Father squeezing her in his arms while Apollo chatted with his sister. Valerian held the reins of a horse that Temi mounted.

"Valerian." I lifted my chin, and he strode over to me. "A minute?"

He grinned. "Have you come to give me your heartfelt goodbyes?" He pressed his fingers to his chest, dimpling his uniform. "Will a few months without my presence in your life devastate you?"

I rolled my eyes. "Yeah, that's it." I pulled my crown off and scratched over my hair. "No, I wanted to talk with you about Epiphany."

His lips parted, and he hesitated a moment before he spoke. "Epiphany?"

"Yes." I plopped the crown back on my head. "I know there is a guard with your group, but I want to ask if you'd keep an eye out for her. She's never traveled independently beyond the city before."

He chuckled. "Are you worried? It's good I'm going on this trip then, isn't it? Should bandits set upon us, think how helpful I'll be?" He smirked. "I mean, someone must mind the horses while Temi and Pip kick their asses."

I huffed a sigh. "I'm serious, Val."

He raised his eyebrows. "I am, too. You haven't seen Temi in action."

A dove fluttered past us, landing in the limbs of a pear tree and shaking a few leaves loose that tumbled to the ground. "Valerian."

He slapped my shoulder and gave the muscle a squeeze. "She'll be fine, Cyn. Honestly. And you don't have to ask me to look out for her. You already know I will."

I gripped his fingers. "Thank you."

He nodded and then clapped me into a hug, and I squeezed him in return. Something about both trips felt like we all stood on the edge of a precipice, looking over, our destiny shrouded in fog below us.

"She'll be all right," Valerian said as he leaned back. "I'll see you again soon."

"Safe travels."

He inclined his head and walked over to his horse, swinging up over her back. Epiphany ambled over, and I drew her into my arms, letting the rose-scented sweetness of her linger on me. "Pip, be careful, please."

She grinned as she pulled away. "Don't worry. I'm sure you'll pray for an utterly boring trip for me." She winked. "I'll do the same for you."

I groaned. "Why do I worry that is not what either of us is going to get?"

"Stop being such a pessimist."

"I'm a realist."

She squeezed my arms again. "I love you, Cyn. I'll see you in a couple of months."

"I love you, too."

She walked over, last of the three dozen that made up their party to take to her horse. They gave one final wave of their hands before guards opened the palace gates, and the group trotted out.

Father crossed his arms, a sheen glittering over his eyes, reflecting the gray of the world. He and Emrin stood side-by-side as the wind rippled their robes around their feet. I separated from Apollo, who had joined me, kissing his knuckles, and stepped over to them. Father shook his head and brushed a finger under his eye. "It's hard watching your children grow up."

I squeezed him into my arms, and he clapped my back before clearing his throat. "And you leave after lunch?"

"Yes."

"Well…" He sniffed. "I'd better not hold you up from any last-minute preparations. I'll see you at the meal."

I nodded. After he had walked away, I turned towards Emrin, an uneasy feeling stringing through me. "Perhaps both of us leaving at the same time was a mistake."

Emrin's gaze trailed to Father's form as it grew smaller, but he shrugged. "It's fine, Cyn. You know I'll help in your absence."

"Yes, of course. I know you will."

He worried his lip between his teeth. "I am surprised he let Epiphany go, though." His face shifted toward the gates.

"Yes, me as well. One more thing to worry about."

He knocked his shoulder against mine. "It'll be okay. Epiphany has a well-trained guard with her. And your group will, too."

"Thanks, Em."

He offered me a serene smile, and it made him look so young. Gods, he was so young. And I was leaving a great deal on his shoulders. But it was for the good of the king-dom. And I had been younger than him when I'd taken over much of the work I did now. In a lot of ways, it had shaped me into who I'd become as a person, for the good and bad. But it also had taken part of my youth from me, forcing me to mature when my friends still spent their afternoons playing sports and sharing jokes while I studied the economic and political realities for our nation. I hated that burden for Emrin.

"See you at lunch?" he asked.

"See you then."

He nodded and made his way across the lawn.

Apollo ambled up, wrapping his arm around my waist. "So, what do we have left to do?"

"Would you come with me?"

His brow furrowed, but he bobbed his head, and I tangled our fingers together and led him into the palace and up the stairs and into my room. Once I closed the door, I pushed him against it, parting his lips with mine, yanking his hips against me.

He laughed against my mouth. "We have a couple hours left to get ready, and this is how you want to spend it?" He sunk his teeth into the dip where my neck met my shoulder, and I groaned. "Not that I'm complaining, but it intrigues me."

I sighed and pressed my forehead against his. A bad feeling had draped over me that morning, and I needed some time alone where I felt safe, and soon that would be ripped away as well. "I hate that we have to pretend on this trip not to be together. It's going to kill me, I'm sure of it."

The veil over Apollo's eyes slipped, and his irises glowed golden, his voice dropping low and husky. "It will only feel that way."

"Also," I whispered, tucking my face down against his

neck, "I worry that I'll lose you. If not with something else, then with your ascension."

Apollo breathed against me, wrapping his arms around my waist, and kissed the edge of my jaw.

But he didn't speak.

He didn't offer false promises.

After all, he didn't like to lie.

"I'm all yours at this moment, Prince," he whispered, breaking the silence. "Have me now, and let the future worry about itself for the time being."

I lifted my face and feathered my mouth over his. He pulled me to the bed, and we dropped together, our fingers peeling clothes away with reverence, like we unmasked the sacred, discovered the untouchable and clenched our greedy hands into it.

We made love the same way, not speaking, as if we never wished for the moment to end, like we'd hold each other into eternity in that manner, hide in the shadows and hope kings and gods forgot about our existence.

When I cried out, my head dropping back against the mattress, Apollo curled his arms around my waist and pulled me against him, resting his chin on my shoulder.

We lay there as the sun shifted over the panels of the wall, silhouettes of tree limbs growing smaller and dancing across the ceiling.

A clock chimed, and I sighed. "We need to get ready for lunch and say our goodbyes. We'll leave soon."

Apollo curled in tighter against me and kissed my neck.

And then he stood and tugged his clothes back on. The absence of his body next to mine sent a shock over my flesh, the cool air raising goosebumps along my skin.

I rose and dressed alongside him, but a bad feeling lingered like a chill I couldn't shake.

7

Artemis

The horses clipped along, occasionally tossing their heads. Several of the guards sang a song together, the words lost in the wind, but the tune carried to where Valerian, Epiphany, and I trotted together. Epiphany's cheeks held a touch of color, and she threw her head back, her dark curls swaying over the navy of her riding outfit.

"Excited?" I asked.

"Yes. But also… I don't know… it's more, I feel… free." She sighed, and her lips parted into another smile. She turned to Valerian, who studied her. "What are you thinking?"

He hesitated for a moment, but then his expression fell back into the teasing one he sometimes donned. "I'm thinking free looks good on you."

She bowed her head, her cheeks coloring again. And I fought an eye roll. I liked them both, but gods if they weren't oblivious.

Gray clouds hovered over a shimmering lake. The rest of the world stretched flat and endless at the bottom of the valley. "Are there no more mountain ranges?"

"Ack," Valerian said. "No. It will get flatter as we continue farther south. And warmer at that."

"Those both sound like positive things to me."

He smiled, his emerald eyes sparkling. A guard trotted up and turned his horse alongside us. "We've found a suitable place to stop for the night near water where we can put up tents. We won't reach any cities until tomorrow at least, and the captain thinks it's a good idea to turn in early today."

Valerian nodded. "Better to not overextend the horses."

"All right," I said. "I'm going hunting."

The guard—a tall man named Theos with thick brown hair that held a touch of a curl and skin that always had a rosy brush to it—furrowed his brow. "How many guards would you like to go with you?"

"None."

He startled and shifted to Epiphany and Valerian, as if they might offer support before turning back to me. "My lady, the king has tasked us with your well-being and safety."

I sighed, but Epiphany spoke up, loose curls of hers wisping across the gray sky like a trail of smoke. "Captain, with respect, my father sent you for my sake. Temi is her own agent and not under your responsibility."

He hesitated for a moment, his features tightening, but he bobbed his head and coaxed his horse forward towards the other guards.

And so, an hour later, I found myself in the cool belly of a forest where moss crawled over boulders and a creek trickled just beyond the dark streaking forms of the tree line. I was relieved to get a few minutes alone. As much as I loved having Epiphany and Valerian on the trip—and I truly did; they already made the traveling more pleasant—

I also still hadn't had time to process everything happening to me.

I wondered if I ever would assimilate it. All that I'd known about myself had turned out to be a lie, and it seemed like my world spun around me, with no place for me to gain purchase and find out how to define who I was now. That's exactly why I had to go to Sappho and seek answers. Until I had them, my life would stay in chaos. It felt normal, at least, walking through the forest, moving alone through the loamy ground beneath boughs of leaves that rustled together.

I'd always felt most myself outdoors, creeping through the woods in the lonely hours of the day. And that was doubly so now that everything felt up in the air.

Something crackled, and I tightened my fingers around my bow, tucking down behind a bush, allowing my breath to whisper its way between my lips. The air shimmered, like glitter flitted on the breeze, a sweet floral scent permeating over the earthy smells of the forest and hair rose on my neck. That wasn't natural.

"What are you doing, Artemis?"

I startled and jumped around. On a hill, tucked between two gray pines, a goddess stood, the gold of her eyes as bright as stars, the silver outline of the high deities hovering over the alabaster of her skin. Her flaxen locks shimmered.

"Who are you?" I asked.

Her ruby lips parted into a cruel smile. "I suppose you wouldn't know me as you don't pay tribute to me as you should. As any *woman*"—she emphasized the word—"should."

"Hera," I breathed.

She stepped closer, her feet crunching over pine straw. "Yes. And I've come here with a warning for you."

She kept easing nearer to me, and I readjusted the bag that held my arrows, hovering my fingers over them. "What kind of warning?"

"You do not know what you seek. You don't realize the prophecies you set in motion with this journey of yours. Stop now before it's too late."

I took a careful step forward, my boot dipping into boggy ground, and I repositioned, finding firmer footing. "I have a right to find out who I am."

"Women who go seeking answers end up hurt," she said, her voice as cutting as a blade. "Did your mother never tell you the legend of Pandora's box?"

"My mother died before I had a chance to hear her stories, but"—a twig cracked as I moved around the trunk of a tree—"I have a feeling she wouldn't have told me that one, anyway. She didn't believe women should be power-less and shamed."

Hera's nose wrinkled, her glow brightening. "Oh, yes," she hissed through her teeth. "I won't forget your mother. For all her supposed bravery, the last look in her eyes, as the blade ruptured her lungs, was terror."

I shook my head. "My mother died in childbirth with me."

She laughed, her shimmering gown dragging over twigs and pebbles. "Is that what you believe?" She came close enough to me that the bright citrus scent of her trailed to me. "Oh, my foolish, naïve child. No one who fucks my husband lives for long. My fate is entwined with my husband's, and I will destroy anyone who threatens it."

I sucked in a breath that sliced at me. "Are you saying that you killed my mother?"

Hera's chin dropped, her eyes taking on a glint, a smile curling up over her cheeks. "Yes, I did. And I will do so much more to keep fate in my favor."

I slapped an arrow out, losing it as soon as it hit my bow. Hera swiped her hand in the air, splintering the wood, and it peppered the forest floor. "Oh, you are as senseless and brash as your mother, believing you can fight a goddess."

She jumped in front of me; her glowing reflected over my skin. My heart lurched, but if I was going down, it would be fighting. I snatched a blade from the belt on my leg and slashed it towards her.

A growl tore from her as she yanked my wrist and pounded us both to the ground with a thud that knocked the air out of me. She pressed her arm into my throat, and I gasped, scratching and jerking against her. She leaned her weight forward, and I dragged a ragged breath into my nose. But it wouldn't pass. My heart pierced with warmth and the sharp edges of panic. Air. I needed air.

She smiled. "Turn around and go home, and I shall let you live."

"I know," I choked, "something... that...." I coughed over the words, my vision blurring. "You... don't."

She lessened the pressure. "And what would that be?"

I gulped in a breath hungrily, like a starving animal offered food. My throat ached, but I scratched my voice out. "If you are so desperate to stop me, you would have killed me before drawing my attention." She glowered, and I spat the sentence at her. "You must believe that I'm a high deity's child, and that the only god who can kill me is Zeus, who holds the spark. But you weren't aware that I suspected that. Which means you're trying to scare me because it's the only move you have."

She clamped her teeth together and jerked the blade from my hand. "That might be so, you filthy half breed, but I know something you don't as well."

I trembled and attempted to grab another weapon, but

she pressed her weight against me, freezing me. "What's that?" I asked.

"You have enough mortal aspects that, while you may not die, you can suffer." And she stabbed the blade into my arm and then ripped it out. Blood, thick and coppery, surged forth, gushing from the wound. She rose, her face speckled in burgundy. She blinked, her features pinched, and then she disappeared, that glittery, floral essence filling the air.

The forest stretched quiet and cool and lonely again.

I stood but then fell to the ground, hitting the exposed roots of a tree with a thump that banged my shin bones.

Blood coursed down my arm, hot and sticky. At the rate it flowed, I had limited time before I passed out. I crawled to my bag and fumbled, opening it with one hand. I pulled out a tunic and wrapped it around the injury. It slipped, and I cursed under my breath, using my teeth to pull a knot tight.

Sweat had broken out over my forehead, and I fell back against moss. The world blurred, a swirl of sage and gray. The sun had already draped down to the skyline. Night would fall soon. I had to get out of the woods.

If I knew what magic I might possess, I could pull on those powers to help me.

But I didn't know.

I stood and stumbled forward, catching my hands against rough bark that scraped up skin.

Shit.

All right. I could do this.

One breath at a time.

I took an uneasy step.

Everything narrowed to the moment.

The squish of my feet pressing into the ground.

The chittering of pine needles clambering together in the wind.

The sway of my hips and the blurring of my vision.

It felt like eternity had passed, the sun burned out, the world birthed itself anew by the time I reached camp. The group had already erected tents, and they fluttered in the breeze, twilight sweeping over them like the sky draped itself over everything.

My steps grew as heavy as stone, but I continued dragging myself forward.

Pip lifted her face up to me as I approached the light of the fire. "Temi!" She gasped and jumped out of her seat. "Oh, my gods, what happened?"

Guards jumped up, rushing towards me. I fell into their arms. Valerian pushed others aside, his eyes doubling in size. "Lay her down over here." His hands fumbled over the fabric on my arm. "Shit. Heat water, now," he yelled. "I need cloth boiled, my equestrian bag, someone grab my shears, so I can cut this sleeve away."

"It's fine," I whispered, my lips growing numb. "It won't kill me. I'm a deity."

And then the world faded to black.

8

Apollo

Our group had stopped for the night, and two separate fires burned against the velvet of the evening sky. Around one, guards hovered, their laughter peeling to us. At the second, I sat by Hyacinth and Len, who both focused on Delon as he spoke.

He leaned onto his knees closer to the fire, his skin warming as he thrust his hands out. "So, she did this thing with her tongue..." He stuck his tongue out, curling it up. "And then she drew it down..."

"That's far too much detail," Hyacinth said, smacking his mouth. "No one wants to hear all of that."

Delon smirked. "Maybe you don't. Everyone else here" —he gestured to me and Len—"seems interested."

Hyacinth looked to Len, who cocked up an eyebrow. He shifted back towards me, and I shrugged. "What? It's an intriguing story."

Hyacinth clicked his tongue, but Delon laughed, clapping his hands together before grabbing a stick and stirring up the fire, sparks jumping into the dark sky. "I told you so.

And don't act like some damn prude, Cyn. It's not like you haven't had your share of companions."

"Maybe Cyn practices the principle," Len said, "that gentlemen shouldn't kiss and tell."

Delon rolled his eyes. "Hyacinth has the whole prince thing going for him. I bet half his partners have just been intrigued."

Hyacinth huffed a breath. "Thank you for making me sound simultaneously easy and yet incompetent at the same time. Obviously, it's the crown I wear that has resulted in anyone ever being willing to sleep with me."

Delon slapped Hyacinth on the shoulder. "Anytime, Cyn."

Hyacinth scoffed, but I draped my hand over his thigh. "It may be the crown that brings someone to your bed, but it's not what compels them to return."

Hyacinth's cheeks took on a flush of color, but Delon and Len both burst into a laugh. "See," Delon said, "this is what I'm talking about."

A star outlined in crimson streaked the heavens, two more following in its wake. I sucked in a breath and rose to my feet.

"What's wrong?" Hyacinth said.

I grasped his fingers. "I'll be back in a moment."

His eyebrows pressed together, but he nodded, and I strode away from the crackling fire and the hum of their conversation. The sky swept out like an inky blanket, draping over the mountains.

"Apollo."

I turned and Ares stood before me, a shadow outlined by starlight. He wore a veil that pulled in his luminescence, and standing there, draped in the dark edges of the world, he seemed somehow small and insignificant.

"How are you, brother?"

He lifted his face to the moon, his cape ruffling around his legs. "I'm busy. Fates are shifting."

I gasped. "War is coming?"

"Maybe." He kicked a rock, and it clattered. "Father hears rumors, whispers, that Jupiter plans to move against him." He let that hang between us, that phrase a shiver of cool air in a humid world. "He sends me to ask if you're involved?"

"I'm campaigning for his sake. Has he not received the offerings we've made to him?"

"He has. And he's pleased but suspicious." Ares' shoulders rose with a breath. "He wonders why his child, who hates him more than any other, would campaign for him."

I chewed the inside of my cheek. "Maybe I'm doing so to have an excuse to push off my ascension."

Ares remained quiet for a moment, and an owl hooted in the distance. "That's a believable lie that I will happily pass along to him for you."

I bowed my head. "Thank you."

"But you won't like the other reason he's sent me."

I raised my face. "What is it?"

"He's holding you to the arrangement you made. A year, Apollo. He wants you to ascend by spring."

My heart ached. My ascension would mean losing Hyacinth, Temi, and everything that mattered to me. But I forced the words to form. "Tell him I will."

Ares huffed a laugh, with no humor. "He won't accept your word for it."

"He's asked for a vow?"

Ares nodded.

"Wait." I stepped in closer to him, gripping his arm, and his muscles tensed. "He's asked me to vow to you?"

"Yes. But you know that's as good as a promise to him. If you break it, you'll be committed in service to me and essentially him through me."

I swallowed and rubbed my thumb over my palm. "All right. I'll vow it."

Ares' veil slipped for a moment, his body glimmering silver. "You will for all intents become Zeus' slave if you don't keep your word or die if you break the vow."

"That won't happen," I said. "Because I don't intend to break it. I will ascend by spring."

My muscles trembled as I spoke. Everything in me wanted to fight it, but my ascension hovered over me like Fate herself breathing down my neck. And making this vow was the only way to guarantee I kept Zeus from looking too carefully at Niria. If he saw us offering him dedications and knew I planned to ascend, it would buy Hyacinth and his kingdom more time. I had promised Cyn when I returned to help him and his country. I had to do it. For his sake.

Ares remained quiet for several heartbeats. "Very well." He pulled a blade out and sliced his arm, his blood leaking out golden and shimmering. He handed the knife to me, and I made a similar cut and then pressed my arm against his, the crimson of my blood glowing against his light.

His magic stung through me, like arrows slicing, and I gritted my teeth. When the ache of it receded, Ares withdrew his arm and pulled cloth bandages out of his bag, handing one to me. I wrapped my forearm. "When will I see you again?"

"If you do before your ascension, it will be because war is coming." He knotted his bandage. "So, hope that you don't."

"I miss you," I said.

He shook his head. "Life no longer allows that for us. Use the time you have wisely." He clapped his arm over my shoulder, and I gripped his fingers.

A moment later, he disappeared, and the maroon stars streaked the heavens.

I ambled back into the camp, rubbing my hand over the bandage.

I'd known this was coming.

I'd known this was what would happen.

But I'd spent my entire life avoiding it, and my mind had apparently gotten into the habit because, now that it felt like a reality, my soul seemed to sink into my feet.

Hyacinth looked back over his shoulder and jumped up, his robe ruffling with the motion. He met me and bowed his head towards me. "What's wrong?" His gaze shifted to the bandage, and he gasped. "What happened?"

Tears bit at my eyes. "Can I not talk about it right now?"

"You don't have to," he whispered and pressed a kiss to my cheek.

"Could we..." I scanned the empty world around us, the dark outline of trees shuddering in a breeze in the distance. I licked my lips. "Could we stay together tonight? We're nowhere near a city. Just our party is here. No one outside will see."

"Of course." His brow furrowed. "Are you sure something isn't wrong?"

"It's nothing to worry about for now," I said, gripping his hand.

I couldn't bring myself to share with him. Not yet.

But I needed to be with him.

Already time ripped away from us, fate snagging Hyacinth from my fingers before I could properly grip him.

And all I wanted was to hold him next to me and pretend I could do that for eternity.

Even if it was another lie that I allowed myself to believe.

9

Epiphany

Temi looked out the side of her eyes at me as I brought a blanket and tucked it over her. She clenched her fingers into the fabric, pushing it down as she leaned against the fallen log she rested against. "Thanks."

"Try not to sound so grateful," I said as I sat beside her.

She rolled her eyes. "I'm sorry. I'm just tired of everyone fussing over me."

Valerian strode over, handing her a mug and her scowl deepened. "I'm not thirsty anymore."

He dropped into the grass beside me. "You lost a great deal of blood. You need more liquid than you probably realize."

Guards exited the woods, mist swirling with their motion from the fog that had settled around us. They raised several dead squirrels in our direction. "Fresh meat for tonight."

Valerian bobbed his head at them. "Good. I think another few nights of rest, and we can get back on the road again."

"We probably don't need a few more nights." Temi slid the bandage down her arm, revealing the thin line of a scar.

I gasped. "That's amazing. You've healed so quickly."

"Yes, well, if my run-in with Hera accomplished anything, it confirmed that I'm a deity."

Valerian kicked his legs out in front of him, crossing his ankles, his boots getting lost in long grasses. "If you need to test that again, let one of us stab you instead, okay?"

Temi frowned at him. "Would you?"

"Well, if the alternative is you facing a vindictive goddess and stumbling around in the woods alone, slowly bleeding out... yes. As a friend, I'd be happy to."

Temi bowed her head. "Thank you for everything you did."

"Don't worry about it."

I grabbed his arm, and his eyes met mine. For a second, we both froze, the world fading around us. But then I cleared my throat. "You were amazing, Val. You saved her life."

"Except I couldn't die," Temi deadpanned.

I side-eyed her. "Well, we didn't know that at the moment, and you certainly seemed to be dying."

"I'm sorry," Temi said. "And I really appreciate it, Valerian. Whether or not I could die, it was terrifying. Having you there made it less so."

He reached across me and patted her hand. "Anytime another deity needs me present to bleed out on my favorite tunic and unnecessarily help, just call for me."

She huffed a laugh and picked up her mug, taking a drink.

Valerian jumped up and dusted his hands off. "Well, I need to go tend to the horses before the sun sets."

He ambled off, and I sighed, leaning back against my arms. Temi huddled into herself. "He's a good one."

"Yeah"—I bowed my head—"he is."

She took another swallow and rested her cup against her knee.

"I've been thinking," I said.

"About?"

"Telling Valerian how I feel."

Temi nodded.

"I've…" My hand trembled, and I tangled it in the patch of weeds on the ground. "Well, I've considered telling him on this trip."

Temi's eyebrows shot up. "Really?"

"You think it's a terrible idea?"

"Not terrible."

I kicked my foot out, and dandelion seeds puffed out in the air. In the distance, the guards started a fire that glowed through the mist, lighting it up like a veil. "You getting injured scared me. It made me realize that life is short, you know?" I huffed a laugh. "Well, I guess maybe it's not for you, actually."

"I remember… how it felt. I always knew how brief my lifespan would be compared to Apollo's. So, I understand."

"I thought, possibly I could say something to him and we'd have a chance to… I don't know… figure out where we stood before my family got involved."

She nodded. "I can see that."

"But you think it's stupid."

"No. Not stupid. Brave, maybe." She bit her lip. "I hate to be a pessimist, but if it doesn't go well? It might make the trip awkward."

"I guess I'll be like you then."

I bumped into her uninjured shoulder.

"What do you mean?"

"Well, we're both asking questions we might not like the answers to. But we can't do anything but ask and see what happens, right?"

She drew in a breath and then leaned her head in against mine. "That's true, Pip."

I reached out and snagged her fingers, and she gave my hand a squeeze.

That night Valerian stepped away, a towel tucked under his arm, and walked down the path that led to the river. I turned towards Temi. "I should speak to him now while he's alone."

She sat before the fire, the apricot color of the flames dancing over her skin. Her features tensed for a moment, but she nodded. "I'll make a distraction. Go into our tent and leave out under the back when the guards are busy."

"Thanks, Temi."

She smirked. "What are friends for?"

"Besides unhelpfully not-saving your life?"

She chuckled. "Go, before you lose too much time."

I hugged her and then slipped into the tent. A moment later, Temi's voice carried to me with a note of panic to it. "Theos, did you see that?"

"What, my lady?"

"On the edge of the woods there. I think I heard something."

The crunch of multiple feet shuffling over dry leaves trailed out, and I lifted the back of the tent and pushed under it and creeped around the side. Most of the guards had joined Theos at the boundary of the forest, the few remaining at the site had their eyes trained on them. I tiptoed across the clearing and eased onto the path.

A breath whooshed out of me when I made it beyond the lantern lights, and I continued walking until I reached the end where a waterfall roared, mist rushing up like a shroud of pastel blue over the stones that peppered the river. Valerian stood at the edge, running a towel through his hair, his bare feet sinking into the mud, a loose pair of pants hanging low on his hips. Droplets of water dripped over the muscles of his chest.

"Valerian," I said as I stepped into the clearing.

His face snapped up. "Epiphany." He cleared his throat and reached out to a tree limb, snagging his tunic from it and jerking it on. Moisture bled through the fabric, causing it to cling to his form. "What… what are you doing out here?"

"I'm sorry to interrupt you."

He pulled at his hair with the towel. "You don't have a guard with you?"

"Temi helped me sneak away."

He released an uneasy chuckle. "I still can't decide if she's a good influence or not."

I grinned but stepped in closer to him, the hush of the falls echoing around. "I asked her to help me because I needed to speak with you alone."

His body stilled, his eyes—shadowed so that they appeared navy in the darkening light—widened. I trembled, my heart racing, and reached out for his hand. His fingers stiffened at my touch, and I bowed my head. "Valerian, I'm—"

"Pip, don't," he whispered.

I lifted my gaze to meet his again. "I must." A muscle in his jaw ticked. Some bird cooed, and I breathed in with the sound. "I'm in love with you."

His mouth dropped, and he shook his head. "Epiphany… no."

I released his hand. "You don't feel the same."

His arm scrambled forward, his fingers lacing into mine again. "It's not that. It's…" He gestured with his free hand towards the water that glistened lilac as if the river could explain everything.

"Are you..." I swallowed. The murk of the riverbed sank into the charcoal shadows of night, and my voice dropped to a whisper alongside it. "Are you not attracted to me?"

"Epiphany," he gasped. He drew in closer, and his eyes raked over me. A chill ran from the top of my head to the base of my toes, swirling along with the curves of my body, making me intimately aware of every inch of my flesh. Valerian's voice barely rose over the noise of the rushing water. "You're, by far, the most beautiful woman I've ever met. And you must know I feel the same as you. I thought" —he hesitated, his eyelashes fluttering against his cheeks— "we've both felt the same way for a long time but said nothing because we knew…"

"We knew what?"

His shoulders dropped, the mist enveloping around him, his eyes reflecting the starlight. "That I'm not good enough for you."

I grabbed his free hand, curling my fingers into his. "That isn't true. Where it matters, you're wonderful. Your integrity, your kindness." I stepped in closer. "A judgment of someone's worth should be based on their character. With that parameter, you're the best person I know. And I'm tired of being in love with you from the sidelines. Don't you feel the same?"

He bowed his head, and his face dipped into shadows. An outline of a leaf fluttered in the breeze behind him. "Of course, I do."

"Then let's stop pretending. Let's"—I whispered my free fingers over his arm, and his muscles stiffened—"be together."

Val froze for several heartbeats before loosening my

hands and turning towards the river, his ankles getting lost in long grasses. "I'm sorry. I can't."

"You can't?"

He shook his head. "I can't disrespect your family like that. Or, more importantly, disrespect you in that manner."

My lips trembled, and words stuck on my tongue, sinking to the pit of my stomach. When they finally rose, they came with heat. "So, you love me but not enough to face the hardships our relationship might cause?"

He shifted back towards me, and the wind rippled his tunic against him. He brushed his knuckles over my cheek, and I shivered. "Oh, Pip." His fingers trailed down my neck and glided along my collar bone before he dropped his hand. "It's just the opposite. I love you too much to burden you with sullying your reputation with mine."

"It wouldn't be a burden to me."

He released a heavy breath. "I don't mean this disrespectfully, but you've always had an elevated status. You don't know what it means to bear a poor reputation."

"But, Val—"

He raised my hand and kissed the tips of my fingers, causing me to freeze. Crickets chirped, their songs overtaking the roaring water. His voice came thick with feeling. "You're a princess, Epiphany. You deserve to be treated with every honor. And I certainly won't be the one to tear that down. I love you far too much to do that to you. Can you understand?"

Hot tears welled up in my eyes and spilled along my cheeks. "And I love you too much to continue pretending to just be friends." I drew back from him, freeing my hands. "If you believe nothing more will come of us, then I'm done."

"Epiphany, please."

"No." My voice shook, but I lifted my chin. "Decide,

Val. Face the world with me, and we'll make it work. Or let me go altogether."

The night had grown dark, and his features lay swallowed in evening shadows. He remained quiet for so long I wondered if he heard me, but then he finally spoke, his form sinking. "I guess it will have to be the latter."

"Fine." I snapped the word out and turned back to the path, my feet thudding against the dirt as twiggy vines whipped against my ankles, cutting them.

"Epiphany, wait!"

I kept my gaze ahead, ducking branches, my heart racing. My chest trembled as sobs racked through me. A branch popped out, hitting my cheek. It stung, and something warm dripped down my face. It might have been blood or just more tears. I wiped my sleeve over it and continued running.

Gods, I was an idiot. I'd been in love with Valerian for as long as I could remember. And now it was all for nothing. I'd lose what we had. My heart thundered with so much hurt that I sucked in air over my teeth to ease it, but it didn't help.

I ran into the tent site, guards lifting their faces up and gaping at me. But I ignored them, flying into my tent and falling against my bedroll, sobs racking my body.

Temi dropped a folio she held and leaned down beside me. "Epiphany?"

"He said"—I choked on the words—"no."

"Oh." She whispered the word like a coo and wrapped her arms around me tight. "I'm so sorry."

I heaved another cry into the rough cotton of my pillowcase. Temi rested her chin against my shoulder and smoothed her hand over my hair.

I wept until my chest and throat hurt and my cheeks puffed miserably. It felt like eternity had passed, a hundred nights of stars and moons and disappointments. Candle-light flickered our shadows onto the wall of the tent. Temi whispered, "Do you want to talk about it?"

"What is there to talk about? The man I'm in love with turned me down. And you were right. I shouldn't have approached him at the beginning of the trip like this."

She clenched her fingers into my shoulders. "No. You were brave. He's an asshole."

I sighed. "He's not. He doesn't want my reputation to suffer by being in a relationship with him."

Temi remained quiet for a moment, her sandalwood smell permeating everything. She huffed. "Fine. I won't call him names. But I will wish him hardships." I gasped, but she continued, "May he always get the finicky horse. May his bread always be stale. May he step in every puddle that crosses his path."

I laughed. "Stop, Temi, that's terrible."

She chuckled, and the warmth of her breath tickled my neck. "I am sorry, though." She paused, and her voice took on a brightness again. "Do you know what the worst part of this happening on this trip is?"

"Umm"—I groaned—"the fact that we have to spend the next few months with him every single day, and it's going to be extremely awkward and even more heart-breaking for me?"

"Nope."

I rolled over to where I could face her. "What is it then?"

"There's no cake to be had."

I froze for a moment before laughing through another sob. "Oh, my gods, you're right. What was I thinking?"

"You were thinking he'd be smart and say yes."

I sunk down into the blankets. "Well, he didn't, and now I have a broken heart and no comfort food."

"You're practically a walking tragedy."

"I am." I chuckled the words out and twined my fingers with hers. For several moments we remained quiet, our eyes directed at the tent's peak where the candle swirled a circular band of gold about. I squeezed her hand. "Thank you, Temi."

"Always," she answered without breaking her gaze.

10

Hyacinth

The carriage bumped along an uneven road that led to a smaller city of the kingdom. Lilac mountains undulated like rippling silk in the distance, the air taking on a bite to it. Our group trotted ahead, the horses' hooves clattering against the road in rhythm. Apollo scowled and pulled his plain gray coat out, looping his arms through the sleeves.

"Glad to have that now, aren't you?" I said.

He groaned but nestled down farther into the thick lining of it. He'd remained quiet since the previous night and hadn't brought up whatever occurred that disturbed him so much. His arm had healed already, but something seemed to weigh on his soul. I readjusted the reins.

"Why don't you wrap them around your hand, so you don't have to keep adjusting them?" Apollo said.

I chuckled. "That'd be a good way to break your hand."

He chewed his lip, and that quiet, insecure expression hovered over him again. "Do you wish you were riding horses like Delon and Len?" He gestured towards them where they trotted ahead, their laughter punctuating the air with clouds of their breath.

"No." I dropped my free fingers onto Apollo's thigh. "I like horseback riding fine, but I'm happiest to sit beside you here."

He nodded, quieting again. His eyes drifted to the scrubs of fir trees that peppered the horizon, but he laced his fingers into mine. I squeezed his palm, a sweeping desire to push whatever weighed on him away filling me.

"Would you tell me now what happened last night?"

He sighed, his shoulders dropping. "Ares visited."

My muscles tensed. "For what purpose?"

Apollo turned towards me and tucked his chin on my shoulder. "Don't worry. It was for my sake. Nothing related to war... yet."

"Yet?"

"My father isn't oblivious, Cyn. He knows something is happening. I think currently he's focused on Jupiter."

The carriage hit a dip in the road, and it jostled us, causing Apollo to sway away from me. "What did Ares have to say to you, then?"

Apollo's veil glimmered, gold shimmering through before his features settled. "Just the usual. He wanted to warn me and remind me of who I am."

A god.

A son of Zeus.

Who had to ascend soon.

"Hopefully we can stall some of that," I said.

His expression tightened, but he bobbed his head.

I parted my lips to speak, but Apollo jerked his fingers free of mine and withdrew his veil. The silver light of him shimmered around me, like we shared it.

"We aren't in the city yet," I said, my hand aching with the absence of his touch.

"We're close enough to be seen. I may not like to lie." He winced. "But I know when it's time to play a part."

I sighed. Yes, yes, he did.

Once we made it into the city and marched through the streets, we went through the temple ceremony, blessing Zeus. It took every inch of my years of training as a prince to do so with decorum as my mind buzzed around Zeus' treatment of Apollo and how he pressured him to ascend. I didn't know what it was like to have a wicked father who you despised. But Apollo would spend eternity with him if he didn't fall. And I wasn't sure how long we had. I liked to think we had my lifetime at least, but between my mortality, the upcoming war, and his looming ascension, it felt as though time eroded like wet sugar and the more we grasped at it, the quicker we ushered it along.

We returned outside the temple to speak with a crowd who gathered around, strands of their hair rippling on a cool breeze.

"Citizens," I began, my voice booming off the sides of buildings as Apollo, with his straight posture and glowing eyes, stood at my side. "Thank you for hosting us today and for your gracious reception. We are honored to have Apollo, son of Zeus, aligning with our country to bring consideration from the gods to our—"

"You whore yourself to gods at the expense of your citizens," a man in the back of the crowd yelled.

Guards shifted towards him, people scrambling out of their way. They snagged his arms, but he continued yelling. "Some of us can't pay taxes as it is, and now you demand higher offerings to Zeus. You're a disgrace of a leader."

A guard drew a sword, but I thrusted my hand into the air. "Stop." Wide eyes lifted to me from the crowd. I cleared my throat. "I wish to speak with this man."

The guards hustled him away from the gathered

people and herded him forward towards Apollo and me. "Not here," I said to the guard flanking me. "Where can we purchase a meal? Somewhere private where we can talk?"

The guard frowned but nodded. Fifteen minutes later, we sat in a public dining house that stretched empty, the fire of the candle on the table in front of us dancing, its reflection weaving over the gritty wood.

The man, who had a mop of unruly walnut hair and large brown eyes, dropped into the seat across from Apollo and me. He pulled his hat off and swallowed, his throat bobbing.

"We haven't properly met yet. I'm Hyacinth."

"Cineas," he said, his gaze lowered, his lip trembling over the word.

I gestured to Apollo who grinned as the proprietor set plates of food before us, the dishes clattering against the table. "And this is Apollo. Now"—I leaned back against my chair, crossing my fingers across my stomach while Apollo poured several glugs of wine into his goblet before tearing off a piece of pie and popping it into his mouth—"I wish to hear more of what you have to say."

"Your Highness," Cineas whispered, "if you plan to punish me, certainly it would be easier to move forward with it."

"I'll tell you something that Apollo"—I nudged him and he frowned at me before taking another bite—"told me not too long ago."

"And what was that?"

"He said, 'If I wished to kill you, you'd already be dead'." I paused, letting that hang in the air.

"That's taken out of context," Apollo said, licking his fingers.

Cineas stared at him. Apparently, a god eagerly digging

into food was more distracting than potential punishment from a prince.

"The point I'm making"—I grabbed the bottle of wine and poured Cineas a glass—"is that if I wished for you to receive a punishment or worse, it would be done. When I say I'm here to listen to you, that's what I mean. If you have grievances you'd like for me to hear, now is the time."

Cineas took a swallow of his drink, his hand trembling as he set the goblet down. His eyes darted to the guards, who watched him with dark expressions. "I'm the eldest of my siblings, Your Highness. I'm not even twenty, but the only man in the house. Six younger brothers and sisters who cannot work yet and my mother all rely on me. How am I supposed to increase my dedication to Zeus?"

I tapped my fingers against the table. "And you thought publicly decrying a prince and a god was the method to deal with this? What happens to your family if you end up in jail, Cineas?"

His color paled. "They would lose their home, Your Highness."

I nodded. "Let me give you some advice. Reacting to a moment out of passion that can have a lifetime of repercussions for not only yourself but those around you as well is unwise." I turned to Apollo. "Anything you want to add?"

He popped another bite of food, swallowing before speaking. "This"—he gestured at the plate—"is absolutely delicious. What do you call it?"

Cineas' eyes darted between the two of us. "It's just a vegetable pie, my lord."

"A vegetable pie." Apollo stretched the words out, and then he elbowed me. "Your kingdom is lacking, Prince. You need to have these."

"This is my kingdom."

70

His eyebrows rose, and he shrugged. "Your city is lacking, then."

I clicked my tongue and turned to Cineas. "That said…" I side-eyed Apollo who ignored me. "It is a priority to me, to know the problems all of my citizens face. So, I'd be happy to discuss with you what hardships you, and others you're connected with, might endure with this new law. While I think making connections with the gods is wise, there has to be some compromise where we don't harm our residents. Do you not agree, Cineas?"

He trembled but bobbed his head.

Later, as we left the city, I turned to Apollo, who hunched down in the carriage seat, his veil tucked back in place. "How did you do that?"

"Do what?" he said.

"Figure out how to put him at ease?"

He shrugged. "For all his stupidity and blathering, he was really just scared. He needed to see us as humans, not evil overlords. And, as I told you, I know how to play a part."

I pulled the reins, steering the horses along a steep, rocky trail. Yes, he knew that. I chewed the inside of my cheek. Apollo, despite not liking to lie directly, was excellent at putting on a face, dipping secrets and worries down beneath his radiance when he wished to.

"You'll tell me when you're ready, won't you?" I whispered.

He sat up straighter, the hood of his coat fluttering in the breeze. "Tell you what?"

"Whatever you're not sharing from your meeting with Ares?"

He sucked in a breath and then released it, his shoulders dropping. "I will. Yes."

I studied him, longing to push for more.

But trust and respect were always what we'd had between us since we'd started our relationship. In our positions, they were essential. They were all we had, really.

"All right," I said, and I clicked my tongue, urging the horses farther into the cooling world.

11

Artemis

"I'm going hunting," I said as I snagged my bow and bundle of arrows. Epiphany had tucked into our tent, and a restlessness swept through me. Valerian brushed down a horse in the distance, his shoulders drooping as they had all day.

Theos jumped up from his seat at the fire, where he sat with other guards, and scrubbed his fingers into his dark hair. Twilight sparkled around him in a hazy plum. "I must insist that you do not."

I sighed. "Listen, this is our final day before we reach the port city and therefore probably my last chance to have some time in the woods before we are on a boat. And I cannot be the only person who'd like to have meat with dinner."

"But, if you run into another god?"

I tossed my braids back behind my shoulder. "I won't. Hera already made her point; there's no reason for her to return. And I can't let her intimidate me away from living my life over one incident."

Theos' lips snapped apart, and he swept his hand out.

Guilt that he'd allowed me to go alone before seemed to weigh on him. I held off a groan. "What if I take someone with me?"

He nodded. "That would be ideal, yes."

I ran my tongue over the back of my teeth, keeping my expression in place. "All right. Valerian!" I yelled. He raised an eyebrow. "Would you go hunting with me?"

He looked at me for a long moment before nodding.

A cool earthiness permeated the woods. Moss clambered along the roots of massive trees, and mist tangled with low bushes as evening light trickled through branches, illuminating the world in a foggy gray.

"I can't decide," Valerian said, his expression drawn, "if you brought me out here because you want to reprimand me or because you're hoping another goddess stumbles upon us and ends me."

"I brought you with me," I whispered, "because you're an excellent shot and I wanted fresh meat to eat. But if you'd like to talk about how you fucked up, I'm happy to listen."

He frowned and crossed his arms. "You know why I can't be with Epiphany."

I stopped walking and turned towards him. "And why is that?"

"I'm not good enough for her."

A bird fluttered at the volume of his voice, and I sighed. So much for hunting. "Look me in the face, Val, and tell me I'm a worthless bastard."

He startled, his eyes brightening. "Why would I do that?"

"Because"—I thrust my finger into his chest—"your story and mine are the same. My father is apparently a god, and he's never claimed me or been in my life. So, I'm like you," I hissed, "a bastard, rejected by her father. And with the way you're acting, that must mean I have no value."

"That's... It's..." He gave his head a shake. "That's a different scenario altogether."

"Is it, actually? Or could it be that you give grace to others you won't extend for yourself? I'd argue it's the latter. But I'm not good at pep talks, so that's all you get from me. I advise you to pull your shit together before you spend your life regretting the choices you made because of someone else's actions you had no control over. But really, it's up to you what you do with it. Now, could we be quiet, so we can actually attempt to not alert every animal within five miles of our presence?"

He blinked several times, hesitating like he might speak, but then he gave his head another shake. "Of course."

We crunched forward over dry leaves, but Valerian sighed, and I turned towards him. "What is it?"

"It's nothing. Let's hunt."

I gripped his arm. "It's going to be all right."

He studied me, the emerald color of his irises sparkling against the shadows of the woods. "Here I'd thought you hated me."

I rolled my eyes. "If I hated you, I wouldn't waste my time on you. If I tell you how it really is, you can know I care about you."

"With that in mind, I'm feeling deeply cared for."

I huffed a laugh. "Good. Now, could we hunt?"

He nodded, and we pushed farther into the forest. We returned with several rabbits, but misery still hung on Valerian like a coat. That entire night as we ate dinner, Epiphany spoke with me but never even shifted her gaze in his direction, despite many sad glances he sent her way.

It prickled at me so much that the next morning, as

Epiphany and I trotted alongside each other, I brought it up. "Valerian is pitiful."

Epiphany looked out from under her long lashes at me, her lip pursed in a pout. "Are you taking his side now?"

I groaned. "I don't like there being sides."

"I can't just go on pretending," she said, swaying along with her horse. "I've spent years—gods—a decade doing that. It's too... awkward... to keep faking it. I'm in love with him." Her eyes welled with tears. "But all he sees me as is a princess." Her voice took a hard turn. "That's all anyone sees me as."

"Not me."

She offered me a small, sad smile. "That's true. And you've made me realize that I'm more than what everyone else tells me I should be. Even my family doesn't see me. Having the last couple of days to think about it, I've realized that the only person who knows who I am is me. Maybe they've known me since birth and share the same blood as me. But that doesn't make them the ultimate authority on me. Only I can define who I am. You know?"

I remained silent for a moment, allowing the clip of the horses' hooves to fill the silence. "Yeah, I guess so."

"Oh." Her cheeks took on a touch of color. "I didn't mean that about you."

"No, but you made a good point. We get to pick what we do with our lives. You're right."

She nodded. "Anyway, I would have liked for something to come of me and Val, but if he can't see me as anything more than a princess, then so be it. I'll define my own life. I can figure out happiness on my own as well. But I'm never going to let who I was born as hold me back from being true to myself again."

"That makes sense," I said, and then we fell into another silence that allowed my thoughts to weave their way through me. Well, Epiphany made some valid points. Maybe finding out who my father was didn't define who I was. Clouds swept across the sky, cloaking the road in shadows for a moment before whisking away again. I swallowed. My father wasn't just a standard issue person, though. He was a god. So, perhaps that was different. After all, my connection to him already brought the wrath of Hera upon my head.

Uneasy thoughts clattered around within me as we continued forward. Valerian kept shifting his gaze towards Epiphany. She never even looked his way.

12

Apollo

Snow fluttered through the air, catching in my hair and melting against my cheeks. I would tell Hyacinth what news Ares had brought as soon as we left the Palace of the Four Winds. I didn't want to distract him before then. Some part of me liked how he could see past the surface of me, though. No one had ever known me like that before. It warmed me even more than the sun fizzling through my veins, lighting me up.

And then the feeling crashed back down.

Because I remembered.

What I needed to tell him.

I'd have to leave him by spring.

Less than six months.

I suppose I could still visit him… some. Much of that depended on how this war may go, anyhow. Who knew what could happen to all the gods under Zeus' power if we defeated my father? Myself included. If Jupiter took the spark of Olympus, he could kill us all and might exercise that. And it wouldn't matter if Zeus found out our treachery and killed us both, anyway. The future stretched out so uncertain and fragile; it was as though we grasped at a rope that frayed with each passing second.

I reached across the carriage seat and curled my fingers around Hyacinth's. He tightened his grip on my hand, like he could push steadiness through that touch.

And it worked. Where I was all chaotic energy, a sun burning its way to its conclusion, Hyacinth was the steady rhythm of the seasons. The warm reminder that though winter may chill and darken the world for the moment, the sunshine of spring waited around the corner.

We trundled over a hill, the horses' feet sinking into snow and jumping it up, creating miniature blizzards with their motion. In the distance, a sharp-pointed castle, glimmering in demure colors of blue and gray, huddled behind wisping ivory winds. The Palace of the Four Winds. I swallowed and pulled my hand back.

Hyacinth frowned and leaned into me. "A week. We'll be here no longer than that."

I nodded.

But my spirit sank.

A week of the limited time we had left together, and we'd spend it here.

And that's exactly why I couldn't tell him. He wouldn't focus on the task he needed to accomplish if I did. I couldn't burden him with that knowledge yet. Instead, it sat alone, a lump of ice in my heart.

After stable hands ushered the horses into a barn, we made our way inside the palace through stretching crystal doors. An iciness permeated the air, leaving my cheeks and nose cold. The foyer held tall ivory walls and an enormous chandelier composed of delicate glass pieces that sparkled silver reflections on the floor.

"Ah," Notus said, walking in with Zephyrus and Boreas shadowing him. Half a dozen hounds followed them, and they clambered around their feet, tails batting against the polished floor, tongues lolling as they panted. "Our honored guests. We are so grateful to have you with us, Prince Hyacinth and Lord Apollo." He grinned, stretching out the golden flesh of his cheeks, his gray eyes sparkling. He bobbed his head towards Delon and Len as well. "When we received your letter, it was quite the surprise. But a happy one, isn't that right, brothers?"

Boreas, who had ivory, crepey skin and ice-blue eyes, gave a sharp nod. But Zephyrus fluttered out his wings, a cruel smile spreading over his face. "Oh, yes," he said, gaze pinned on me. "We're delighted to act as hosts."

Notus frowned at Zephyrus' tone, but Hyacinth stepped forward, shaking Notus' hand. "We appreciate the hospitality."

"Well, on that note, please join us for lunch." Notus gestured towards the door, and they ambled through it, the group following. Zephyrus strode up to me, his mouth taking a hard turn. "Last time I saw you, your face looked like a storm cloud. Did you get tired of Daddy beating you around?"

I clenched my teeth. "And last I saw you, Zeus still hadn't invited you into the throne room. Did you get tired of being treated like a nymph?"

His wings shuddered, the feathers fluttering together, and I held back a grimace. Hyacinth had slept with this man. Zephyrus had touched him, known him in a way that felt sacred to me. My fingers curled, and I forced them to smooth out. "Do we intend to stand out here and stare at each other all day?"

Zephyrus glowered. "Please, follow me to the dining room."

I smirked and tossed my head, but a hot, swirling

feeling in me wanted nothing better than to punch him. I took a deep breath. "Thank you."

We ambled into a multi-story space made up of stone walls and a massive fireplace at the end that filled the chamber with the crackling and warmth of a fire. Notus gestured at the table and everyone found seats. Hyacinth chose the spot beside Zephyrus, who offered him a smile, his eyes lingering and skimming along Hyacinth's form.

Oh, gods, this was going to be a long ass week. I sank beside Delon as attendants strode in, placing food on plates, flat discs of bread, yams so dark their flesh almost shined garnet, and legs of chicken. I grimaced as an attendant set one on my plate. The smell hit me, causing bile to rise into the back of my throat.

Delon snatched it and dropped it on his dish. "I've got you."

I blew out a breath but inclined my head to him.

"So..." Boreas ripped into his bread, steam rising around his fingers. "We'd love to hear more about the purpose of your visit. Your letter was vague, Prince Hyacinth."

Hyacinth shrugged, the silk of his robe glimmering in the firelight, his hazel eyes sparkling. Gods, he was beautiful. My heart gave a painful lurch as I shifted my focus back towards my plate. "We're just hoping to strengthen connections," Hyacinth said, his voice a hum that curled up in my stomach. "I don't think my father or myself has interacted with any of the wind gods since the decade dedication."

Boreas nodded. "I believe that's true. How goes trade in the Southern regions?"

Hyacinth dove into discussing trade routes and politics and economics and other topics, throwing in several gracious comments about the importance of the wind for the country's prosperity. Zephyrus grinned as though he achieved the triumph of Niria single handedly and anger sparked in me. After the summer, I knew how hard Cyn and his father worked to ensure that success and the weather only played some small part. But Hyacinth kept Zephyrus' gaze each time, offering him undeserved smiles.

When dinner finally ended, attendants ushered me into a sitting room with another fireplace that washed the space in shades of apricot. The blue of evening pressed against the windowpanes, snow whipping by, darkening the space. And for just a moment I stood alone, cherishing the quiet. Hyacinth walked in and sidled up beside me, handing me a glass of wine. The jasmine scent of his swirled through the air, and I breathed it in, my fingers twitching, longing to reach out for his hand.

"Notus said to help ourselves"—he nodded to the drink—"so I'm taking him up on that."

I took a swallow and then hesitated for a long moment. "The wings are not intriguing."

Hyacinth's lips twitched, but he kept his gaze ahead on the storm outside. "Is that so?"

"Zephyrus is obnoxious."

"Are you feeling jealous, golden boy?"

I scoffed. "No. Because there's nothing to be jealous of." Hyacinth hummed his response, his mouth pinching at a smile. The fire crackled beyond us, and I ran my thumb along the bumpy spine of my glass.

"Apollo?" Hyacinth whispered, his voice feather-gentle. "Hmm?"

"You know…" He paused and that v-shaped dimple formed between his brows as he drew in a long breath. "You mean… so much to me. This with Zephyrus is just a game. You know that, don't you?"

I sighed. "Yes. I do."

Hyacinth fiddled with a ring on his hand and then shifted towards me. "By the way, I wrote a poem for you… in your folio."

My lips parted. "When?"

"Last night. While you were asleep." He grinned. "Does it bother you that I got into your bag?"

I considered that. "If it was anyone else, it would. But no. Anything of mine is yours."

Hyacinth smiled again, the most beautiful expression in the world. "Save it to read when you need a reminder of how I feel about you."

My heart picked up at his words, sending a spark of warmth into my stomach. Sometimes the depth of my feelings for him would rush over me like that, stealing my breath.

"Hyacinth," Zephyrus called as he walked in with Notus at his side. "I hope you'll join us for a drink or two." He winked. "Or maybe more, if I'm at all convincing."

Hyacinth released a quiet sigh, his shoulders firming, and bobbed his head to me before walking across the room, joining them. Zephyrus shifted towards him, leaning in closer, his posture taking on a possessive angle. My fingers curled into my palm until my nails bit into my flesh, and I took a long drink of my wine.

It was a game. That's all. I could make it through the week.

Hyacinth laughed at something Zephyrus said, the hazel of his eyes sparkling honey-gold in the firelight.

I scowled and tossed my goblet back again, swallowing the last of my drink. That was unfortunate.

Boreas ambled over, joining me, his bushy eyebrows inching up his forehead. "So, tell me, Apollo, how does the Golden One fare?"

I shrugged. If there was anyone I didn't want to think

about more than Zephyrus, it was probably Zeus. "He's as well as he ever is, I suppose."

Boreas studied me for a moment, his wings stretching and trembling the fabric of his ivory coat, which brushed against the floor. "I hear rumors that once you ascend, he will hold power over all the elements."

"That's the funny thing about rumors." A nymph with sage eyes walked up, offering more wine. I held out my goblet, and she refilled it. "They are often variations on the truth."

Boreas tapped his finger against his glass and took a sip. "Do you not intend to ascend? That's another rumor I've heard."

"You seem well informed."

"You know how gossip carries on the wind."

A hound ran in, skittering its claws over the stone floor before curling up at Boreas' feet. He bent and scruffed his fingers over its head. I needed to be careful about what I said. Hyacinth wanted us to get information about where the wind gods and their connections might fall in a war between Jupiter and Zeus. But I didn't want to give away everything I knew in case they fell on the wrong side of things. "Well," I said, "perhaps I wonder what benefit my father would find in me ascending when he already has such vast holdings?"

"Your words belie your reputation as a devoted son."

I laughed. "If that's my reputation, it surprises me."

"Does it?"

"Mmm." I finished the second glass of wine, the liquid warming my blood. "I've scarcely devoted myself to Zeus. In fact, he sent me to spend time with Prince Hyacinth"—I gestured to him where he stood listening to Zephyrus, who had taken a step closer—"hoping his devotion and obedience would rub off on me."

Boreas nodded. "And has it?"

I sucked in air over my teeth. "I'm not sure. But I can say one thing I've gained from the visit."

"And that is?"

"A new perspective or two."

The dog yawned and curled up, laying on Boreas' feet, wrinkling the hem of his coat. "What might those be?"

I shrugged again, like the words had no actual weight, as though they fluttered out onto the air like petals on a breeze, fluttering away and already forgotten. "Hyacinth is a man of change. He's mortal and doesn't perceive the world from an eternal mindset. He sees an issue—something that doesn't sit quite right—and he moves to alter it. I have to say, I respect that."

Boreas crossed his arms, the lines around his eyes deepening. "And is there something that doesn't sit right with you?"

"Many things, Boreas. But"—I offered a grin, all playfulness and teasing—"I'm young. What do I know?"

Boreas hummed, his wings pulling in tighter. "I'm unsure. I've often found the younger generations see the world in a fresh manner."

I smiled again, like I didn't catch the subtext of our conversation. Zephyrus grazed his hand along Hyacinth's arm. The expression washed from my face, and my heart thundered. I could deal with Hyacinth leading him forward for information, but Zephyrus touching him was another thing.

Hyacinth chuckled but stepped back, sliding his fingers over his lapels as if he needed to smooth out his impeccable outfit.

"Our mortal prince is a rather attractive young man, is he not?" Boreas said.

I sucked in a breath and cleared my features. But it was

too late. Boreas' eyes twinkled as he studied me, and I sighed, trying to shift the conversation. "He's damn aware of it too, I assure you."

"Well, as you said"—he bobbed his head to Hyacinth —"he's a mortal walking amongst gods. It likely makes him conscious of how limited his time is. I hope"—he bent and patted the dog's side, and the creature jumped up, stretching and yawning before ambling on—"he seizes the day he has." Boreas nodded at me and then walked out of the room.

Mortal.

I'd never hated a word as much.

And Hyacinth didn't know yet.

How little time we really had.

Hyacinth shifted his eyes to me, for just a moment, half a heartbeat, but his gaze said everything. Feelings swelled and thundered through me. I couldn't stay in there for another minute and watch Zephyrus eye him like a hunter marking a deer. I handed my goblet off to the nearest attendant and strode out of the room.

13

Epiphany

The sun sank into the sea, and I leaned onto the rails of the boat we had paid for passage on. Hair fluttered free from my braid and whipped out ahead of me, but I didn't bother to tuck it back. The warmth of the air kissed over my skin and I closed my eyes, breathing in the ocean's saltiness.

One of the horses nickered, and I shifted in their direction. Valerian had tied their leads along the other end of the boat, and he stood by them, his hand resting on Meadow's shoulder, but his eyes, the welling emerald color of them, trained on me. And so much sadness swept over their surface I couldn't breathe for a moment.

I turned back towards the rocking waves again. I couldn't face him. I could barely think of him without wanting to burst into tears. Temi leaned down beside me, her muscular shoulders bare in the sleeveless tunic she'd donned. "The captain says we should be there in a few hours."

I swallowed back the last of my sadness. I'd been caught up in my drama too much. Temi deserved a better friend who was more focused on her. This trip was big for her, and I didn't want my issues impeding that. "Good. How are you feeling about it?"

She shrugged, her eyes reflecting the rippling highlights of the water. "About the same." She pulled in closer to me, her arm grazing my dress. "And how about you?"

I bit my lip. "The same also, I guess."

She nodded. Words died between us, but it was a comfort to stand with a friend as we faced the uncertainty of the future together. I leaned against her shoulder, and she dropped her head against mine. The sun slipped its way into the sea, painting the water in shimmering oranges before disappearing.

Darkness had fallen, and stars glinted in the sky by the time the boat docked. The torches and lamps the crew lit illuminated the boundaries of a jungle where tangling leaves clambered together, sharp edges of palm trees chittered in the breeze, and a short stretch of sand sat gleaming ivory beneath the moon.

Sailors lowered the gangplank down to the empty stretching walkways of the port and Valerian led two horses forward towards it, but they tossed their heads, the whites of their eyes showing. They pulled against the leads and whinnied. Valerian frowned. "There's something on the shore that's disturbing them."

Temi's brow furrowed, and she nodded to Theos. "Should we go check it out?"

He cleared his throat. "Of course." He gestured to guards that followed alongside Temi and Theos down the gangplank. Some held torches, and the fire flickered over the sands, casting strange shadows that danced and drifted about as they stepped away from the walkway and onto the beach beyond it.

The world chirped and snapped and tittered. Temi

swept her gaze over the jungle slowly, her fingers resting on her knife belt.

"Are you certain"—Theos turned back towards the captain—"that this is the correct location?"

The captain bobbed his head. "Aye. The path to Sapphos' residence lies just beyond the palms there."

I swallowed and my gaze followed his pointed finger to where a dirt divot broke up all the scrambling wild shrubs. Theos frowned. "How often have you..."

A snarl cut off his words as a growl burst out over the chittering bugs of the forest. Leaves crackled, and a massive ebony cat jumped onto the sand. Half a dozen more snapped through the trees and landed next to him.

They growled again, and hair raised on my neck. "Shit," Valerian whispered beside me. The horses whinnied, jumping and pulling at the leads. Valerian turned to face them, but my gaze remained frozen on Temi, who stepped back towards the ship in front of the guards.

One cat leapt forward and Temi whipped a blade out, catching it in the shoulder.

It yowled and then a clear light glimmered over it and it transformed. A man crouched in its place, the blade sunk deep into the tan muscle of his shoulder. "Fuck. That hurts like a bitch."

Another panther shifted into his human form, a hulking person with dark skin and golden irises, and he thrust his hands out towards Temi, who held another knife at the ready. "Let's talk."

Temi drew a second blade. "Who the hell are you?"

"We're the panthers of Dionysus, and we guard this land. I'm Atara." He narrowed his eyes. "Who are you, and why are you on Sapphos' island?"

"Fucking Zeus' wife," the other man said as he pulled the blade out. "Hades with tits."

"Troshon, enough," Atara said.

Troshon glowered. "How about you pull a fucking knife out of your shoulder and then give a lecture?" He wiggled the bloody blade around. "And damn, has she got a throwing arm on her. That went straight to the bone. It will probably take two days to heal properly."

Atara sighed and turned back towards Temi. "You didn't answer me. To what purpose are you here for?"

Temi frowned. "Maybe if you hadn't fucking attacked us before..."

The man bared his teeth, long ivory ones that dimpled his lips. The others behind him who had shifted forms drew weapons, and I tucked around the horses, running down the ship. "Pip," Valerian called. But I didn't turn back to him. I kept moving until I reached the guards and slipped beyond them, my feet sinking into the sand.

"Hello," I said in a breath. "I'm Princess Epiphany of the Kingdom of Niria. And this"—I gripped Temi's arm—"is Artemis, sister of Apollo, son of Zeus. We're here to speak with Sappho, hoping she may have answers for us. We don't intend to come aggressively."

Temi side-eyed me, her nose wrinkling, but she remained quiet.

Atara raised his hand, and the others drew back, lowering their weapons. "Why did you not announce your visit before coming?"

"We did," Temi growled. Atara's features tightened again.

I cleared my throat and squeezed my fingers into Temi's arm. Please, for the love of the gods, stop talking. "We sent a letter. Perhaps it was lost. I'm afraid we didn't wait for a reply as we have a limited amount of time."

Atara studied me for a moment. "Princess Epiphany, I

met your father and brother at the decade dedication. How do they fare?"

"They're well. Thank you."

He drew in a breath and scanned over the several dozen members of our group, Valerian, who still stood on the edge of the ship, his fingers tangled into the horses' leads, the captain and his crew that watched with crossed arms. "Glad to hear it," he said. "We will guide you to Sappho's residence and leave it to her. But"—he jerked his face towards Temi—"keep your weapons away."

"I'll carry a weapon if I damn well..." I clenched my nails into Temi's arm, and she winced.

"Thank you, Atara," I said. "We'll do that."

He frowned but bobbed his head and nodded in the path's direction. The other panthers shifted back into their animal form, their lithe bodies disappearing into the jungle. Except for Troshon, who had wrapped his shoulder with his shirt, leaving the muscles of his chest exposed. He grumbled curses under his breath but joined Atara.

"Our horses," I said. "We wish to bring them as well."

Atara hesitated again, his jaw shifting. "Very well. You may bring them. We have stables that can accommodate them if you stay."

Valerian's shoulders dropped and he led the mares to the gangplank. They eased down, but their ears pressed back against their heads. He cooed and murmured words against them as he urged them down. And his voice, so close, so tender, made my stomach ache. But I shifted towards Temi and joined her on the path.

She scowled as she ducked under a palm frond and stepped onto the trail. The darkness of the jungle swallowed us. "I could have handled them."

"Really?" I asked. "Because I was trying to decide if

you intended to get us killed or chased away, so you didn't have to face the answers we came for."

She blew out a breath that covered the sound of some chirping frog for a moment. "They started with aggression."

"And you planned to finish it, obviously."

"I would have if I'd had to."

"Thankfully"—I stumbled over a vine and braced myself against her arm—"it didn't come to that."

Her expression eased, the warm light of the torches washing over her skin. "No, because we have a diplomat with us."

My cheeks flushed. "I'm not that at all."

"That's what I saw just now."

I bit my lip, uncertain of how to respond. But at that moment we turned a corner in the path and Atara gestured ahead to a large building with a straw-thatched roof, illuminated by hundreds of torches. "Welcome to the residence of Sappho."

14

Artemis

Atara led the group around a covered walkway. Trellises that walled off sections of it bloomed with ivory flowers that perfumed the air. Epiphany tucked in closer to me, and I grasped her arm into mine.

Atara stopped at an entrance flanked by two guards, whispering to one, who disappeared inside. The door opening allowed a golden splash of light and enthusiastic music to trail out and pool around us. A moment later, a woman stepped through the entry. She had a head of dark curls clasped in various places with gold fasteners and beads. Her tan skin shimmered like glitter in the torchlight, her gauzy dress draping over her form and skimming like a puddle at her sandaled feet. "Now, who do we have here?"

Atara gestured to us. "This is Artemis, sister of Apollo and Princess Epiphany of Niria."

Sappho took us in, her eyes grazing along our forms. "I've heard you injured one of my guards."

"I wouldn't have done so if he hadn't threatened to attack us first."

Sappho kept her gaze on me for a moment before

bursting into a laugh. "Just so. I have to say, I love a woman who can handle herself." She shifted to Atara. "And how is Troshon?"

"Pissy, but he'll live."

"Good. Tell him I'll make it up to him."

Atara bobbed his head and turned, exiting down the long walkway.

"So, you wonder if you're a goddess?"

I sucked in a breath. "How do you know that?"

She skimmed her eyes over me. "Consider it a guess, sister of Apollo. I bet you love being referred to by that."

I didn't reply but couldn't help the frown that pressed into my face.

She laughed. "Just so. Now, you two must join me for dinner." Sappho grinned like a cat who'd cornered a group of mice.

An evening breeze off the ocean swept through the trellises, and Epiphany shivered beside me. I firmed my stance. "We'd love to, but we have one other person who will join us."

She cocked an eyebrow. "A servant?"

"No," I said. "He's a friend."

A muscle in her jaw jumped, but she nodded again. "Very well." She gestured to a guard. "When you retrieve your friend, return here, and Esson will lead you into the dining room. And"—another grin slashed across Sappho's mouth—"I hope you brought your appetites."

I sighed as she returned into the house and pulled Epiphany with me. "Come on," I whispered. "Let's get Val."

Epiphany shuddered. "I don't feel good about this place."

"Me either. Which is part of the reason I want us to stay together." We clambered across a lawn and into the stables, a weathered stone building that didn't hold the grandeur of the barns at Epiphany's palace.

Valerian swung himself out of a stall and gestured to one of our guards, who led a mare farther into the barn. "No. She needs to be by Meadow. She's had an anxious disposition on this trip. Let's put her beside another horse that might calm her."

"Valerian," I said.

He turned around and brushed his hands through his hair, his gaze darting to Epiphany, who bowed her head. Valerian studied her for a moment, his eyes shimmering, before he shifted back to me. "Yes?"

"Come to dinner with us."

His mouth dropped. "I... I can't. The horses... and..." He cleared his throat. "I have nothing to wear."

"Don't you have one of your good uniforms?"

"Well." He scraped his fingers over his jaw. "I do."

"Great. Wear that. Leave the insignias off."

He sighed again but then nodded, his gaze catching on Epiphany, who hadn't lifted her face. "All right. Give me a moment to instruct the men on what else to do here and let me change."

Twenty minutes later, the three of us strode back to the house and allowed the guard to usher us into a large hall decorated with shimmering gold silks and tiled marble flooring. Esson gestured into a space where the sharp sounds of flutes trailed from.

"Thank you," Epiphany said. And we stepped in.

The room held hundreds of silk fabrics in as many colors that laced across the ceiling and draped over the walls. A low table hugged the floor, and large cushions sat tucked beneath it. In the corner, musicians played and the pattering beat of a drum and bright notes of a stringed instrument blended together into a barrage of sounds that dominated the space. A warm, spicy smell permeated the air.

"Ah." Sappho stood at the head of the table, clapping her hands. "Our guests. Let me introduce you to my partner, Phaon." She gestured to a woman with auburn hair, bundled up under a headband, her skin sparkling, her large brown eyes trailing over us.

"Lovely to make your acquaintance," Epiphany said, curtsying, and I joined her.

"Please, find seats, so we can discuss what you have visited us for." Sappho draped back down on her cushion. Phaon leaned in against her, resting her head on her shoulder, and Sappho smirked, snatching a grape off a platter and feeding it to her.

Epiphany and I trailed to one side of the table, lowering onto large cushions and Valerian took a seat across from us, next to Sappho. She grinned again and leaned into him. "My, you are a beautiful specimen. Which of these ladies is your lover that dragged you in here like a cat bringing a bird to my feet?"

He coughed. "I... Well..."

I tapped my fingers against the table. "He's my friend. Thank you for inviting us to dinner. King Magnes' advisors have told me you may have answers to some of my questions."

Sappho clicked her tongue and wagged a finger at me. "No questions until I've properly fed and entertained you. No one visits Sappho's island without leaving with a story to tell." She smiled again, her eyes reflecting the candlelight.

Hair raised on the back of my neck, and something sunk down in my stomach. The king had said he trusted this woman. I understood his hesitance now. Everything about her implied she knew things she wasn't sharing.

There was little I liked less than manipulative people. And her reputation was not stellar. Maybe it wasn't fair to jump to conclusions, but something about her made me hesitate. And my intuition rarely led me astray.

But I settled into my seat though every muscle in my body tensed and the weight of my knives pressed against my leg. King Magnes felt comfortable enough with Sappho to let Epiphany come along. He didn't expect her to harm us seriously, or he never would have agreed. He was protective of his children—overprotective, really. So, if he didn't think Sappho would poison us or have some other nefarious intent, I could sit and eat a meal. But I trusted this woman about as little as I esteemed a god.

Epiphany raised her chin. "Thank you for hosting us. You have a lovely home."

"That's kind of you, my dear." Sappho reached across Phaon and patted Epiphany's hand. She paused and frowned. "Oh, but not such a good time for you, is that right?"

Epiphany's brows furrowed. "What do you mean?"

"Are you not heartbroken? Or have I read you wrong?"

Epiphany blushed, and her lips gaped. Valerian's cheeks warmed also, and he swept his napkin off the table and into his lap. Sappho's eyes darted between the two of them. "I see," she said. "Hmm… you all have come bringing stories for me as well. This makes me so happy. A good story is what I live for. I'm a poet, after all. I thrive on the nectar of heartbreak and"—she pressed a kiss to Phaon's cheek, who smirked at her—"romance. On that note…" She clapped her hands three times. "Welcome to my island. Let me not hold up the pleasures for you any longer."

The music began again, a man pattered drums, another person strummed that bright, chirpy stringed-instrument. A woman rose to her feet and sang, her voice blending in with the melody. A flutist started as dozens of servants walked in, placing dishes on the table in front of us.

A servant placed a roasted pig in the center. Others set out breads, jams, three different soups that swirled their spicy smells out into the air, trays of vegetables and grilled fruits, two platters of seasoned rice.

"Did you know we were coming?" I asked.

Sappho laughed. "No, my dear. We are night creatures here." She tangled in against Phaon again. "You just arrived for our large meal of the day."

I nodded and accepted food dished out onto my plate as another servant poured wine into my glass that was so heady it perfumed the air. The room heated with all the bodies pressing into it, the music gaining volume.

"Now, sit back," Sappho said, "enjoy your dinner and some other pleasures I offer."

She clapped again, and servants blew out candles; the smoke joined the spicy, rich scents of the food. The melody picked up pace and dancers swept into the room. They wore shimmering ebony tops that exposed the skin of their décolleté and stomach. Jewels and beaded strands decorated the top and the belt around their hips where fabric split into different directions, the smooth flesh of their thighs peeking through.

The women swayed to the music, their arms tangling, flesh gliding together. They brushed their fingers over the other dancer's cheeks, allowing their hands to skim each other's forms, tease along their breasts, and tangle into the fabric at their hips.

Valerian's eyes widened, and he dropped his attention to his plate where he picked at his food. Epiphany stared, her face turning a deep crimson. I elbowed her, and she coughed before picking up her wineglass and taking a long swallow.

"So," I said over the music, shifting to Sappho, my voice coming dry. "Is this how you get people to tell you things? Distract them, so that they drink too much strong wine." I nodded at my glass. "And then shock them into letting their guards down?"

Sappho smirked and popped a grape into her mouth, chewing before answering me. "Ah, but you're a clever one. It won't work on you, then, will it?"

"It will not."

She snagged another bite and then draped back against Phaon, who tucked an arm around her. "I've found it to be extremely effective. Even with gods. Give them something to talk about—something unseemly for a human woman— and you'll be amazed at the secrets you hear."

"Is this how you got your reputation as a witch, or do you actually practice magic?"

The dancers continued their undulations, and Valerian bowed over his plate like he wished to sink into the floor and disappear. Sappho leaned in across the table, the bracelets along her arms clattering together. "Let me tell you something I've learned."

My heart picked up, and I draped my hand over my dress where my knives rested. "What's that?"

"Men"—she allowed the word to hang in the air for a moment—"who fear intelligent, capable women, call those they cannot control a 'witch' to dissuade others from seeing her light." She leaned back again, crossing her legs, the draping material of her dress puddling around her. "I've been called far worse. Witch is actually one of my favorite insults. Because it acknowledges two things about me."

"What's that?" I said before taking a swallow of my wine.

"That I have power and that people fear me."

"Is that what you wish, to be feared?"

She shrugged. "You tell me, Artemis." She curled her voice over my name like it held secrets in it. "She who desires to find out if she holds the powers of the gods. Do you wish to be feared?"

I pressed my lips together. "I wish to be respected."

The dancers' bracelets clattered as they moved, ringing in time with the music. "Are those not the same things in a way?" Sappho said.

"I don't think so."

She cocked up an eyebrow. "Interesting." She clapped her hands, and the women stopped dancing. "A beautiful job, my dears. That's enough for tonight, though. Wonderful. Weren't they wonderful, Phaon?"

Phaon bobbed her head. "Yes. Lovely as always."

Sappho snapped, and attendants lit the candles, illuminating the rippling silks of the room again. Valerian fiddled his hands over his meal, his eyes glued to his plate. Epiphany sighed and pressed her fingers into her cushion. Her shoulders hunched, and she weaved towards me.

"Are you all right?" I whispered.

"Yes, I'm f..." Her words blurred together, and she swayed, falling against me.

I wrapped my arms around her as shock coursed its way down me. "Epiphany?"

Valerian jumped out from his seat and ran behind the table, bowing beside us.

Sappho clicked her tongue. "She'll be fine. She just can't handle the wine because she's human."

I lifted my face. "You intentionally gave her a drink that you knew would harm her?"

"She isn't harmed. She's only asleep. However, it's confirmation for you."

"Of what?" I bit the words out through my teeth.

"That you're a half-deity." She drifted her eyes to Valerian, who swept Epiphany into his arms. "And what of you? Are you god-born as well?"

He frowned. "No. I'm just a servant. I know better than drinking on a job."

"Ah." She smirked. "A wise man and a compassionate one. I like you better and better." He glowered at her in such a manner that it was clear he did not share the sentiment, but she continued speaking as if nothing had happened. "Let me allow some attendants to show you to a suite."

"No, thank you," he said, his voice as cold as ice. "I plan to stay with the horses tonight, and I'll keep Epiphany near me and her guards."

"Very well, if that suits you."

Valerian bobbed his head, his jaw jumping, and strode out of the room with Epiphany in his arms, the silks rippling as he passed them. I jumped up to join him, but Sappho grabbed my arm. "No, let them go, my dear. You know he'll look after her. You and I have things to discuss. We've already confirmed"—she nodded to my wine glass —"that you're a deity. I'm sorry to tell you I don't have the knowledge of who your father is, but"—her eyebrows inched up her forehead—"I know someone who will."

My eyes darted to the passageway Valerian had disappeared with Pip to. I hesitated, but then shifted back towards Sappho. "Who?"

15

Hyacinth

Zephyrus stepped into the dining hall, grazing his hand over the olive skin of his jaw and then brushing his sandy hair back. He sat in the chair beside me, his wings fluttering as if he stretched them out for the first time that morning. Apollo lifted his golden eyes up to us. They pinched for a moment before he dropped them to his plate.

At the head of the table, Boreas took a sip from his glass, his attention caught in a letter in his hand. Notus ripped up pieces of meat from his platter and tossed them to the hounds that scattered around his chair, their tails wagging. A mumble of conversation hummed through the air from farther down the room where Delon and Len sat together.

"Do you still ride?" Zephyrus said.

I startled. "What?"

He grinned above his goblet. "Horses. Are you still as proficient as you used to be?"

"I don't ride as frequently as I once did, but I imagine I could still keep up."

He smiled, his eyes lingering on me. My throat tightened, and I forced the muscles on my face to stay relaxed. He leaned in towards me—too close—his breath trailing over my cheek. Goosebumps rose on my skin and my stomach twisted with discomfort. Apollo had lifted his face to us again, but I refused to meet his gaze, afraid too much would show in my expression.

Every moment I spent with Zephyrus made me long for Apollo. How I wished to lie in the safety and surety of his arms, knowing I could be fully myself and loved for that. How I longed to have his eyes skim over me as a wicked grin creeped over his lips. To press my mouth to his and swallow that smirk, run my tongue over his, shudder as sparks snapped between us with our touches.

"Well?" Zephyrus said, raising his eyebrows.

I cleared my throat. "Forgive me. I missed what you asked."

"Would you want to take a few horses out today, explore the mountains?"

I took a taste of my drink to stall my words. Because no, no, I did not. I set the glass down with a clink. "Yes, I'd love to."

His smile widened, and he leaned in towards me, his crystal blue eyes glimmering, his wings behind him stretching out, curling in my direction, and I fought a shudder as his feathers traced over my shoulder.

Notus smacked his hands together, the hounds at his feet whining. "Sorry, loves, I'm all out." He turned in our direction. "Now, where are you two headed off to?"

Zephyrus frowned. "I thought I might take Hyacinth to see the peaks. They're beautiful this time of year."

Notus nodded. "Mmm, that they are. It's a shame Euros isn't here. He adores a good morning out on horses." He laughed. "But autumn is his season, is it not?"

"It is, that," Zephyrus said dryly, annoyance coloring

the pitch of his words as if Notus had reminded him the two of us weren't alone together.

"Horseback riding never intrigued me, but wouldn't anyone else like to go with them?" Notus raised his voice, gesturing to the table. "How about your companions, Prince Hyacinth? Hmm?"

Delon cleared his throat and looked at me. I gave the subtlest shake of my head, and he shrugged. "Len and I already made plans today. Inside plans that don't involve snow." He scowled.

"Well, there's that." Notus draped against his chair and rested his chin on his fingers. "And, you, Lord Apollo?"

Apollo's lips parted, but I spoke before him. "I'm afraid Apollo doesn't ride horses."

Zephyrus grinned again, shifting towards Apollo. "What a shame. The high deities always believe they're above simple, human pleasures, but truly they miss out."

Apollo cleared his throat and rose. "I think I'll spend the morning in your library, if you don't mind, Boreas."

Boreas raised his face. "Of course, of course. Make yourself at home."

Apollo nodded to him, and then his golden eyes met mine for just a moment, a heartbeat, but they held so much. Hurt seemed to ache through them. I pulled in a deep breath and had to brace myself against running after him. He knew this was all for show, didn't he? I didn't invite him because me getting Zephyrus alone was part of the plan. And he was aware of that. But a queasiness settled in my gut as he rose from his seat.

His shoulders dropped as he disappeared past one of the cavernous doors. My heart ached and tore at me. I needed to figure out a way to get Zephyrus to talk, and fast, so we could leave.

Zephyrus scoffed. "Apollo is such a moody character.

It's a wonder you could tolerate being around him all summer. Was it a terrible punishment?"

I readjusted in my seat, my gaze longing to shift to the hall Apollo had walked down. I allowed a gentle smile to trail over my lips and leaned in towards Zephyrus. "A punishment is exactly how I described it when I first received word from Zeus. But we can't deny him, can we?"

Zephyrus' expression darkened. "No. I suppose not." He stood and fluttered his wings out, stretching them wide, so they reached the length of four chairs. That was compensating if I'd ever seen it. "Are you ready to go?"

I bobbed my head and followed him. Once we made it out of the stables and had trotted on horseback far past the palace, reaching a peak where sun peppered through fog, casting the world in a wash of peach that reflected in shimmering colors over the snowbanks, we dismounted and stood together, taking in the valley below. My cheeks ached from the crispness of the weather, but warmth from the ride still pumped through my blood as my breath laced into the morning air. "The horses," I said, "are remarkable. They handle the cold so well."

"Ah." Zephyrus grinned. "Yes, we created them for the ice and winds. One of my particular projects." He bobbed towards the horse. "Their fur is thicker, keeping them warm for longer, and they have stockier bodies that help conserve heat as well."

"Clever of you."

Zephyrus leaned against a tree that stretched leafless limbs against the crisp blues of the sky. Clouds shifted, and rays of the sun draped across the frigid world below us. Apollo would one day control that light and warmth. And that's what he was to me. Comfort. Home. The opposite of Zephyrus, with his overly handsy manners and icy smiles.

I longed for Apollo to my marrow.

And it was stupid.

Because we had a few more days with the wind gods, and we could be together again.

But somehow a fleeting sense peppered through me, like I'd never truly grasp ahold of him. It would always be snatches of him I'd have, like trying to capture sunshine itself in a jar.

"Apollo is enamored with you," Zephyrus said, those icy eyes darting to me. He scanned along my form, and my stomach soured. "Not that I can blame him."

Panic flitted through me—worry that my feelings for Apollo had been too obvious—but I shrugged, attempting to keep my mannerisms relaxed. "I'll take that as a compliment."

Zephyrus stepped in closer to me, his breath warming my cheek, and my heart jumped around in my throat. "Hyacinth, you must know what a beautiful man you are. I suppose I'm not the only god you've ever been with."

He traced a thumb down the sleeve of my jacket, and I struggled to remain still and not recoil from his touch. Being with him was one of the highest mistakes I'd ever made. I had been young—too young, really—and he'd focused only on his own pleasures and desires. At the time, it had seemed exciting to have his attention. Now that I'd known the gratification of reciprocal lovers and had experienced the attentions of Apollo with his fingers eager to please, his eyes gleaming with my happiness reflected in them, I realized Zephyrus was the worst kind of man.

I laughed, and it echoed against the mountain ringing back, false even to my ears. "It feels like you want me to account for my partners. That wouldn't be terribly gentlemanly of me, would it?"

Zephyrus clicked his tongue. "Who said anything about being a gentleman?"

The horses shook their heads, their manes tossing in the wind. "I certainly don't find myself in the bed of every god I meet, if that's what you're asking."

He smiled again, leaning in closer to me, and dread sunk into the pit of my stomach. I cleared my throat. "I heard that you married. How does Flora fair?"

Zephyrus studied me for a moment before shrugging. "She's fine enough, I suppose."

I pulled in closer to him though my skin crawled. "And does she take issue with whom you invite to your bed?"

"I can't say I've asked her opinion on that. For one thing, I doubt it would bode well for marital felicity."

I chuckled and ducked my head.

"What would you do in my place?" he whispered. "If you were married but ran across someone so beautiful you couldn't take your eyes off of him?"

I met those eyes, the intensity of his gaze, and forced another serene expression on my face. "Well..." I shrugged and stepped away. "I can't say I would ever marry a woman." I smirked. "So, I probably don't know."

He huffed a laugh that clouded the sky like mist. "My marriage is political. Not romantic."

"Political?"

He hesitated, shifting back towards the sun that stretched out over the valley. It was as though Apollo watched us, and I fidgeted my fingers inside my gloves. Gods, if he was hearing this conversation, he would not like it. I'm not sure if he'd be more hurt or angry, but either way, it ached through me again. Perhaps this entire idea had been a mistake.

Zephyrus sighed. "Not every god wishes to patronize Zeus and his continuous greed for power and hunger, you know."

A zip of energy slid down my back because this was

exactly the information we needed, and I took a slow breath to pace my words before speaking. "I hear not every human does either."

Zephyrus side-eyed me. "An interesting opinion for someone who has allied himself with Zeus' son."

"Certainly, you're aware Zeus and Apollo do not get along."

He huffed a laugh, with no humor. "That's the damned truth, isn't it?" His expression soured as if he'd taken a bite of something putrid.

I tapped my thumb across the lapel of my coat. "But, who would lead if Zeus didn't? I suppose there must be a hierarchy of leadership, even amongst the gods?"

Zephyrus' fingers curled up into his palms. "Who deemed Zeus the ruler, though? He grabbed it for himself. Killed others to achieve it, in fact. Is that leadership you might admire?"

"Well, it's not how I intend to lead."

"No." His voice softened, and he pulled in closer to me, trailing his gloved hand over my jaw. "You're a far kinder leader than that, aren't you?"

I smirked but took a step back, my boots sinking in snow. "I suppose a god might see that as a character flaw?"

"I doubt I could see any flaws in you."

He drew in closer again, his lips parting, and I laughed, turning towards my horse. "Let's see if I can best you in returning to the palace, and we'll discover if that remains true?"

Zephyrus frowned at me for a moment, as if he saw past the veneer and bright smile. Then he clicked his tongue. "These horses are my creations, Prince Hyacinth. You won't have a chance."

"We'll have to find out."

He shook his head but climbed onto his mount, urging

it into a gallop. I cleared my throat and rubbed my shoulder over my jaw where his fingers had trailed along my skin. Logically, I shouldn't have cut that conversation short. He was sharing exactly the information we came here for.

But I couldn't let him touch me. Beyond my personal revulsion, it felt like a betrayal to Apollo. I had to figure out some way to find out what plans he knew about, though. It sounded as though there were gods who wished to dissent from Zeus, and Zephyrus had connections with them. But I wasn't sure what cost that information might come at.

Another cringe ran down me, but I leaned in closer to the horse and took a deep breath. A few more days. I could manage it.

16

Epiphany

I took a deep breath and rolled over, rubbing my eyes. Morning light poured in wide, open windows, the sweet smell of hay filling the air. I didn't know where I was, and panic bubbled its way through my veins. My fingers pressed into the straw beneath me, and a horse nickered. I was in the stables somewhere. The last thing I remembered was the dinner with Sappho, the blaring music, the smoke, and feeling woozy.

"Epiphany." Valerian dropped to his knees beside me, dust jumping with his motion.

Despite the discomfort that had played out between us, seeing him was like a cool breeze on a blistering day, and my heart slowed. I lay on a pile of blankets on the ground in a stall. I sat up and peeled grass out of the ends of my curls. A horse snorted and shuffled somewhere in the distance. "Why am I here?"

"I'm sorry," Valerian whispered. "I didn't want to leave you alone after last night."

"What happened? Wait"—panic swelled within me like a wave again—"where's Temi?"

"She's fine. Sappho gave you a sleeping drug in your wine."

I gasped. "She did what?"

Valerian frowned. He had dark circles under his eyes, his beard holding a scruffy edge to it, his color wan. I wrinkled my fingers in the blanket I lay tangled in. "So, you brought me out here?"

"Yes. Again, I apologize if that's not what you would have wanted. I couldn't stand to leave you in her house."

I peeled the cover back. Underneath I wore only my cream shift, the thin fabric scarcely covering me. I clutched the blanket over me again. "Did you undress me?"

Valerian's skin blushed furiously, his nose turning a deep crimson. "No… no… of course not. Temi was here most of the night, and she did."

"Oh."

He coughed and looked over his shoulder. "I finally convinced her to lie down. She apparently has some goddess she's going to meet tonight that will know who her father is, so I told her to get a few hours of sleep."

I swallowed. "It doesn't look like you did."

"Well, one of us ought to." He scratched his jaw.

"Besides me, you mean?"

His emerald eyes shifted to me, a hint of a sparkle glittering across them, the corner of his lips turning up. And despite everything, the longing for him whipped through me. "At least someone carried that burden for us."

I fumbled over the blanket and stood, sweeping it around my shoulders. "You took care of me last night. Thank you."

"Of course." He scanned over me. "Do you feel all right?"

"I do."

He frowned again but inclined his head. "I'll give you some privacy, then, if you'd like to get dressed."

I nodded, and he strode down the stable, calling to someone and pulling the door shut. My dress from the day before lay folded over the stall, and I pulled it on. Someone had tucked my bag into the corner, and I found my brush and tugged it through my tangled curls. When I finished, I stepped out into the bright sunshine of morning. Palm trees swayed in a breeze, the ocean shimmering in the distance.

Valerian stood between a couple of horses, combing down their backs. I walked up to him. "Val?"

He lifted his face and so much swelled in his eyes, so much he wouldn't speak. And gods, was I tired of that between us. It was like a music we'd learned to play so well we couldn't find another tune. But I was ready to learn one. "Do you know what I thought when I saw you first thing this morning?"

"What?"

I swallowed, and my curls, loose and still slightly tangled, wisped out on a breeze. "I thought about how much I missed you. How I'm tired of avoiding you."

His shoulders slumped. "I'm tired of being avoided."

I stepped in closer, our arms brushing. The earthy smell of the horses enveloped us. "I've been thinking a lot about what you said."

He studied me for a moment but didn't speak.

"You stayed up all night for my sake." It wasn't a question, and he didn't deny it, though his already piercing gaze intensified. "You've told me you love me. So…" My voice grew fierce. "Make me understand why you don't want to be with me."

He blinked rapidly and thrust his hand out towards the

blue skies. "It's not about what I want. My life has never been about that, Pip. It's about doing what's right."

A breath puffed past my lips. Why was everything in my life always wrong? My desires and hopes and dreams never lined up with the path everyone else wanted me on. I'd always felt like with Valerian I could truly be myself and share the desires of my heart. He didn't see them as foolish or hopeless.

Except for this.

"Why am I wrong?" I said, my voice catching.

He pulled in closer, the sweet grassy smell of the stable filling the air between us like the ghost of touches we both denied each other. "You're not, at all. But you're a princess. And I am not appropriate for you."

Heat flushed my cheeks and filled my chest, and I wanted to scream and stomp my foot and kick something. I was a princess. Of course. My entire life, I had felt trapped by something I had no decision about, something that was decided for me from the moment of my birth. I hadn't even taken a breath yet, and I had already been labeled as royalty, untouchable, different. And no one understood.

If I complained, most people would see me as ungrateful. What did I have to complain about, after all? I had a loving family, money, and security. But I was also trapped in a box that seemed to grow smaller by the minute, and it was going to suffocate the life out of me, I was sure of it.

I eased in closer, and my fingers grazed over the back of his hand. His muscles tensed, but he didn't pull away. "Valerian, surely you understand what it's like to be born to something you have no control over. To be labeled one way and for your destiny to be set without you getting a say in it."

A muscle in his jaw ticked.

"I want the right to choose my destiny. And if I could pick anything in it, I would choose you."

"Pip," he said, his voice trailing off.

My heart pounded so hard against my chest it vibrated, my arms trembling, but I leaned in, brushing my nose against his. He released a shaky breath, and I pulled in closer and let my lips whisper over his.

His fingers swept out, trailing along my arm, and my stomach heated, warmer than the humidity of the day hovering around us. His mouth captured mine, his coarse thumb grazing my cheek. After a long moment, I drew back, letting my nose linger against his.

"Epiphany," he whispered against my lips, his voice gritty. "You're killing me."

I snagged his hand and squeezed it. "Then stop fighting this and be with me."

"I'm not sure it's that easy."

"Of course, it isn't easy." I tightened my grip. "But I think it would be worth it."

Valerian didn't speak, but he grazed his thumb over my knuckles, the rough edges of his touch sending spirals of warmth through my body.

"Well?" I said.

"I…" The horses shuffled as guards strode up, and I dropped Valerian's hand.

"Your Highness," the guard said, inclining his head as he walked past.

I shifted back to Valerian. "I want you to seriously think about what I've said. Maybe it wasn't fair that I put you on the spot before. But we're on this trip." I gestured to the island, the dark clouds puffing together far beyond the shore. "You have time to consider it—consider us. So, do that, please. Will you?"

Valerian released a breath that dropped his shoulder. "I

will."

"All right. I'm going to see if I can find Temi."

I turned, but his voice, a whisper of a sound, paused me. "Pip?"

"Yeah?"

His brows furrowed, and he swallowed hard. "I'm glad you're okay. I was worried... last night."

I hesitated for another moment. Love rippled from him like a current. And to know that, for it to sit in the air between us like a golden ray of the sun, present but untouchable, was going to break me. "Thank you, Val."

He bobbed his head, and I stepped out from behind the horses and over toward a group of guards. Theos jumped to his feet. "Can I help you, Your Highness?"

"Do you know where Temi's room is?"

He nodded.

"Would you take me to her?"

"Yes, Your Highness." He gestured to three others who joined us, and we ambled towards the house, which sat demure and bland in the sunlight, all brown, grainy siding topped with a thatched roof. It looked nothing like the foreboding and magical villa it had appeared under the moonlight and in the glow of a hundred torches. We reached a doorway where Sappho's sentries bobbed their heads to us before we stepped into a hall.

Silks lined the walls, but in the light of day, it seemed empty and austere. The space stretched vacant of furnishings or other decorations. Morning sunshine splashed its way around, brightening the passage. Theos turned down another hall and stopped outside a doorway. I knocked.

"Who is it?"

"It's me," I said.

"Come in."

I inclined my head to Theos and then entered the

room, letting the door close behind me. Temi rose in the bed—the only piece of furniture in the suite. Her blankets fell with the motion and draped down over her lap. She pulled a silk scarf off her head, and her braids dropped against her shoulders with the gesture. "Epiphany," she breathed out my name. "You're okay."

She patted the space beside her, and I eased into it. "I'm fine. Though distract me quickly before I start to actually think about what happened last night. I'll be so embarrassed, I'll die."

Temi chuckled but pulled me into a hug. "Well, then, I'll tell you why I'm here instead of in the stables with you."

"Why's that?"

"Because Val was guarding you like a mother lioness. I think if I'd stayed another moment, we might have come to blows."

"You're kidding."

She smiled, the ivory of her teeth glinting in the sun. "Of course, I am. Well, about the fighting part. Not about Valerian acting like some sort of overprotective creature. I was stressing him out by being there."

I dropped my head back against the wall, and silk fabrics on it grazed over my neck. "It was foolish of me last night to drink that wine. I know better than that. Even with my father approving of me coming, I should have had my guard up."

Temi nodded and shifted towards the window where sunlight flooded its way in and landed in a bright puddle on the bed that warmed my legs.

"Val told me you have some goddess you're going to meet with that may have answers for you."

"Oh, so you're speaking to him again."

The feeling of his lips against mine swept through me,

and I scrunched my fingers into my dress. "Maybe. I don't know. You're getting off topic, though."

Temi shook her head, and her braids rattled over her shoulders. "Sappho has a connection that she swears has a method to find out who my father is, but she can only come at night."

"Why didn't you see her last night?"

Temi jerked towards me. "Are you serious? Sappho poisoned you, as far as I'm concerned. I spent the night with you, and fuck her."

The heat behind her words shocked me. "You're mad?"

"Are you kidding me? Yes. But,"—her voice lowered—"I guess, stupidly, I want answers badly enough that I'm still willing to stay here and find out."

I dropped my head against her shoulder. "It's not stupid. When will we meet this goddess?"

Her muscles tensed, and she didn't speak for a moment. "Actually, I'd rather you didn't come." I sat back up, but the expression she wore—all heavy eyes and down-turned lips—stalled my words. "Last night reminded me you're mortal. Humans have gotten hurt"—she swallowed hard and her voice came shaky—"killed, even, around Apollo and myself before. I don't want you to get mixed up in it any more than necessary."

I chewed the inside of my cheek, but what could I say? I'd already drank wine that could have poisoned me. She had a point. But everywhere I turned, walls trapped me in. And I was growing tired of it. "Would you tell me who the goddess is, at least?"

Temi fiddled her finger along the hem of the blanket which had missing stitches, the raw edge unfurling. "You know how it's rumored that Sappho is a witch?"

"Yeah?"

"Apparently the goddess we'll meet tonight is where that rumor came from."

"Do you think it will be dangerous?"

She sighed and stretched her legs out. "What about this trip hasn't been dangerous so far?"

I suppose she had a point there. I released a sigh as well but nestled against her shoulder again, and she curled up beside me. We both fell into silence, the weight of our thoughts pressing into the empty room until it felt almost unbearably full of unspoken things.

17

Apollo

The library at the front of the palace had massive curved windows that overlooked the side of the mountain. Standing up against them, it almost seemed like falling and my heart dropped into my stomach. I had considered opening the poetry folio in my bag and reading whatever Hyacinth had written in it. But I wanted to save it as he'd suggested. So instead, I stared out ahead at the drop of the cliffs. The fire crackled behind me, popping and spitting, but I almost felt the icy winds whipping across my skin, the snow-covered rocks sweeping towards me.

"A beautiful view, is it not?" Boreas said.

I jumped and turned around. "It is. Yes."

He cocked an eyebrow up but found an armchair in front of the fireplace and sat in it, dropping a basket onto a table while two of the hounds who had trailed with him into the room curled up by his feet. I chose a chair near him and lowered into it.

"Can I ask you something that is very curious to me?" he said.

"Of course."

"Tell me this. Why would a young god who is in love with a mortal stand back and say nothing to him?"

My mouth gaped. "I... that is..."

He raised his crystal eyes and smirked. "I see that I'm right. Zephyrus suspects your admiration of the prince as well. He's always been a jealous sort."

Oh, shit.

This was not the direction this should go.

I had gotten too caught up in my own troubles. But Hyacinth was counting on me. I couldn't mess this up. My interactions here had his welfare on the line, and that of his people. I had to smooth things out.

"Hyacinth's focus right now is on the wellbeing of his kingdom."

Boreas chuckled and grabbed a poker, placing a piece of bread on it and guiding it into the flames, the crust growing golden. "Is that so? And yet he is here, visiting with us, spending his morning horseback riding with Zephyrus." I winced. Watching the two of them leave earlier from a window had ached at me in a way I'd never experienced before. Every moment they remained gone made the discomfort grow. Boreas sighed. "What precisely does he believe we can do to help him with his kingdom?"

I swallowed and fidgeted my fingers together. "Well, as you said, gossip spreads on the wind."

"Hmm." Boreas pulled the toast back and blew on it. "That it does."

"It seems this may be the best place to visit if one wishes to hear news of changing fortunes or futures."

"I would think the best for that kind of inquiry would be the Fates." I cringed, and Boreas laughed. "So, you've met them?"

"Only once. It was enough."

He hummed a response and wiggled the poker. "Would

you like a toast?"

I shrugged. "Sure."

He popped another piece of bread onto it and handed the poker to me. He dipped his hand into the basket on his table, retrieving a jam jar, and he spread the glistening, auburn jelly over his slice. "I've always found the simple pleasures of life to be the best ones, don't you think?"

I twisted the iron in my hand. "I wish I could focus on them."

Boreas took a bite of his bread, chewing it slowly. A dog at his feet whined, and he ripped a corner off, tossing it to him. "I am not a man of high ambitions, Apollo. I don't approve of all these changes I hear about on the wind. And I suppose you coming here, rather than visiting your father—and with your human prince, at that—only confirms the gossip we keep hearing."

I pulled the toast back, blowing on it, but I struggled not to freeze. "And what gossip is that?"

He took another bite, his eyes fixed on me. My heart thundered, but I picked up the jam jar and spread some on my slice. "I've heard that Jupiter," he said, "is no longer a friend of Zeus'."

"I would think anyone describing themselves as a friend of my father's likely overstates the relationship, anyway."

Boreas nodded. "Too true. Zeus has always set his mind to his own benefit. But most of us have been wise enough through the ages to not cross him. What about you, Apollo?"

I let the toast rest on my fingers, the heat of it burning my flesh, and shrugged a shoulder. "I doubt anyone would use the word 'wise' to describe me."

He hummed a response and popped the last bite of bread into his mouth. He smacked his fingers together and rose. "A word of wisdom, then, from someone who, if not wise, at least has more life experience?"

"That is?"

"Letting your heart get involved"—he fixed me with a look—"will often impede your ambitions and plans. You should choose one or the other."

"Thankfully, as you said, Hyacinth doesn't appear interested in me."

He scratched behind the ear of a hound. "I did not say that though I believe Zephyrus thinks that. He's always been a fool." His voice lowered. "But an ambitious and vindictive fool. Keep that in mind."

"What ambitions does Zephyrus have?"

Boreas' expression broke, and he whistled, calling both of the dogs to his heels. "As I said, I don't get involved in such things. Ambitions are not for men like me. However, I will do this much for you. I'll host a dinner, and we can invite many of the connections that you and the prince are wishing to make." He nodded towards the fire that sputtered, sparks of flames clambering against the dark stone of the chimney. "Have as much toast as you'd like. It's a simple pleasure, but one I greatly adore. I'll leave you with your thoughts now."

I sank into the chair.

Damn it. Boreas had seen through our ruse. I wondered if he would tell Zephyrus that he suspected we were together. That would fuck any chance Cyn had of unearthing secrets. A selfish part of me wished that would happen. I was already over pretending to not care that Zephyrus hovered around Hyacinth like a fly. But we needed that information. This was a smart move. It's why Hyacinth was the decision maker of the two of us.

Zephyrus would have knowledge we didn't, though. He was—as Boreas had said—ambitious and well connected with many of the lower deities. But Boreas' expression had held a discomfort. Zephyrus must have ideas he didn't approve of. And that concerned me. He was only a wind god. He couldn't possibly plan to have ambitions against Zeus himself. That was a fool's errand if I'd ever heard one. But something disturbed Boreas about his plans. We needed to figure out what they were.

Those thoughts sunk into me throughout the day and even during dinner. The only thing that broke my focus on it was when Zephyrus kept touching Hyacinth, a finger over his knuckles, a hand grazing his arm.

The sun within me burned.

I rose from the dinner, bad feelings surging through me. Delon jumped up and threw an arm around me, leaning in and whispering. "Len and I plan to play a few rounds of cards tonight. Interested in joining us?"

I shifted towards him. "I guess I could be up for that."

"We're gambling."

"Even better."

He grinned and smacked my shoulder. "I knew I liked you. Meet us in the library in half an hour. I'm going to see if Cyn can get loose from"—he rolled his eyes—"the wind god."

"That seems unlikely," I said, and I couldn't hold back the way my voice sank.

"Well, I have to try, at least."

I nodded and headed down the halls to the library to wait. Len had already made it, and he bent over by a fireplace, stacking logs.

"Would you like help?" I asked.

He gestured to the wood.

In a short time, we had a roaring fire going, and a table dragged closer to it. Delon arrived, bringing not only a stack of well-worn cards but also several large bottles of spirits, his other hand clutching a group of glasses that clinked together.

"Any word on Cyn?" Len said.

"He doesn't think he'll make it."

I frowned and snatched up the cards Delon dealt to me.

"You look like you could use a drink." Delon lifted the glass in my direction. I nodded, and he smirked. "Excellent. I plan to take all of your money tonight."

"I'm a half-god. It takes a lot to get me drunk enough to play poorly."

"Then you are welcome to as much as you like." He grinned.

I huffed a laugh, the first non-miserable moment of the day. "Who starts?"

An hour later, the three of us had drained our glasses a sufficient number of times that my blood warmed with it and we all laughed heartily, the cards hitting the table with heavy smacks. "Ha," Delon crowed, smacking his fist down and dragging gold coins towards him. "My round again."

"Damn you," Len said.

Delon grinned. "I warned you both I planned to take your money bags to bed with me tonight."

The library door opened, and we all froze. Hyacinth stepped in, a floral-embroidered robe on, and he clicked the door back in place before walking over to us. Delon jumped up, clearing the seat next to mine, which Cyn eased into.

Delon took another swallow of his drink. "Didn't think you'd make it."

"Me either." Hyacinth groaned and dropped his head into his hands.

"Hope you have money on you if you want to play."

Hyacinth lifted his face, his brows drawing together.

"Are you serious?"

"Yup." Delon shuffled the cards as the fire crackled beyond him.

"I'm the crowned prince. You should assume I'm good for it."

"You could die before you return. I need my money tonight."

Hyacinth's mouth parted. "Hades' realm, it's nice to know that's the words of a friend."

"I'll cover him," I said with a chuckle. I turned to face Hyacinth, my heart pattering. He seemed so miserable, and it made me ache for him. "Delon is set on taking all of my gold, anyway. That will double his chances."

Delon laughed and sloshed out more drinks for us all, adding a fourth glass, but Hyacinth smiled, a gentle expression, like flower petals unfurling. He looked back over his shoulder and then leaned into me, pressing his lips to mine, combing his fingers into my hair. "I've missed you," he whispered.

I trailed my thumb along his jaw, every piece of me warming. "You seem stressed."

"I am. Hera's lot. I'm ready to get the hell out of here. But"—he nodded towards the game—"this is a pleasant reprieve at least. Have you had any luck with Boreas or Notus?"

I snatched up my cards, arranging them. "Actually, Boreas intends to host a dinner on our behalf and invite some deities they know."

"That's good."

"And he said something to me today that made me think Zephyrus has plans in motion too, but he wouldn't reveal what those are."

Len dropped cards, and Delon snatched two up. Hyacinth frowned. "I get that feeling as well." He snaked his fingers over my leg, gripping my thigh. "I'll see if I can find out what it is."

I grazed my knuckles over his, and our eyes met.

"Yes," Delon crowed, dropping a winning hand onto the table.

"Fuck," I said.

"Oh, Cyn." Delon's smile stretched his cheeks out. "Please stay and distract Apollo all night."

I frowned at the cards as I threw my set down, but Hyacinth kept his gaze on me, his voice whisper-sweet. "Gladly."

Feelings whirled within me like fresh snow, all hope and unspoken promises. The door opened. Hyacinth snatched his hand back as Zephyrus strode across the carpets and paused at the table. "I heard there was a to-do in here tonight. Do you mind if I join?"

Hyacinth's posture curled inward, like he wilted. Delon's gaze flipped between the two of them but landed on Cyn, who gave him a subtle nod. Delon took another sip from his tumbler. "Do you have a money bag on you?"

Zephyrus laughed and pulled a leather purse out of his pocket.

"Then pull up a chair," Delon said.

Zephyrus grabbed one, placing it between me and Hyacinth.

Hyacinth's jaw tensed like he'd clamped his teeth down, but he lifted his drink. "To a good game."

Zephyrus accepted a glass for himself and clinked them together.

And I dropped my attention back to my hand. Well, the best five minutes of the week had passed. Time to shift my focus to the cards instead. But the laughter had died out, like a fire draped with water, only the sizzling smoke of a pleasant evening remaining.

18

Hyacinth

The formal dining room in the Palace of the Four Winds held hundreds of different beings who mingled together, glasses of wine in their hands they had carried from their abandoned seats after the dinner. Most of the deities in attendance lacked the glow of the high gods, their skins glimmering with a more subtle shine. A few other human city leaders peppered through the crowd.

And many of the gods in attendance were from Jupiter's court. Though not all. Which was interesting. I didn't realize how many of the low deities from Mt. Olympus intermingled with those from the west.

Silvanus—a slim man with a pinched expression who had sat by me at dinner, tightened his fingers around the stem of his glass. "The thing is, Prince Hyacinth, most deities are low deities, and they grow tired of the politics and upheaval that the high gods cause."

"I can appreciate that, on a smaller level, perhaps."

His sage eyes twinkled. "I imagine so. It's not so different, being a prince and being a god, is it?"

My gaze slipped over to Apollo, who stood glowing and

golden, a thick cloak draped over his shoulders. A tremendous smile dominated his features as he spoke with a group across the room. He seemed as at ease as a person could be. And it was the fakest I'd ever seen him. Perhaps Silvanus had a point that being a royal and being a god were more similar than one might think.

He continued speaking. "Wars happen, and for you, a city is burned down. For me,"—he swept his free hand up against the draping tunic he wore—"a forest is decimated. And in both situations, what did the creatures that live there do to deserve their fate?"

"Fate," another god said, stepping up beside us. He shimmered silver, his eyes glowing golden. A high god. "What an interesting topic."

Silvanus cleared his throat and lifted his goblet in the god's direction. "Janus. A pleasure." He bobbed his head to me and turned, absorbing into the press of bodies.

"You see, Prince Hyacinth, that's how many humans and gods alike react when fate comes for them. But not you." His eyes scanned over me for a minute as the hum and chatter of the crowd swept us up. "How interesting."

"Forgive me, I haven't made your acquaintance."

He didn't respond for a moment but scratched his fingers over his thick, curly beard. "Janus, god of transitions, the past, and the future."

"Do you see the future?" I said and only realized after the words came out that my voice sounded too eager.

He continued to stare at me without speaking, and a shiver slipped down my spine. I longed to shift towards Apollo. I suddenly wanted someone by my side—someone I could trust unhesitatingly. But I forced myself to keep my gaze off Apollo—as challenging as that was.

"I do," Janus finally answered. "But I don't disclose it,

not even to Jupiter himself, much to his unhappiness. Do you know why?"

I had a strong feeling I didn't wish to learn the answer to that, but I forced a congenial smile on. "Why?"

His eyes bore into mine. "Because most beings—even the resolute ones like yourself, Prince—could not bear to hear what all they will face on the path they walk along."

I couldn't help it at that point. I shifted towards Apollo, who already studied me, a note of concern in his expression. He gave me the slightest nod before turning back to his conversation. If he was aware I was uncomfortable, I must show too much. I stilled my muscles. "I suppose every path has it ruts."

Janus smiled, an eerie look on him. "A clever response. I think you believe that if it would change the outcome—if it would protect the people in your kingdom—you'd be willing to hear the tragedies stalking you."

My skin crawled, and I longed to leave the conversation, but he was right. "I would."

He chuckled then and took a swallow of his drink. "No. You only believe you would. It is too much to bear, the heartache of a lifetime all at once. Especially for a man who walks a particularly tragic path."

Dread snaked over me. Perhaps that was his aim. He wanted to throw me off. He didn't feel like a friend. "I suppose we have to make the best decisions we can and keep moving forward."

"Indeed. Your father certainly shares that perspective. He saw war coming for your kingdom and decided, if one must face down destruction and death, he might as well use the opportunity to remove your people from the tyranny of Zeus."

"How many other gods know about that?" I clenched my teeth together. Damn it. Janus had me continuing to blurt out things I didn't intend to. I looked over my shoulder, but no one else seemed to pay attention to our conversation as the attendees laughed and chatted, the glowing of the gods swirling through the room.

"Not many. My temple doors, you see," Janus said, "are only open when war is on the horizon."

I paused a moment before answering, not wanting to let my thoughts pour forth again. "And they're open now?"

"Oh, they've been open for several years, Prince Hyacinth. The major players are just finally realizing it." He lifted his glass towards me and walked away.

I took a deep breath, my robe shifting over my shoulders with the movement.

The conversation had left me rattled. Which was not helpful. I had already felt overwhelmed trying to decide who to speak with in the room and how much information to share. And I was wary of speaking to any of the high gods. Apollo told me they could see into the heart of mortals and past the ruse I played here. It was lucky that few high gods attended, probably due to earth sickness, an ailment the lower deities didn't share. I suppose it didn't matter with Janus as he saw everything. But he had given me nothing but puzzles and disquiet. My life would be tragic—how shocking for a prince in a kingdom heading up a war and involved in a relationship with a being who would far outlive him. And warfare was coming. I assumed those things and had seen the fear of my mortality reflected in Apollo's expression.

Apollo had left me in the summer to avoid that fate for me.

But I was caught up in this war between gods even before he got involved.

I gave my head a shake. Janus was just distracting me. Thinking about that wasn't helpful. I needed to seek someone who may have answers about who we could connect with. And I knew who that might be.

I took a sip of my wine, letting the tang of it sit on my tongue, and walked up to Zephyrus, who spoke with a goddess with curly, sable hair and bright green eyes. "Ah, Hyacinth," he said, pulling away from her. "Have you met Flora yet?"

Oh. His wife.

"I have not," I said, offering her my hand. "It's a pleasure to meet you."

She gave me a half-hearted smile and then skimmed her gaze down me, stopping on my outstretched palm but not accepting it. "The pleasure's mine, Prince Hyacinth." She flicked flaming eyes towards Zephyrus before bowing and turning, disappearing into the crowd.

I clenched my fingers around the stem of my glass. "I'm afraid I've offended your wife."

"Yes, well." He tossed his head to the side. "That is often the case when a woman meets her husband's past lover, is it not?"

I cleared my throat. "Even in a political marriage?"

"Things are usually more complicated than they seem, especially in politics, don't you think?" He took a swallow from his goblet and set it on a low table near him that held a vase full of dried flowers. "On that note," he whispered, "there's a topic I would like to discuss with you, but alone, perhaps?"

Alone.

I did not like that.

But that was likely the only circumstance he'd share the things I wished to find out.

"Of course," I said, but my heart pattered around. I trailed through the crowd behind him. Apollo laughed at something a nymph commented to him, his curls bouncing with the motion. How I longed to slip away with him instead.

He lifted his face to me again, for a heartbeat, and so much coursed between the two of us it stole my breath. I snapped my head forward and found Delon where he stood flirting with a woman in a long cream dress. Our eyes met, and I gave him a firm look. He nodded once and returned to his partner.

Zephyrus trailed down a hallway that sat in shadows and opened the door to an equally dark room. He stepped inside and lit an oil lamp that bounced light over his features, exaggerating them. "Before I get to the topic at hand, I heard an interesting rumor tonight that concerned me."

I turned towards the shelf where stacked scrolls sat interspersed with small statues of horses. "What's that?"

"That Apollo has vowed to Zeus to ascend by spring which will complete Zeus' control of the elements."

My breath caught, my heart aching. That couldn't be true. Apollo would have told me. Though there was something in his conversation with Ares he hadn't shared. But, no, he hadn't met with his father that night. And Zephyrus probably lied to me to try and spark jealousy or uncertainty in me. Relief flooded through me. That had to be it. Apollo would never keep something that major from me. I almost felt ridiculous for even entertaining the idea. I shrugged. "He can't deny his father. Zeus has the power to end the high gods."

Zephyrus released a weighted breath before responding. "Yes, that's true." He sounded disappointed. So, he was baiting me by making up lies to try and get me to react. I swallowed back every ounce of emotion and chastised myself for allowing him to make me doubt Apollo.

Zephyrus could say what he wanted, but he would not pull anything from me.

I turned around to face him where he leaned against the desk. "Your conversations with many of those in attendance tonight has surprised me."

"Is that right?"

He shrugged, the flame flickering over his wings, making the feathers appear as though they fluttered. "I thought I may have information that interests you. But one can't be too careful," he said darkly. "Zeus has spies everywhere."

This. This was what we traveled for. I swallowed back the excitement that wanted to peel through my voice and kept it even instead. "So I've heard."

Zephyrus' tone came heavy and charged with something that seemed to lace through the surrounding air. "Do you know much about the spark of Olympus?"

I stepped closer to a bookshelf, tracing my finger over the scrolls. "It's the source of the high god's powers, is it not?"

"Yes." Zephyrus frowned. "Zeus holds it, but it doesn't belong to Mt. Olympus."

I turned to face him where he leaned against the desk, his wings draping over the shining surface of it. "I have not heard that before," I said.

He shrugged. "Zeus has worked hard to keep it that way, I assure you. But the spark isn't the property of the most powerful god; it goes to the god who has exercised the most power."

I crossed my arms. "Isn't that the same thing?"

"No. Because another could take it. If they could overpower Zeus."

"Who could possibly do that, though?"

Zephyrus studied me, his face half lost to shadows.

"Surely you believe someone can, as you seem so eager"—he paused, his wings stretching out—"to form connections that stand against him yourself."

I fiddled my thumb against one of my rings. I felt a wariness in this conversation. Zephyrus was clearly not loyal to Zeus, but for whatever reason, that didn't make him feel like an ally. I couldn't discern if it was just our personal history and my dislike of him, or something else. "Who might take Zeus' place if he fell anyway, though?"

Zephyrus shrugged. "The Fates willing, not another high god."

"Why?"

He scoffed. "The high gods are all so removed from the mortal world, from human experience, they make terrible leaders."

I smoothed my robe out. "So, a low deity is who you have in mind. Someone like you, maybe?"

He smirked and pushed off the desk. "Maybe." He crossed the rug between us, sauntering, his feathers ruffling. He reached me, his arms brushing over mine, and my heart picked up again. "Perhaps," he whispered, drawing a finger across my shoulder, "it's not a bad idea, if you're looking to make connections, to start with me."

He pulled in even closer, and my skin ran cold, but I kept my voice light. "That was precisely my thinking when I decided for us to come here. I always knew you were ambitious."

I didn't always realize he was foolish, but that was rapidly becoming apparent if he thought he could take Zeus on and had revealed those ambitions so easily to me.

But he was foolish and well connected and generally liked, which he had shown with his connections with the crowd that evening.

That was a problem.

"That's one word to describe me." He leaned in close enough that his breath brushed my cheek. The door flickered with golden light, and I cleared my throat. He bent down, his gaze on my mouth.

A knock came. "Prince Hyacinth?"

Zephyrus frowned, his jaw jumping, but he pulled back and gestured to the door. I walked over, opening it. Delon stood in the hall. "Apologies, Your Highness, but Lord Boreas is looking for you. There's something he wishes to discuss with you."

"Of course. That's no problem."

I tossed an apologetic smile to Zephyrus, who nodded before I strode out into the hallway alongside Delon. Once we made it several doors down, I leaned in towards him and whispered, "It took you a fuck of a long time to come get me."

"Making sure you had a chance to get what you needed." He smirked. "Why? Are you finding the wings less intriguing now?"

"That's not... wait... where did you hear that from?"

He grinned. "It turns out Apollo is very honest when he drinks."

"Hades' realm." I blew out a breath and smoothed out my robe.

"Put your game face on," Delon said. "There's more than a few beings aware that you left."

"Thanks for your indulgent levels of compassion."

He rolled his eyes. "I already faked it in front of the feathered guy. You won't get me to kiss your ass like that again anytime soon, so be grateful."

I sighed. "Thank you for saving me."

He clapped my shoulder.

And we continued down the hall, back towards the party. But worries strung through me. Zephyrus' plans seemed bigger than I had imagined. And the way he had interacted with the hundreds of deities in attendance felt more of a show of his popularity, on his part, than any desire for me to make connections.

I had to find out what he had in motion, but the idea of being alone for another minute with him, of him touching me, sent chills of revulsion through my gut. The crawling sensation of that settled on me as we continued down the hall together.

19

Epiphany

I climbed a ladder up to where the ocean breeze whipped through open windows, and dropped in the hay beside Valerian. The stables differed from the ones at home, the walls a cool gray in the moonlight. But the space held a grassy sweetness that permeated the air that felt familiar.

"I thought I might find you up here," I said.

His gaze stretched ahead, his eyes lost in shadows. "We were never very good at unique hiding places."

"Our one spot always worked to avoid others." I tangled my fingers together in my lap. "We've never wished to hide from each other before."

An owl hooted, and Valerian turned towards the sound. "That's true," he whispered. "Has Temi left with Sappho?"

"Yes." I chewed the inside of my cheek. "I wish I could have gone. I'm tired of everyone treating me like I'm untouchable."

Valerian's eyebrows drew together, and he shifted closer to me, his dark hair gleaming in the spill of ivory light that trailed in. "Do I treat you that way?"

"Until recently, no. But since I told you how I feel, yes. It's like I don't get to decide things outside of what I was born as. As if it's a prison sentence I'm shackled to."

Valerian's jaw jumped, and he bowed his head.

"Have you considered what we discussed?"

His eyes caught a glint of light that reflected like water shimmering at night. "Epiphany," he whispered, as if the word and the meaning it held were too sacred to enunciate. "That's all I've thought about this entire trip. But... I can't... How am I supposed to...?"

I reached out for his hand, sliding my fingers between his rough ones. "I love you."

He winced, but his voice came steady. "I love you, too. I have for a very long time. But, feeling that way and acting on it have different repercussions."

I leaned in, my heart thundering like hooves galloping across an expanse and into a future I couldn't determine. I let my nose brush his, and he sucked in a breath. My lips feathered against his, so soft we barely touched. Valerian shivered, his fingers tangling into my hair, his mouth parting.

Kissing him again sent sparks flying through me. I wrapped my arm around his back and pulled him in tighter, deepening the kiss. When we peeled apart, I bowed my head into his shoulder. "Don't you want this?"

"Of course, I do. But..."

The hay crunched as I leaned towards him. A cool feeling slipped down my limbs like I stepped out on starlight, trusting magic to hold me aloft as I found my voice. "Can you stop thinking about what's right, for once, and just give in to what you want instead?"

He released a breath, and the warmth of it caressed my neck. His heartbeat thundered against me. He closed his eyes for a moment, wrinkles sweeping over his forehead. When he opened them, he met my gaze. "You're making it very difficult to try and do the right thing."

"Then don't."

Val studied me in such a way that he could have touched me and had less impact. Something in his gaze changed, and he reached out and brushed his thumb over my cheek and then pressed his mouth against mine. The kiss came rough and needing, unlike any touch we'd shared before. He gripped his fingers into my arm, pulling me against him until our heartbeats pounded together.

I didn't know what I was doing, but I knew Valerian. I knew the way his eyes crinkled when he laughed, the feel of his calloused hands in mine, how sweat beaded over his bare chest. Heat burned in my stomach, and I pushed him down.

His muscles tensed, his hands lingering by my side. I straddled my legs over him, and he swallowed, the sound like a stone hitting a well as it echoed against the rafters. I lowered my face to his again and kissed him. "Pip," he drew away from me, "we have to be careful."

"I'm so tired of being careful."

"I mean…" His fingers snagged mine, his other hand finding the dip in my lower back. "You could get pregnant if we go too far."

I laughed and let my fingers trail along his neck, trace over the sharp edges of his collarbone. "Val, women know how to prevent pregnancy. There are herbs you can take to keep that from happening."

His lips parted. "Are you taking those?"

"I am."

"So, you planned on something… like this… happening between us?"

I kissed the edge of his collarbone, and he shivered. "Maybe I hoped it would."

His chest rose against me with his breath. I rolled his shirt up, and he leaned forward, allowing me to peel it off of him. He fell back into the straw and then winced.

"What's wrong?"

"The hay." He chuckled. "It's kind of sharp." He shifted, sitting up, holding me in his lap. I brushed my hands over his broad shoulders, peeling bits of the grass off his skin. He lifted his chin and kissed me deeply, his arms tightening around me, as if his touch could make sense of us two, the way our lives intertwined like the braids of the crowns he'd always made me.

I drew back and trailed my fingers along the muscles of his chest. He trembled, tensing as I allowed my hands to slip down his form. How many times had I watched him shirtless and longed to feel his skin under mine? I lifted my dress up over my head and dropped it with a chuff that made bits of hay jump.

Valerian whispered his fingers along the flesh of my exposed midriff like he touched something priceless. "Gods Epiphany, you are beautiful."

My arms quivered, but I raised them and untied the band covering my breasts. The fabric drifted down into our laps, but neither of us shifted it. Valerian released a breath, his thumbs tracing up along my side. His hands shook, and I put one of mine over his to steady it. "Are you nervous?"

"Yes," he said.

The trembling in his muscles picked up, his gaze darting between my eyes and my bared body. I gasped. "Wait, have you never?"

Valerian's fingers froze. "No, I haven't."

"Oh." I fumbled for words, warmth sweeping up my cheeks. "I thought you had... I mean, Hyacinth and Delon and most of your friends... well..."

"Just because I'm their friend doesn't imply that I do everything they do."

"Oh," I said again. The word hung in the air, our bodies frozen aside from thundering hearts and shaky breaths.

"Have you?"

"No." I braced my hand against his chest. "I haven't. I just thought one of us would know what we're doing."

Valerian chuckled breathily. "I'm sorry to disappoint you."

"You haven't." I rested my forehead against his, and my nipples grazed his flesh, sending a flood of warmth through me again. "I shouldn't have assumed. But I thought that with you being Cyn's friend..."

Valerian scoffed. "Are you seriously going to tell me you think Cyn is the authority on how to pleasure a woman anyhow?"

I raised my face. For a moment we stared at each other, two shadows dipped in moonlight, unsure of our next move. Then we both burst into a laugh. My shoulders eased, and I kissed his jaw. "We'll figure it out, Val. We don't have to do what anyone else does. You know? We can just do whatever feels good to both of us, right?"

He nodded. "You'll tell me if anything doesn't feel good for you?"

"I will."

His mouth met mine again, and a new energy swept into his touch, like he'd been holding back. His hands grazed my flesh hungrily, and I moaned. "Here," he breathed. He freed one hand and smoothed out our discarded clothing. He rolled me over onto it. The hay still crunched against my skin, but then his body hovered over mine and I didn't care. I pulled him against me. He paused, though. "Stop me if there's anything you don't like."

"I will."

He nodded, and his flesh burned against me again. Stars winked in the ebony silk of the sky just outside the window. They sparkled as our fingers discovered the planes and curves of each other. I gasped and closed my eyes as our bodies joined.

Valerian froze, pulling up away from me. "I'm hurting you."

"Val." I cupped my hand against his cheek. "Please... I promised you I'd tell you if I wanted you to stop. And I will. But I don't want you to."

He swallowed and pressed a kiss to my collarbone, which sent a shiver down me. I clenched his shoulders and drew him to me. And our bodies joined again, the warmth of him coating me.

I clasped my hands into his flesh and breathed him in, felt the weight of his body against mine, quivered as his fingers traced over my flesh, his movements lingering whenever I whimpered.

Once sweat slaked both of us and we trembled from the pleasure of it, Val cried out, his face crumpling, and pressed his forehead into my shoulder. He tucked against me in the hay, his dark lashes fanned out over his cheeks. When my heart slowed, I shifted towards him, but his gaze already fixed on me, his lips pursed, his brow furrowed.

"What are you thinking right now?" I asked.

He parted his mouth to speak, but a door to the stable opened, a salty breeze trailing in with it. Stable hands spoke, their voices echoing around the space alongside the nickering of a horse.

"Shit," I whispered and sat up. Val peered over the side, and I peeked out behind him, attempting to stay in the shadows. The two men grabbed supplies off a shelf and headed towards the exit. I picked up my clothes and began pulling them back on. Valerian lifted my dress and brushed it out, smoothing the wrinkles, but it still looked thoroughly rumpled. I snagged it over my head. "Sorry. I should return to my room before our guards realize I've slipped off. They're already on edge."

The stable hands exited the barn, the door thudding shut behind them. Valerian bowed his head, his shirt crumpled between his fingers.

"Val."

"Forgot the shovel," someone said from below, and more footsteps echoed up to us.

"You should go." Valerian swallowed. "Getting caught... like this..."

"Yeah." I grabbed his hand. The last thing we needed was rumors about us. They could reach my father and brothers before I could speak to them. Or, worse, Galeson or someone connected to him. And what if that affected his country's alliance with Niria? Plus, there was Valerian's mother and the other stablemen he worked with. We had to keep things quiet until we had time to think about how to tell others. "We'll talk tomorrow?"

"Tomorrow."

I nodded and waited for another moment to make sure silence stretched around the stable before I climbed down the ladder and slipped through a side door and back into the shadows of the yard.

20

Apollo

The hallway Hyacinth and Zephyrus had disappeared down together sat huddled in darkness as the party continued humming and tittering around. I cleared my throat hard and turned to a window.

I should attempt to make connections for our cause, or at least try to overhear discussions, gather the perspectives of attendees. But I had tried all night. And fuck if I knew how to execute a plan. Already the politicking caused a headache to build in my temples.

And then Hyacinth had left with Zephyrus.

Alone.

I should carry on.

Continue working the room.

But I couldn't do it.

My heart ached.

"I have to say," a silky voice that rumbled like a purr whispered, "it surprised me when I heard you would be here, Apollo."

I turned to face the woman who had bundled her dark curls up. She wore a creamy gown with a furred cape that highlighted her porcelain complexion. "Kalliope." I cleared my throat and bowed. "I should say the same to you."

Her eyebrows rose. "Oh." Her eyes darted around the room for a moment. "Is that right?"

"Was I to expect you?" My blood coursed through my veins. Damn it. This was probably some other detail I'd neglected to pay attention to. Shit. I was terrible with specifics.

Kalliope's lips pinched. "I should have known that damn Zephyrus is a liar."

"Zephyrus?"

"Oh, yes." She smirked. "He invited me, saying that you would attend, and that you were keen to see me. His letter"—her expression deepened, her eyes twinkling—"held certain implications."

Zephyrus.

The fucking bastard.

So, he thought to distract me with someone beautiful, so he could have Hyacinth to himself. Rage washed through me. Hyacinth was mine. Zephyrus had no fucking right. I hated this plan and had been over it from the moment we stepped into this godforsaken palace in the middle of the ice mountains like some sort of glass prison for the exiled. I wanted us—Cyn, in particular—out of this place and away from here.

I coughed and shifted back to Kalliope, where she stood watching me curiously. Well, it wasn't her fault. "I'm very sorry for any miscommunication… I didn't intend to offend—"

She chuckled and wrapped her arm around mine. "Apollo, stop. I should have known the last time I saw you that your interest in me had waned. I'm not offended… by you, at least."

I patted her hand.

She lifted her glass of champagne and swallowed the entire flute. "I mean, I am now a woman scorned, and I had expected to have a carefree night in the hands of someone"—she side-eyed me, her lips pinching again—"who knows what he's doing in the bedroom."

Heat rose to my cheeks. "My apologies."

She began walking us around the party, both of our silver glows reflecting on the floor like a puddle of moonlight. "So, who is it Zephyrus is trying to keep your hands off, then?"

"That's making some big assumptions." Hyacinth and Delon walked back into the room, Hyacinth's features tight. My heart ached. Something was wrong. And he'd been alone with Zephyrus for an extended time. How I wished to go to him, hear whatever burdened him, feel his fingers long and rough against my own. To know that he was safe and protected.

Hyacinth's gaze met mine and then darted to Kalliope before he shifted into the room, walking over to Boreas.

Kalliope squeezed my arm. "Ah, our mortal prince. And he is very handsome, too."

"Well, that's true enough."

She chuckled. "So, tell me, Apollo, what are mortals like in bed as you take such keen interest in them in that department?"

A smile slipped up on my face. "Do you want to find out?"

"I'm intrigued," she said, clinking her nails against her empty glass.

I swept her through the crowd until we approached the person I looked for. "Delon."

He turned towards us and bowed, his eyes lingering on Kalliope.

"Let me introduce you to Kalliope, a muse with a voice of the likes you've never heard before."

He nodded. "I'd be honored to hear it sometime."

Kalliope opened her mouth. But I spoke first. "Sadly, tonight, that isn't the foremost issue. She's been snubbed by an arrogant asshole of a god who she'd planned to spend the evening with."

Kalliope's lips pinched at a smile, and she ducked her head, but Delon clicked his tongue. "He must be an idiot."

"I assure you," I said, "he is. I promised Kalliope that mortals have better manners, and I knew one would be happy"—I emphasized the word, cocking up an eyebrow —"to enjoy her company this evening."

Delon nodded again. "I would be most honored."

Kalliope turned and patted my cheek. "Apollo, you're a lamb, as always."

Delon inclined his head to me, a bright smile flooding his face as the two swept away from the crowd together. An attendant passed, and I snagged a glass of wine. Thank the gods. This trip was going to kill me. A feat for an immortal, but I was starting to think it wasn't impossible.

"Run off the one person in this room that's interested in you?" Zephyrus said, walking up to my side, his wings blocking the light of the chandeliers and casting us into shadow.

"Perhaps." I took a deep breath. "Did you do the same?"

He scowled at me, his eyes flitting to Hyacinth. But then a cruel smile slipped up on his lips. "Do you know what's so interesting about Prince Hyacinth?"

My stomach swirled, but I swallowed another drink and kept my expression neutral. "What's that?"

Zephyrus leaned in closer to me until his breath

brushed against my ear. "He not only smells like jasmine; he tastes like it, too."

My mouth snapped open, an ache surging through me like hailstones, like a dam breaking and flooding my limbs.

Zephyrus smirked and lifted his goblet in my direction before ambling into the crowd.

Across the room, Hyacinth smiled at something Boreas said, the smooth tan of his skin glowing in the candlelight. I swallowed hard and knocked back the last of my drink. I grabbed another glass from an attendant passing by. Fury and jealousy warred within me like dueling gods. And I was growing fucking tired of shoving them back. I tossed back the next drink and faded back into the edges of the party.

21

Artemis

The moon, full and round and so close to the ocean it seemed ready to dive in, glimmered like a pot of cream sat on the sea, its light shimmering over the beach. Waves roared as they crashed against the shore.

Sappho, who had donned a long, dark tunic, withdrew a key on a necklace and wrapped the chain around her hand.

"Did Phaon not wish to join us tonight?"

Sappho sucked in air over her teeth. "It's a bit of a sore spot for her."

"For Phaon?"

She chuckled. "No. For the goddess we're about to summon. We may have once been"—she looped her fingers in front of her—"a couple."

I gaped. "You're calling a past lover of yours?"

She shrugged. "Yes. So, Phaon being here would not be a welcome sight." She raised her eyebrows and leaned in towards me. "Mind you, Phaon and I didn't come together until a year after we'd broken up, but for an immortal…" She gave her head another shake. "That is but a heartbeat."

Dark palm trees resting in shadows shimmied in the breeze, their fronds rattling. For the love of Zeus' child. Deities were often vindictive creatures. I knew that well enough from many life experiences. Now Sappho was about to summon an audience with a goddess she had spurned. That's exactly what we needed. One more vengeful deity paying too much attention to me and Apollo. "What makes you think she will even appear when you call her, much less help us?"

Sappho ran her thumb down the key. "She once made a blood vow to me that she would always come if I called for her and that she would always be on my side."

"And you broke up with this person?"

Sappho scowled. "It was a complicated situation. But she's going to help. Even if it might be begrudgingly."

I crossed my arms, my sandaled feet sinking into the sand, the cool silk of it slipping between my toes. "How often have you called on her since you separated?"

"Never."

I shifted in her direction. "Never? So, why are you doing so for my sake?"

"A few reasons." She set a bowl on the ground, dumping herbs into it. "For one thing, I like you. I understand after drugging your friend to sleep that feeling isn't presently mutual, but I'm used to being unliked. It doesn't put me off. Secondly"—she lifted her face to me, her eyes glimmering in the moonlight—"there's something important happening here. I can… feel it. I haven't spent decades interacting with gods to shirk my part when the time comes."

I sighed but nodded, and she snapped flint and rock together, the small scrap of fabric catching flame, and she dropped it into the bowl. The sweet scent of the herbs tangled with the salt of the sea, and she placed the key against the dish.

"Hecate," she whispered, her voice trembling, "keeper of keys. Hecate, goddess of crossroads, woman of wisdom and death. Hear me and appear to us."

For a moment, nothing happened. Sappho kept her head bowed, her eyes closed. The smoke from the bowl wisped across the beach.

And then a rumble shook the ground, vibrating through my body.

Sappho trembled but maintained her bent posture.

A woman stood on the shore, her glossy auburn hair glimmering in the light of the torch she held. A snake curled around her shoulders, winding over her arm and up along the torch. It stuck its tongue out, smelling the air, before twining tighter.

The woman's crimson lips parted, her eyes heavy on Sappho for several heartbeats before she shifted to me. She tapped her free hand against her thigh. The breeze rippled her gown against it, the outline of a knife holster pressing against the fabric.

My heartbeat picked up, and I struggled against reaching out to touch my own weapons.

Hecate frowned and shifted back to Sappho. "It has been some time."

"It has," Sappho said.

"For what purpose have you called me? As you know, it's Autumn. I'm presently in the underworld with Persephone for the season."

Sappho nodded. "I hope she makes you happy."

Hecate's frown deepened. "Why did you summon me?"

"It was not for my sake." She grasped my arm. "Meet

Artemis, daughter of Leto. She is a deity but does not know who her father is."

Hecate's expression transformed, the snake slithering around her waist, its tail gliding along her collarbone. She walked closer to me. "Daughter of Leto?"

"Yes, that's right," I said. It surprised me when Sappho said my mother's name, but I suppose she knew my brother and therefore would know of her with how interconnected she was with the gods and their lives.

Hecate stepped in close enough to me that the heat from her torch warmed my skin and the snake leaned out, darting its tongue in my direction. "We knew your mother." She nodded towards Sappho. I fought the frown that wanted to press into my face. So, Sappho had more knowledge than she'd let on. Though it didn't surprise me, it still annoyed me. "She was a powerful priestess. Always deeply involved with the gods. Most mortals"—Hecate's gaze turned to Sappho once more, before speaking—"are too afraid to get as deep as she was."

"You knew her well?" I whispered.

She nodded and ran a finger down the back of the snake. "I know a piece of your prophecy as well."

I gasped. "You do?"

"Yes, because your mother once told me I shared some features her future daughter would have."

"What are they?"

She lifted her face to the sky, her long hair trailing out in the wind. "The dark side of the moon is one thing I am the goddess of." She smiled. "And you are the goddess of the moon itself."

I gasped. "I am?"

My mouth gaped. Goddess of the moon. That was... that was a sky deity. That was tremendous, the role of the highest of gods. The weight of that crashed into me like an icy wave. I wasn't just divine. I apparently had as elevated of a position as my brother and even Zeus himself. Shit. That complicated everything. If I was some mid-level deity, others might not look my way. But a sky goddess? That was going to draw attention… a lot of it.

"That is your prophesied role when you ascend. Twin to your brother's sun. Your mother knew this. And she was aware of the cost of getting involved with gods."

My voice broke, and I crossed my arms, rubbing at the goosebumps that had risen over my flesh. "Her death."

"Yes," Hecate whispered, so close to me that the warm, spicy smell of her filled my senses. The snake settled against her shoulder, and she trailed a finger over its scales. "Do you know what I am the primary goddess of?"

"I'm afraid not."

She smiled gently. "That's all right. I'm not a terribly popular deity, nor do I try to become one. Few worship me. But it's no burden to me to lack renown." She turned her head towards Sappho for a heartbeat. "I never longed to have the center of attention." She shifted back in my direction. "I only ever desired a few intimate companions who truly knew me and accepted me for who I am. You see, I intimidate many."

"Because of what you rule over?"

She nodded, and the snake looped across her shoulders, tangling down her arm. "Yes. I oversee many things that mortals and gods alike don't want to look at too closely."

"Such as what?"

"Night, for one thing. Dark magic. But primarily"—she took a deep breath, her posture straightening, an ebony color flashing over her eyes like spilled ink—"I'm the goddess over death."

The way she said the last word sent a chill down my

spine, but my voice came even. I had spent my childhood learning how to hide emotions from gods, after all. "Like Hades?"

She chuckled. "No. He guards the underworld. I can pierce the veil of the afterlife and communicate with the dead."

"I didn't know that was possible."

She shrugged as a wave crashed against the shore, reaching our feet and dampening the hems of our clothing. "As I said, it's frowned upon. I bring that up for this reason. How would you like to speak with your mother?"

I sucked in a breath and stumbled back from her. "You could do that?"

"Yes. Though it's draining. Five to ten minutes is all I can manage before the magic wanes."

I considered that. Paused. Soaked in the quiet hush of the breathing of the sea, the world before everything in my life changed. I had never known my mother. All my years I'd believed she had died at my birth. Now, Hera claimed it was actually her doing. Regardless of the cause, I'd never met the woman. The only thing I knew of her was what Apollo had told me. He'd been generous with his stories and songs. He understood how I craved a connection with her. But I wouldn't even recognize my mother if I saw her. This was my chance. It surprised me that fear gripped me over it. "Okay."

Hecate nodded and then raised her hands. Sappho tensed, cowering into herself. Puffs of plum smoke swept out around Hecate, the gold of her eyes brightening, over-taking the flame of the torch in her hand. The haze surrounded us, darkening the world, so that only our breathing and Hecate's light remained.

She snapped her wrist.

And the torchlight died.

For a moment, darkness consumed us.

My eyes ached against it, struggling to find a drop of light.

Then an ivory mist rose, and an image of a woman with silver, depthless eyes, smooth dark skin, and a long neck shimmered, like the figure struggled to appear.

"Artemis," she said.

"Mother." I trembled over the word.

She smiled, the smoke parting for a moment, causing her form to disappear and then slowly pull back together.

"I never thought I would get to meet you," I said, my throat choking with tears. "All my life I've longed to."

She blinked twice. "The fates prophesied this meeting to me. So much of life is at a crossroads right now. A heavy task lies before you and your brother. But an important one."

"What is it?"

"You must both ascend to your rightful places and undo the wickedness your brother's father has wrought in the world."

"We're supposed to take down Zeus?"

She nodded. "It's a tremendous responsibility, but you were both born for it."

"I… I'm not sure if I can… or if I even want to."

Her lips pressed together, thick full lips like my own. "It's a fearsome thing to walk amongst gods. But you came into this life screaming violently, your fists balled up like you demanded justice from the world alongside your breath. And I knew your father had blessed you with the courage and constitution you needed for your task."

I stepped in closer, my feet dipping into the sand, and the fog moved again, Mother's image fading and then reconstructing. "Who is my father?"

Her depthless eyes flashed. "One of my children has a

155

father, the god of the sky. My other child, a god of the depths of the sea."

"You mean Poseidon?"

"I do."

The vision sparkled and shifted, and Hecate's voice sounded out. "It fades."

Mother tilted her head. "Be strong, Temi. You are brave and good-hearted. You were born for this."

I swallowed, my fingers reaching out towards the image. "You know my nickname?"

Another smile trailed her lips. "Of course, I do, child. I gave it to you."

"Before you go." I gasped, a cry building in my chest that I had to fight. "Is it true Hera caused your death?"

The smoke-form of my mother studied me for a moment before she spoke again. "Yes. Your father veiled you before your birth. And until we separated, that veil extended to me. After you were born, Hera sought me out."

"I'll make her pay."

"No." Mother's voice came stern. "Don't let vengeance distract you. That's always been Hera's shortcoming. Focus on your task and trust that Hera will face the consequences of the life she's led."

"I need to ascend?"

She inclined her head, her long lashes brushing her cheeks. "Seek your father, have the veil removed, rise to power, and help your brother do the same."

"That last part may be the most difficult."

The corners of her lips turned up. "I don't doubt it. But they are all tasks you can manage, my daughter. Do not forget who you are. And don't lose sight of the goodness in your heart."

The image disappeared as the fog receded.

Only the navy darkness of the beach, the outline of the jungle, and the two women standing on the shore by me remained.

I released a breath and hit my knees.

Sappho dropped beside me. "Are you all right?"

"I'm fine."

Hecate slumped. "I shall take my leave now. If you ever need me again"—her golden eyes pierced into me—"you may call me."

She reached out, handing me a bronze key on a chain.

"Thank you," I said, accepting it.

The earth shook.

And Sappho and I sat alone on the shore.

I sighed. Sappho wrapped an arm around me, her palm circling my back. "Is there anything else I can help you with, my dear?"

I clenched my teeth, my fingers digging into the key, but then lifted my face to hers. "Do you know how to call on Poseidon?"

22

Hyacinth

"May I walk you back to your room?" Zephyrus said, his eyes flaming with a desire that left me feeling queasy, my palms growing damp. "To pick up our discussion?"

The party had cleared out, deities finding their ways to bedrooms. Lights had dimmed and fires glowed low and peachy in hearths. "Of course," I said.

As we weaved our way through the few lingering souls in the rooms, I searched for Apollo. But he wasn't anywhere on our path. He must have already turned in for the night. For the briefest moment, I thought of the goddess that had her hand tucked around his arm and had draped in towards him, whispering. He couldn't be with her, could he? I gave my head a shake. That was ridiculous. I trusted Apollo and letting jealousy—unfounded at that—color my views of things because I missed him and longed for him, was senseless. He was probably asleep.

I wished to seek him out, hold him, feel the coarse texture of his curls as they brushed against my fingers, listen to whatever burdened him and share in turn.

But we were leaving the next day.

And tomorrow night I was spending several hours in his arms, regardless of where we stopped for the evening. I was ready to scream our relationship to the mountains, solely so I could hold his hand.

"You can see, after tonight," Zephyrus said, stealing into my thoughts, "how close many of the low deities are."

We turned to the hallway that led to my room, torchlights flickering over tapestries that covered the gray stone walls. "Yes, I noticed that. It appears that their loyalties lie in a different direction than I had expected."

We reached my door, and Zephyrus sighed. "Zeus has been losing support for decades. He cares only for his own power. Others grow tired of it." His eyes grew piercing. "It seems that even human followers of his begin to turn away?"

I hesitated, but the moment for declarations was now. I didn't trust Zephyrus, and whatever his own agenda was—the lower gods against the high ones—would certainly cause issues for my father and our plans to align with Jupiter against the reigning high gods. But I had no belief that he'd disclose us to Zeus as he didn't wish to unnecessarily draw Zeus' attention to himself for his own means. And for Zephyrus to believe that we were on his side—regardless of reality—until I had time to discuss this new information with Father, would give us the upper hand in deciding.

"Our kingdom grows weary of Zeus' demands and punishments as well. You're right." I shrugged. "This is the reason I traveled here."

Zephyrus' expression glittered with excitement, his shoulders rising with a breath. "You came to the right place, then."

"I hope we can consider you friends."

"Or perhaps more, even?" He traced his finger over my shoulder.

Shit. I cleared my throat and grabbed his hand, sliding my fingers over his even though it sent a jolt of revulsion through me. "Zephyrus, I think, if we mean to be potential allies, it would be best if we kept things professional between us." I gave his palm a squeeze before dropping it. "Even if we had a lovely night together in our history."

His lips pinched, and he paused for a moment. I waited, afraid I'd given myself away. Worried that he'd see through everything, but he sighed and bobbed his head. "You're right. Though that's disappointing."

I offered him a smile. "Good night."

"Sleep well." He bowed and clipped back down the hall.

Exhaustion wrapped around my muscles as I stepped into the room and closed the door behind me. Hades' realm, the day had lasted for a hundred lifetimes. I peeled my robe and shirt off like I could remove the place and the trip from my flesh. Gods was it a relief to finally be away from all the people and politics and worries and Zephyrus. Especially him.

Flames from the fireplace reflected in the mirror, its apricot sparks dancing around the ivory bricks, casting warmth over all the textures of the room.

A knock sounded, breaking into the peacefulness.

It was well past the moon rise, and I didn't know who might visit me so late.

Unless it was Zephyrus and he had changed his mind.

My heart picked up, and I clenched my jaw.

I rose, the stool scraping the floor, and approached the door, opening it a crack. "Yes?"

Apollo stood in the hallway, a veil swallowing his luminance, his chin raised, his eyes in shadows. I snatched his arm, dragging him in, and shut the door closed with a thud. "Apollo," I breathed. "What are you doing here?"

He frowned, his nose flaring. "Why?" He skimmed his gaze down my bare chest. "Expecting someone else?"

I sucked in a breath. That comment ached through me after an already endlessly long day. And I had spent a huge portion of it worrying over him, at that. "Is that a serious question?"

"You tell me, Cyn." He crossed his arms, lifting his chin where he could take in the rich fabrics and tall ceilings of the room. "You and Zephyrus seemed almost cozy by the end of the night."

A puff of a breath passed my lips. Annoyance tangled in my heart, buzzing and zipping through me, heating my blood. But there was something in the jut of Apollo's chin, the way he held his posture, the clench of his jaw. Something insecure draped in the mask of defiance.

And that was a soothing balm to my own rankled pride. I had just wondered about the woman he spent part of the evening with, after all. And I'd decided that jealousy wasn't because of a lack of trust in him, but because I had missed him, longed for him. Apollo had to feel the same for me in reverse and that was what this was really about.

I took a deep breath and sauntered over to him, the rug scraping against my bare feet until I stood close enough that his tunic grazed my chest. I brushed my nose along his cheek and whispered against the grit of his jaw. "Are you feeling jealous now, my lord?"

He growled and gripped his fingers into the back of my neck, bruising his mouth against mine, his touch bitter and possessive. His tongue parted my lips. He jerked his hands free, snagging my hips and shoving me against the wall. I grunted at the impact, and his veil slipped, his golden eyes glowing brighter than the fire.

"Yes, Cyn." He kissed me hard again, his hands roaming my body hungrily. Our mouths parted, and he frowned, hissing the words out. "I am. Are you enjoying my discomfort?"

I smiled, feathering my fingers down his arm. "Well, presently, with how this is playing out, yes."

His eyes roamed me, and he tangled against me, snagging my lip between his teeth. He kissed me hard, the rough texture of his hands scraping along my skin. He leaned back, his gaze piercing. "You're mine."

I studied him. "Am I?"

He growled again, and the sound vibrated against me. "Do you not wish to be?"

I trailed my fingers over his thighs, up along his hips, under the fabric of his clothing, over the panes of his stomach. I pulled the tunic off of him, letting it fall to the stone floor. His expression drilled into me. "Come." I grasped his hand. "Let me show you what I wish for."

He followed me to the bed and dropped with me onto the mattress. His mouth found mine again, his touch holding an edge to it. He shoved me down against the blankets, but I flipped him over and shook my head. "Oh, no, this isn't how this is going to go."

His eyes flashed. "It's not?"

I traced my finger along his jaw, down his neck, over the sharp line of his collarbone. Gods, was he beautiful. And him wanting me so desperately was twining in with my desire and love for him, fueling it. "You came into my room seeking me out." He parted his mouth, but I pressed my lips to his to stall his words. When we peeled apart, I cocked an eyebrow up. "You're in my domain, Apollo. And you'll follow my desires or not at all."

His heartbeat pounded against my skin. "And what is it you desire, Your Highness?"

I grasped his jaw and kissed him once more. "It's been a few days since I've had a deity on his knees before me."

His eyes darkened, and he kissed me hard again before rising off the bed and kneeling on the floor. He gripped my hips and jerked me forward. A grin slashed my mouth, and I ran my fingers into his curls.

He pulled the remaining fabric from both of our bodies and began kissing my ribs, his tongue trailing my skin like fire burned down me, his teeth nipping and causing me to gasp. He trailed down my body, exploring every ridge, his rough hands drifting behind, scraping against my flesh.

I stroked my hand over his hair, and his voice rumbled, vibrating against me. I gasped and kicked my head back. He took me into his mouth, and my mind blanked. My fingers gripped into the blankets. For five minutes, every thought swarming through my brain disappeared.

Right as my muscles all tensed and I sucked in a sharp breath, Apollo eased back from me, his lips glistening in the firelight, his eyes holding their own flames. I snagged his arms and pulled him up, shoving him against the mattress and straddling him, his legs banging against mine.

I traced my thumb down his chest. "I should return the favor, don't you think?"

"Yes," he whispered. "I'm inclined to agree with that idea."

I laughed against his hip bone.

And I returned the favor. Right to the detail of pulling up short just as his face crumpled.

He groaned and dropped against the bed. "Damn it."

I chuckled and rose along his body, kissing him hard. "Not enjoying the dish you love to serve up?"

"Hmm," he hummed into my mouth. He gripped his fingers into my shoulder blades and rolled me over, every inch of our flesh sparking against each other. Our hands and mouths and bodies grabbed at the other. We tumbled around the bed, wrecking it, like a flame slowly consuming hay, licking up wood, building into an inferno that no amount of water could extinguish. We kept drawing each other to the point of release only to pull back, passion sweeping over us in waves, rising higher with each crest until we couldn't hold back, and we finished like a hurricane smashing cliffs, our cries echoing against the ceiling.

After, we glistened with sweat, and the blankets and pillows lay in heaps on the floor. Apollo tucked into my arm, resting his head on my shoulder, and I pressed my lips to his forehead.

"Feel better?"

He moaned his response.

"You know I only desire you, don't you,"—I grinned—"golden boy?"

"No nicknames right now," he breathed, his words mumbling together.

I kissed the top of his hair. "You should return to your room before anyone realizes you're missing."

"Don't ask me to leave, Cyn. I want to sleep by your side."

"If you get caught—"

"I'll pull a veil."

I sighed but tucked in closer to him. I wanted him to stay as well. "And if someone notices that you aren't in your room?"

I could practically feel his eyes roll. "They already assume gods are assholes and won't be surprised at all that I'm out doing what I wish instead of what is expected."

I chuckled and kissed his temple. Several moments passed, our heartbeats slowing. The fire had burned down to a burgundy glow, shadows flickering along the walls.

Apollo's shoulders rose and fell in slow undulations, and I whispered in case he'd gone to sleep. "Apollo?"

"Hmm?"

"You know I wouldn't cheat on you, don't you?"

His breath hitched, and he lifted his head, resting it where he could meet my gaze. He hadn't fixed the veil, and his eyes glowed like twin suns. "I'm sorry, Cyn. I'm an idiot."

"Don't be." I kissed him, gently, the steam of the previous hour spent. "But, I love you. I would never—"

"I know." He bowed his face, his curls mussed and illuminated with burgundy highlights from the fire. "Hyacinth, you mean everything to me. I can't stand watching Zephyrus parade around like you're another conquest. He doesn't deserve you." He leaned farther into the bed, causing it to dip, and his words came out in a whisper. "Neither do I."

I lifted his hand and kissed his fingers. "That's not true. But you could work on your patience and temperance some."

He cocked an eyebrow. "Do you regret me coming tonight?"

I brushed my nose over his cheek. "Definitely not. But we'll only be here for one more day. And then it's me and you together against the world again."

He bobbed his head. "As long as we're together facing it."

I pressed another gentle kiss to his mouth, and he curled up against me. The fire crackled and the heavy weight of satisfaction draped over me as we drifted off to sleep beside each other.

23

Epiphany

My feet slipped over the silky sands of the beach, causing me to tumble forward along the path, and I thrust my hands out to steady myself. A guard who walked with me reached over, placing his hand beneath my elbow, and I offered him a smile.

The coast stretched out, wild and undulating, as if humans never came upon it. The sands dipped and curved, shadows washed in coral colors from the sunrise peeking above the sea. Flaxen grasses tumbled across the expanse, caught up in winds that skittered sand as the waves crashed against shore.

Temi sat facing the water. She had her legs crossed, her posture straight and still. Only her braids moved as they tousled together with the breeze. I gestured for my guards to pause as I continued pushing through the sands until I approached her and lowered beside her.

She reached out for my hand and tangled her fingers into mine but didn't break her gaze from the navy silk of the sky where the moon still hung round and heavy.

For several minutes I remained quiet with her,

breathing in the salt as the winds chapped my cheeks. When I spoke, I kept my voice low, letting it sink in with the world around me. "Theos tells me you never went to sleep."

She blinked at the moon before dropping her face. "I couldn't. I had too much on my mind."

"Do you want to talk about it?"

She sighed, her shoulders easing. "Sappho's friend, no... her ex-lover actually..."

My lips parted. "The goddess you met last night was Sappho's—"

"Yes. And she's slightly terrifying in a way. But I really liked her. There's no guile about her, you know?"

"Well, I don't, but I'll take your word for it."

She smiled and leaned in closer to me. "Her name is Hecate." She swallowed. "She had a lot to say and to... show me. I've sat here all night, thinking about everything I learned, and I can't help but feel there is more than what appears on the surface." She lifted her knees against her chest and wrapped her arms around them. "And the only way to find out is to meet my father."

My breath caught. "Did you find out who he is?"

She nodded and dropped her chin to her knees. "Poseidon."

"The god of the sea? He's... he's one of the three major gods."

"I know." She shook her head. Seagulls swooped out beyond, diving until they reached the surf and landing, hobbling away as another wave rushed in. Temi sighed. "I'm the goddess of the moon, Epiphany. A sky deity. That's a major thing."

I sank my fingers back into the sand, the grit of it sliding under my fingernails. "Well, I think that's comforting to me."

Temi looked at me. "Why?"

"I'll think of you now every time I look at the night sky. Maybe the dark will seem less so with you at its helm."

She studied me for a moment and then released a breath of a laugh. "A very romantic perspective, but okay."

I shrugged. "I guess I'm a romantic."

"On that note"—her eyebrows inched up—"did you talk with Valerian yesterday?"

Heat swelled over my cheeks, spreading across my nose, and I snagged a loose curl, tucking it behind my ear.

Temi laughed. "So, you did more than talk?"

"Temi."

She clicked her tongue. "Don't '*Temi*' me."

I smoothed out my dress, brushing sand off of it. "Maybe so."

"I'm happy for you."

I cleared my throat. The previous night rushing through my mind. "So, when do you meet your father?"

"Sappho sent an invitation for him to come to lunch. Apparently, gods don't enjoy being summoned."

"Oh. Would I be able to summon you?"

She scowled. "I just told you deities don't like to be summoned."

A crab scuttled across the sand in front of us, its shell wobbling with its movements. The sun had risen higher and splashed light and warmth around. I nudged her. "You'd make an exception for me, right?"

She narrowed her eyes, but then her lips parted into a smile. "Yeah, for you only."

"What about Apollo?"

She clicked her tongue. "He'd better not summon me if he knows what's good for him." We both burst into a laugh, folding back against the other. We sat and watched as the sun smeared over the sky, dimming the light of the moon, the world shifting again.

Temi's throat bobbed as she stared out across the sea again. "Epiphany…"

I frowned. Something in her voice worried me. "Yeah?"

"I don't want you to come with me when I meet my father."

I stilled. "It's personal, of course."

"It's not that."

Wind swept over my brow, cooling the sweat that had broken out there. "What is it, then?"

She turned to face me and grabbed my hand. "This is bigger than I realized it would be. I understand now Apollo's hesitance to grow close to people. You're mortal, Pip. And I already have one vengeful goddess after me. This is all becoming dangerous."

"You encouraged Apollo to make connections."

"I did." She bowed her face. "But I see his reasoning more now."

"You need friends through all of this, and I want to be here for you."

"I want that too. Which is why I don't want you taking part in this. Something happening to you because of me…" She gave her head a shake. "I couldn't live with it."

A hurt pierced through me. But this wasn't about me; it was about Temi. Supporting her in a way that actually felt helpful was what mattered. And if me not being involved is what she needed, then so be it. "Okay," I whispered.

"Have I upset you?"

"No. It's fine." I lied. But she shouldn't have to worry about me on top of everything else going on.

She looked at me as though she didn't believe my words. "It's just for this. Nothing is changing between us."

"Of course."

We stared at each other. Everything was changing, our relationship included. And I had no control over the situation. I'd just have to appreciate what friendship we had and accept that her fate pulled her away from me. That sliced through me, though. I hated it. But what could I do?

When we parted ways after the sun stretched out bright and golden in the sky and Temi went inside the residence to sleep for a few hours, I made my way out to the stable. Valerian scooped barley into a feeding trough, the sweet smell of it sweeping into the air as a horse dropped its snout towards the meal.

"Val," I said.

He turned, color draining from his face, and he wrung his fingers around the scoop. "Hey, Epiphany."

My guards shifted, their feet scraping against the gritty ground, and I moved back to face them. "Would you wait outside for me?"

Their brows furrowed, but they bobbed their heads and strode out of the barn. Once the space stretched empty, the earthy smell of hay and crunching of the horses eating the only thing remaining, I walked closer to him and grabbed his hand.

He swallowed, his eyes trailing over me. "Did you sleep well?"

I hadn't, actually. Temi wasn't the only one up most of the night. I'd lain in my bed, sore in ways it'd never been before, my mind drifting back to Valerian, his body bared, his flesh scraping mine. I shook my head, my cheeks warming. "Okay considering. You?"

He chuckled. "I suppose I could say the same."

Tension hovered between us like something palpable, an energy we could reach out and grasp greedy handfuls of, tuck it into our pockets. I tightened my fingers. "I guess this is kind of awkward."

He kneaded his neck with his free hand. "A bit."

"About last night…"

"I'm sorry," he whispered.

"You're sorry?"

He dropped my touch and combed both of his hands back through his hair. "We shouldn't have, I mean… Obviously."

Blood drained from my face and down my limbs, leaving my body feeling cool and tingling. "You regret it."

"Do you not?"

"Of course I don't."

He blinked at me for several heartbeats. The horse nearest us huffed a hot breath, and Valerian sighed alongside her. "Soon we'll return home. You'll be back to your life… to your future. And that doesn't include me."

His words came like a smack, bringing blood rushing to my cheeks, my face warming. "What do you mean it doesn't include you?"

He frowned. "You're going to marry, aren't you?"

"Yes. But I thought…"

"You thought what?"

"I thought you and I… might… I mean…"

Shock colored his expression. "You believed we would get married?"

Warmth swept over me again but no longer with the bite of anger. Suddenly I felt ashamed and young and foolish. "You don't want that," I said, and my words came so pitifully mewling that I wished I could cram them back into my mouth and swallow them.

"Oh, Pip." His eyes glazed. "I would want that more than anything in this life. But"—he wrung his fingers together—"we know that isn't possible for us."

"I don't know that."

Sunshine spilled in through windows, bouncing off walls and making his emerald irises sparkle despite the sadness draping over him. "What was your plan, then?"

"I'd talk to my father about us."

"And if he didn't approve?"

"Then I'd leave. You and I... we can go somewhere else, start a different life together. You once told me you'd love to have a chance to go where no one knows you. Maybe that's my dream as well."

His brow furrowed. "You'd give up your family? Your father and your brothers? Your friends? Everything?"

I hesitated at that. I loved my family. And they loved me too, deeply. I wasn't sure I would give them up. But I didn't believe they'd disown me. I couldn't imagine my father casting me aside forever. "I'd give up being a princess without hesitating."

His frown deepened, and he leaned away from me. "So, you'd plan to join me as part of the working class? Have you truly considered what a life always fighting against falling into poverty entails? Will you learn to mend clothes and do without? How would you look at me when your hands cracked and bled from cold and work? When you lost your friends from my reputation? When you suffered," he said so fiercely I trembled, "and I couldn't do anything to ease it?"

"I wouldn't care if that happened because we'd deal with it together."

He dropped his face to mine. His nose brushed my cheek, and his lip quivered against my flesh. "You would care," he whispered so quietly it scarcely rose over the chewing, shuffling sound of the horses. "You just don't know it yet. I've seen my mother suffer like that because of me. I won't see that for you." He moved back again, the warmth of him receding, and bowed his head. "So, yes, I regret last night. Because you deserve far better, and I acted on my emotions, compromising your reputation and status out of selfishness."

"So, you plan to just stand by and watch me... what? Marry Lord Galeson?"

A muscle in his jaw jumped, but he nodded briskly. "Yes, Epiphany. That's exactly what I plan to do."

I stared at him, my mouth gaping. "So, last night meant nothing to you, then?"

"That's not how I intended that."

"No. You've made everything very clear to me. You feel guilty for sullying the wife of Lord Galeson. That's all I am —even to you—isn't it?" He parted his lips to speak, but I cut him off, anger sluicing its way through me. "A princess, a trading piece, a political move for the kingdom."

"That's not what I said."

"You've said enough." Fury thrusted through me, like a phoenix catching on fire and taking flight. Over everything. Over my childhood of meeting no one's expectations. For the way my father and brothers hovered over me like I was some sort of gem to protect rather than a person. Because of the way Temi had pushed me out of her life that morning. And now Valerian. After the previous night, it was the ultimate betrayal.

He'd just taken a memory that had been perfect in my mind and ruined it, shadowed it with his guilt and regrets.

Gods, that's what I was to him.

One giant regret he wished to get away from.

I was never just Epiphany to anyone.

I was always something else.

A princess.

A mortal.

A sister.

And I was fucking tired of it. "Saddle my horse."

Valerian's eyelashes fluttered. "Can we talk about this? I don't feel like I've come across the right way and—"

"No." My voice firmed, ice and steel sliding into my bones. "I'm the princess as you've insisted on continuing to remind me. And I just gave you an order."

"Pip."

"Do not. You have no right. Do as I say. Saddle my horse."

Valerian's eyes widened, some mixture of terror and worry swirling over them. "Let me alert your guards, so they can get their horses ready."

"No. I want my horse now. And I want to take her out alone."

"Epiphany, please."

"Now."

He hesitated for another heartbeat before bowing his head and walking over to the stall, leading Meadow out.

24

Apollo

Waking up next to Hyacinth, watching his chest rise and fall with his breath, had tempered me. We'd already had a final formal breakfast and would leave as soon as we made polite goodbyes to all the deities and other guests who milled around the receiving room, some still rubbing their temples or yawning from the long, alcohol-filled evening.

Hyacinth chatted with Boreas and Janus, his eyes wrinkling with his smiles. His outfit was perfectly smooth, his posture straight. After seeing him pulled apart and ruffled the night before, I admired that version of Hyacinth—the polished, sharp-eyed, and commanding prince. A veil he wore for others.

Gods if he wasn't beautiful. I shouldn't have watched him as intently as I did. But we'd leave within the hour, and I couldn't help it. Hyacinth was the most attractive being I'd ever seen. That he chose me as a partner left me speechless with gratitude.

Zephyrus sauntered over, his fingers curled around his goblet. "Sulking by yourself, Apollo?"

"Drinking so early in the morning, Zephyrus?"

His eyes narrowed. "You know, for someone who is part of a group that is wishing to make connections with us, you're rather obnoxious."

"Wouldn't you be disappointed if I were otherwise?" Knowing we'd leave soon had me in a good mood, and I found it easier than I'd expected to respond playfully to him.

He took a swallow of the drink, his golden locks glimmering in the window light. "What are your designs with Hyacinth?"

I shrugged. "What does it matter to you?"

"I mean," he said, ignoring my comment, "it's embarrassing how desperate you are for his attention. And he doesn't even spare you a glance." He tapped his finger against his glass. "You're the same lost little boy god, hungry for recognition that no one cares to give you, brooding by yourself because your daddy doesn't love you. What man would ever pay mind to someone as ridiculous and pitiful as you?"

My heart picked up, and I clenched my fingernails into my palm but took a slow breath. We were leaving. I could ignore him. "You're probably right."

He scowled. "Has your father beaten you down to where you're too weak to even speak up for yourself? You stand back and allow me to pursue the man you're clearly interested in. I wonder if you'd just stand back and watch while I fucked him as well?"

My blood ran cold, and I cleared my throat hard. "Are you in love with him?"

Zephyrus gave a sharp, piercing laugh. "No, I'm not as foolish as you, Apollo. Love is for idiots who have no real ambitions."

Hyacinth darted his gaze towards us before shifting back to his conversation, but his brow furrowed, the v-shaped dimple rippling into it. A sigh slipped between my lips. I could keep my mouth shut for Hyacinth's sake. I wouldn't stir up trouble, even though in that moment I'd happily ascend solely to bring the fire of the sun down on Zephyrus' head. "It's well known that I'm not as ambitious as you, Zephyrus. I've never denied that."

"Lacking ambition among a hundred other things. You know, I almost worried the first few days you were here that you might act as a spy for Zeus. But gods"—he laughed—"how foolish of me to assume you had such complicated motives. You're a love-sick fool pining after a man who can't bother to look at you. And who could blame him? Does he know about your past? Does he know how you caused the slaughter of a village of humans out of your foolishness? Or does he just dislike you because of who you are?"

He stepped in, his spicy scent tangling with the wine and making my stomach clench. "Why would a man as beautiful and worthy as Hyacinth bother with a god-castoff like you? He wouldn't. And, one day, when the tides shift, he'll be on his knees before me, in one manner or another."

My nose flared, my breaths coming heavy and weighted. I had never loathed someone as much as this being, my father being the one possible exception. Zephyrus stirred up a lifetime of pain for me with a few pointed words like a poker coaxing sparks from a fire. But I would temper myself. I'd let it go. I forced my face to remain placid.

Zephyrus turned and walked away, his jacket whirling out in the air. I moved farther into the room, slipping into an alcove behind the curtains ensconcing it. Three massive windows allowed a view of the sunshine and blue sky contrasting against the painfully bright ivory of the world around it.

"You've made a valid point about Zephyrus," someone said on the other side of the curtain.

I stilled, tucking tighter into the corner.

"I know you thought it was foolish," a second person said.

"Zephyrus isn't who we might have considered an ideal candidate. But he clearly has deep connections."

"I've heard rumors that his wife is Jupiter's daughter."

"Yes, and the mortal prince?"

"Hyacinth."

The first person hummed in agreement. "Clearly, they're close as well. Imagine a future where the divinities of Olympus, the gods of the West, and humans all inter-connected. I never thought it possible, but—"

"I agree. It surprised me too, but Zephyrus holds himself with more dignity than I would have once expected."

"Yes. I've heard he can be vindictive with past lovers and alliances that have gone sour. But that isn't the image I see."

"You know how rumors grow."

The two shuffled away, their voices fading.

And that's when it hit me.

This party, the deities and nymphs and human leaders Boreas had invited here.

Zephyrus used it all to position himself as favored by both gods and humans.

To take over Zeus' role.

No matter what those two foolishly believed, there wasn't a hope in the underworld Zephyrus could pull it off.

Others could kill him—maybe not easily, but he lacked the advantage of the high gods where only the holder of the spark could cause their deaths. No, Zephyrus couldn't manage it.

Snowflakes fluttered past the windowpane, and my heart surged along with them. Zephyrus was a coward. He wouldn't take on Zeus himself. Which meant he gathered all this support as a buffer.

And he intended to use Hyacinth to achieve that end. Things were in motion for the future I hadn't even considered. If Zephyrus began his own war, stirring up trouble to distract Zeus, Hyacinth's kingdom would suffer amid that. Did he plan to sacrifice Cyn's people as a step to his ascension? I didn't doubt he would do so without hesitating.

In the unlikely scenario that he took Zeus' role, he'd be a tyrant, as bad as my father. That was not the future we fought for.

My blood glittered with sunshine, with energy, with fire, as if my magic offered answers to me.

"If I could have everyone's attention," Zephyrus said. I stepped out of the alcove. He stood near Hyacinth and draped his fingers against Cyn's arm. "I'd like to take a moment to thank each of you for visiting with us."

Zephyrus shot me a dark look. He was about to say something to cement all of his plans. Hyacinth's expression brightened, worries flitting across his eyes. His eyebrows pressed together, that v-shaped dimple rippling into his flesh. He wanted Zephyrus to stop but didn't know what course to take to pause him.

Cyn had to know what I did—that Zephyrus was about to use this speech to make every soul in the room believe Niria had aligned with him. I had no idea what Hyacinth's thoughts or plans were with that.

But I could tell from his expression that he didn't want Zephyrus to move forward.

And I knew how to stop him.

I smiled.

Because I'd had enough of fucking hold back, anyway.

My feet snapped against the floor as I walked towards the two of them.

25

Artemis

I had always found the sea soothing in a way.

I'm not sure I ever would again.

I stood alongside Sappho whose blush gown fluttered in the salty breeze, and Phaon, who reached over and took her hand.

The sea rippled, the waters parting.

My heart stuttered.

This was it.

No going back.

I swallowed hard. But I could never live with not facing it.

From the waves two stallions rose who towered twice the height of normal horses, their coats shades of indigos and emeralds that shifted in the sunlight like velvet. They tossed their heads and manes like seaweed slapped against their necks as their riders dismounted.

One was an elderly woman with long gray hair that she wore braided, her dark skin glimmering, her clothing made of rippling layers of aqua fabric.

The man at her side had warm brown skin and golden,

glowing eyes. Silver light shimmered over his form. He wore a tunic that glittered like fish scales, and the fabric bunched up at his shoulder, held with a golden clasp. I shuddered and stepped back. Suddenly I wished Epiphany was there, that I hadn't asked her to stay at the house. I could use a friend at the moment.

The man bowed. "Artemis?"

I swallowed. "I am she."

He took another step forward but then paused like he thought better of it. "It has been a long time that I've hoped for this day."

"Is that right?" I curled my fingers into fists. "You have an interesting way of showing that."

The years of his absence sliced at me, cutting through my heart. I'd spent an entire childhood without so much as meeting him. He was a high god. He could have traveled to visit in a heartbeat. It would have taken no effort on his part at all, but he still shirked his duty, allowing me to wander the world without knowing who I was. And now he stood here saying he'd hoped for this day. The bastard.

He raised his chin. "You're angry. That's understandable."

"You don't get to say how I feel," I hissed.

He chuckled. "You have your mother's spirit. I'm glad about that."

I clenched my teeth. "My mother, who you allowed Hera to kill."

The gold of his eyes, so similar to Apollo's when he removed his veil, flashed. "Leto knew the choices she made, and she was aware of the consequences. She had her reasons, and I hope you will give me the opportunity to explain."

"Maybe, if you had bothered in the last nineteen years to—"

Sappho swept forward and bowed. "What gorgeous horses you have, Lord Poseidon."

Poseidon kept his gaze on me for a moment before turning towards her and patting the side of one creature. "Thank you. I take a lot of pride in them." He weaved his fingers into the stallion's mane. "Horses are my creation. If you ask the wind gods, they will claim them, but they merely altered my existing idea."

Waves crashed against the shore, and the animals stamped their hooves. "They're lovely. You know how I adore the horses here at my home," Sappho said.

"You take excellent care of your creatures."

"I thank you."

"May I speak with my daughter alone?"

Sappho hesitated a moment, her eyes darting to me. I nodded, and she bowed. "It's an honor to have you on my island, Lord Poseidon. You are welcome anytime."

"Thank you," he said.

She grasped Phaon's hand and walked up the sandy banks, meandering towards the house.

And then we stood facing each other, the gray-eyed woman who held the horse's reins studying us both. Poseidon gestured to her. "First, let me introduce you to Amara, your guardian."

"My guardian?"

He nodded. "She is the reason you're veiled so firmly. She transferred her divine nature to you, to cover you."

I sucked in a breath. "Does that mean you gave up your divinity?"

Amara stepped forward, pressing her wrinkled fingers together. Her crepey skin hung along her jaw. "I did, child," she said. "And I'd do it again without hesitating. You are our future."

Poseidon winced. "We may be getting ahead of ourselves, Amara."

She nodded and reached towards me but then paused, drawing back and grabbing the horse's reins once more. Poseidon's features tightened, and he gestured with his jaw. "Let us walk together, Artemis."

I clamped my teeth down, but I bobbed my head and ambled alongside him. He remained silent for a while, his golden eyes ahead of us on the sandy divots of the beach, the smooth forms of driftwood where gulls that swept through the sky landed on limbs, causing them to tremble.

"Your mother," Poseidon said, tucking his hands behind him, "had a prophecy as a young woman from the Fates."

I ran my tongue against the back of my teeth. "How did she meet the Fates?"

"I suppose you know every half-deity has an audience with them as a child."

I nodded. Apollo had gone and returned, refusing to speak for a week. That had been years ago, but the memory of his anxious eyes and furrowed brow pierced my mind through with clarity.

"Your mother—Leto—was gifted from childhood. She was but a mortal and yet had magic in her blood. Likely a grandparent of hers was a half-deity, but that connection is lost." He swept his muscled arms out, rippling the robe he wore. "Her skills as a seer became apparent by the time she was three. And so, the high priestess of her village made an appeal to the goddess Hebe." He paused and shifted towards me. "Are you familiar with her?"

"She's one of Apollo's siblings."

"Yes. Hebe arranged the meeting for your mother, and when she turned ten, she received her prophecy."

Sandpipers scuttled by, their long legs peppering into the sand as they raced the tide. "What was it?"

Poseidon cleared his throat and stopped walking. Standing there bathed in sunlight, he looked like a god of the sea, the curves of his muscles gleaming in light, the ocean roaring beyond him, his strong jawline highlighted as he lifted his face towards the heavens. "What I tell you changes your fate. Or perhaps seals something Leto set in motion many years ago."

"I know."

He nodded. "She was to be the mother of a new era. A time comes"—he paused, frowning—"where the old high gods fade, and new ones rise to take their place."

I leaned away from him, my toes dipping into the warmth of the sand. "Are you talking about me?"

"I am. You and your brother."

"We're to replace the old gods? Do you mean yourself?"

"Yes, and Zeus, among others."

"You're saying this like it doesn't matter to you."

He sighed and stepped closer to the shoreline, so that his feet dipped beneath the tide as it swept in. "I've lived a very long time. Far longer than you can presently imagine. I've seen entire human civilizations come and go, stars spark to life and burn themselves out, galaxies form and dissolve. This world and its pettiness have long exhausted me. It doesn't bother me in the least to see it handed off to someone else, to face whatever reality may stand for gods after our deaths."

"And Zeus?"

"Will fight to maintain his authority, even if the cost is the torture and pillaging of every soul remaining on this planet, divine or otherwise."

My sandaled feet sunk into the damp sand as another

wave washed forward, a scalloped shell biting my toes. "How does he accept the Fate's prophecy, then?"

Poseidon clicked his tongue. "He doesn't know it. At least not all of it. The Fates have long since held back futures from him. For all his power, he cannot usurp them. They reveal only pieces of destinies to him, bits they have selected."

"So, not about me or Apollo?"

"They've told him Apollo is to ascend and become the sun god. He believes that to be in his favor. But he also fears it won't. Zeus is not a fool." He shifted his sharp gaze back to me again. "Keep that in mind in your future."

"Maybe I don't want this future. Have you considered that?"

"I have not. What you wish for is irrelevant."

I scoffed. "Is that right?"

"It is. I understand why that offends your mortal sensibilities, but much more is at play here than your feelings."

I crossed my arms. "You know, I had imagined meeting my father for my entire life. I always thought I wouldn't like you, but I'd stupidly hoped it would be different."

His lips pursed, and he remained quiet for a dozen heartbeats. "I imagine the story you would like to hear is that your mother and I were very much in love. She made a mistake with Zeus, and she and I pledged ourselves to each other. Her death has haunted me since then, and I've spent the last two decades longing for you." He pinched his mouth together again. "But none of that is true, Artemis, and I would do you a great disservice to lie to you. Besides…" He flicked his wrist, and the waves swept back with the motion. "You have the resolution to handle reality."

Tears bit at my eyes. "That no one loves me? That my father doesn't feel a drop of affection for me. He abandons me to be raised by strangers in our mother's village, leaves me to think that I'm a mortal. And then he meets me," I growled, my mouth foaming with spit, "only to look me in the eye and tell me he couldn't care less?"

Poseidon cocked his head to the side. "I never said no one loved you. Your mother's feelings for you were fierce. And your brother—for all his flaws—is deeply devoted to you. Furthermore, I care very much about you. The world's future rests on both of your shoulders."

My nose flared. "You're concerned about my prophecy, not me."

He considered that, tapping his thumb against his arm. "That's true."

"Really? You're not even going to deny it?"

He blinked twice. "I won't lie to you. If that's what you're longing for, you will find yourself disappointed."

I blew out a breath and turned back to the sea. Dark clouds rumbled over it in the distance, wind picking up and peppering salt spray over my skin. "Fine. Tell me what I need to know then."

"Amara gave up her divinity to shield you, so that the other high gods did not recognize who you truly are. Otherwise, Zeus would have killed you at your birth. As you saw Amara earlier, you know she sacrificed much to do so. She can pull the veil back and restore your powers. She longs to, in fact; the magic calls for her. But"—his jaw tensed—"you must be ready for what you'll encounter. If, once she unbinds your veil, the gods discover a future high deity with a prophecy of ruining them walks the earth, you will face a great deal of wrath."

I clenched my fingers into fists. "You already told me I'm resolute enough to face it."

"That you are."

"Fine, then. Release the shield and let me get back to my life, and you back to yours."

"It's more than that, Artemis. You and your brother must move when the time is right. You need to take the spark of Olympus for yourselves."

I leaned back from him. "Neither of us has any desire to be the reigning gods."

He reached out, placing a large hand on my shoulder, and my muscles froze. "Which is precisely why you must be the ones to take it."

Feelings swept their way through me. I was pretty sure I hated this man. My father. Apollo had always liked him, but he hadn't known who he truly was. And he probably had looked out for Apollo for my sake. Not for me—Temi's —sake, but me—the prophecy holder's—sake. And that made me furious.

I was a goddess, though.

And unlike Apollo, that future didn't scare me as much as it did him.

"Unveil me, then, and leave."

"Very good." He nodded back at the shore we'd walked from. We returned in silence. As we approached Amara, Poseidon bobbed his head, and she stepped forward. I studied her as she took my hands in hers. She'd said I was her hope. And the way she looked at me, it made me feel exposed and found wanting. How many deities knew of me and my prophecy, and counted on me for answers? That weighed on me much heavier than the idea of ascending.

"Are you ready?" Amara said.

I nodded because I couldn't get words to form.

A sparkling sensation, like a glass of champagne fizzing, washed over my skin. And then a silver shimmer slipped over my dark arms. Energy swelled through my body, filling my limbs. I felt buoyant, as if I could float over the surface of the planet.

I released a breath as Amara dropped her hands. Her eyes glowed golden, the divine luster surrounding her once more. I twisted my fingers in front of me, the silver light blurring through the air above the khaki sands.

My heart thundered.

I'd known I was a goddess, had accepted that.

But this.

This was real.

And I suddenly wanted to throw up.

I was a high deity.

Goddess of the moon.

And prophesied to end Zeus' reign.

It seemed like a bizarre nightmare. Just a few months before, I'd been Temi, the huntress who helped the women in my village. Now, I held the fate of the world in my hands. The nauseous feeling grew.

Glitter swept through the sky, a floral scent filling the air.

My arm ached in memory of the last time I had sensed that.

Poseidon lifted his face. "Amara and I must leave. Hera has come to Lesbos." He studied me. "Do you wish to go with us? It will take some months before you can ascend, and until then, you remain vulnerable."

"She's already attacked me once. She won't return for me again."

He frowned. "Then she's likely after your mortal companions you traveled here with."

I sucked in a breath and shifted towards the rippling palm trees that stood in front of Sappho's residence. Epiphany and Valerian. Gods. "Would she harm them?"

Poseidon fixed me with a look. "She would. It's a

burden of being a high-god. No human around you is truly safe."

"I have to go after them and warn them."

"Very well." Poseidon bowed and took the reins to his horse from Amara's hand.

I swept back towards him, my braids thunking against my shoulders. "You won't help me?"

The gray of the clouds beyond silhouetted him. His expression scarcely shifted. "It is not my place to intervene with Hera. More is at stake here than the lives of two mortals. I'd advise you to not allow her to bait you with them. Their deaths—if it came to that—will be a noble sacrifice to the future."

"Are you serious?" I gasped so hard it hurt. "You're a monster."

He sighed. "I'm a god, Artemis. An old one, as I reminded you. You need to consider the destiny that rests on you and your choices."

I studied him for another breath, the nobility and power that radiated around him. And then I turned and ran up the path towards the stables, my feet chuffing against the sand.

Fuck Poseidon.

I'd tear the world apart before I let Hera harm Valerian and Epiphany.

I may know nothing about myself, my powers, my fate.

But I knew about loyalty.

I knew friendship.

And love.

The floral smell in the air deepened. My breath came heavy as I threw myself faster along the trail.

26

Hyacinth

Zephyrus leaned in closer to me, his eyes sharpening like a predator's. I had no idea where he was going with the speech he gave, but my mind was spinning trying to figure out how to stop him from continuing. Control slipped out of my fingers, and I didn't know how to grasp a hold of it. Whatever point he was about to make, he hadn't informed me of it, and my thoughts whirled, trying to calculate his angle. However it landed, I feared my people would bear the burden from it. Despite that, words wouldn't form. I didn't have time to consider a course of action.

Zephyrus draped his fingers along my arm, and I fought a cringe. "The last few days have provided an opportunity for us to make and reaffirm alliances," he said loudly enough that his voice carried through the room to everyone who watched us. Boreas frowned, crossing his arms as Zephyrus continued. "A new day comes where—"

Apollo strode up, wrapping his arm around my back, pulling me out of Zephyrus' grasp, curling his fingers over my hip.

I froze. And then Apollo leaned over and kissed me

hard, our teeth clinking together. My mouth gaped, and I jerked away.

What the fuck?

He peeled away from me, glaring at Zephyrus. Everyone in the room tittered and laughed, and Zephyrus glowered.

I had spent an entire lifetime learning to act appropriately in tense situations.

To know how to fake authority and calm in front of a crowd.

But at that moment, I couldn't force my mouth shut. I couldn't stop gaping at Apollo.

He had just forced himself on me to embarrass Zephyrus.

He had just... used me.

Boreas cleared his throat, swallowing his drink before turning and exiting the room. The crowd's voices had dropped to whispers covered by hands.

Everyone stared at us.

Our plan—all the careful maneuvering and work from the past week—was fucked.

But that wasn't what draped over me like a cloak of misery at the moment.

Apollo had violated me for vengeance.

I sucked in a sharp breath as Zephyrus spoke, his mouth twisting up like he swallowed back bitter wine. His voice came as a stinging whisper that punctuated the air as he snapped at Apollo. "I knew if I pushed you hard enough, made you jealous enough, you'd show your hand. I didn't realize you were so foolish to do so in front of a crowd of gods who will carry your secrets into the world and undo you. But I suppose you've made a fool of me as well. Congratulations," he hissed at him before shifting towards me. "I presume, as you remain in his embrace, that you two are together?"

I sucked in a breath and jerked away from Apollo, who crossed his arms. We stared at each other for a moment. There were so many things I should say, so many actions I should take to smooth this out. But I couldn't find the words. Apollo had betrayed me.

Zephyrus leaned in towards Apollo, his eyes glittering. "I hope my shame is worth what all it will cost you in the end."

"Fuck you," Apollo growled.

Zephyrus' features tightened, and he shifted to me. "And, as to you, Hyacinth. You can forget everything we've discussed. I wouldn't align myself with someone as manipulative and traitorous as you for anything. Best of luck to you with your purpose." He turned, his coat rippling out behind him, and he swept out of the room.

The laughter among the crowd picked up. My cheeks flamed, and I shifted back to Apollo.

Words.

Come up with words.

But they froze on my tongue, painful icicles that stung through me.

He'd used me.

Without my consent.

Publicly.

Flora walked up, her lips spread wide, her teeth glimmering, and she lifted her chin towards Apollo. "I must say, Apollo, you've vastly improved my day."

She bowed and sauntered away.

Notus covered his gaping mouth with his hand. "Wait," he said. "Are you two fellows together? Gods,"—he smacked his forehead—"that does make sense, I suppose."

The laughter picked up again. Some deities rolled their

eyes while others pushed out of the room, eager to separate from the shame and drama of it all.

"Cyn," Apollo said.

"Let's go," I growled. I couldn't talk to him about it. Not there in front of everyone. I inclined my head to Delon and Len, and they both fell in alongside us. Eyes trailed our group as we left.

Once we made it to the stables and guards hitched up our horses, Apollo approached me again. "Cyn, listen…"

"No. Not here."

He nodded.

I tossed my bag into the carriage. I couldn't even look at Apollo. How could he? How could he possibly have done that?

Trust was what we had between us.

That and respect were the foundation of our entire relationship.

And he'd just set it on fire, shamed me, destroyed everything because of his petty jealousy. I wanted to sink into the snow and let it swallow me whole. I wanted to scream until my throat turned raw. I wanted to throttle him.

Instead, I hopped up into my seat on the chariot and kept my eyes ahead when Apollo joined me. As the horses trotted out into the ice of the world, my heart sank. I didn't understand how he could have done that, and I had no idea how to handle it. My soul ached as we trundled out into the ivory of the day.

27

Epiphany

Meadow's feet clattered along the path, seashells and pebbles jumping by her feet as she galloped along it. The wind whipped over both of us, brushing my hair away from my face. The trail we took curled alongside a densely forested mountain that swallowed the view of the house and the beach and left me feeling—for a moment at least —alone in the world.

My guards had startled when we'd trotted out of the stable and left without so much as me looking over my shoulder as they cried out. They'd probably given Valerian an earful. A tinge of guilt pinched at me. But, no. I was so mad at Valerian I hoped they tore into him.

I tried to make sense of everything Val had said. But warmth swept up over my cheeks again. He'd regretted it, wished he could take it back. I bet my brothers never had their lovers telling them they had remorse over joining their beds.

No. It was because I was a princess. Fucking double standard.

I dug my heels into Meadow's side, and she picked up

her pace, darting along the forest path and farther into the mountain, causing bushes to tremble as she turned corners and smacked against them.

My whole damn life I'd been treated differently, and I was freaking tired of it. I wanted one person who really saw me beyond politics, rules, and connections.

I had thought I'd found that in both Temi and Val.

But, no.

Now that Temi knew she was a goddess, maybe she didn't want a mere mortal as a friend. No. Not just a mortal. A princess—a shiver of equal parts frustration and revulsion coursed down me—who might stir up international issues. Who wanted to be friends with a high-profile but useless person like me?

And Valerian... The heat returned to my face, warming my neck. Meadow's rhythmic clattering filled the spaces between our breaths. Valerian wanted me married off to some Lord where he didn't have to bother with the shame he felt about me anymore.

He was in love with me—had sex with me—but wasn't willing to risk anything for our sake. Or for mine.

It hurt.

Beyond all the anger burning through me, that deep ache of betrayal was the actual emotion. I felt so lost and so incapable of doing anything about it.

I turned a corner and passed a large tree that wept towards the ground, its branches scraping into the sandy path. We'd already passed that tree. Which meant I sent us in circles around the damn mountain. Just like my life. I felt like I was making progress, doing something important, but it was all a game.

I clacked my teeth together hard enough that it hurt as we took another bend.

And then I jerked on Meadow's reins hard, pulling her up short to avoid hitting someone standing in the path.

Meadow snorted and tossed her mane.

The woman standing before us smirked as she lifted her face.

Her golden, glowing eyes bore into me, and a shiver ran down my spine.

"Well," she said, her voice silky. "It's convenient for you to come to me, and alone at that. Saves me the trouble of killing off your guards."

Searing light took over my vision, and I gasped, falling from Meadow and hitting the ground hard, my shoulder screaming in pain.

28

Apollo

Hyacinth had remained quiet since we left the Palace of the Four Winds, and the silence stretched between us like ice, cold and biting. I felt like I should speak, but I wasn't sure what to say. And I could barely turn to face Hyacinth with his furrowed brow and pinched lips highlighted by the brightness of the sun's reflection on the snow.

Hyacinth pulled the reins, and the horses stopped, prancing their hooves and chuffing up ivory powder that danced into the breeze. Hyacinth gestured at his guards and Delon and Len, a dark look flashing over his eyes, and they inclined their heads, trotting away from us.

Hyacinth turned towards me. "What the hell was that?"

"You didn't hear the people talking like I did. If I hadn't—"

"Oh, I'm certain," he bit out, "that we've given them all a great deal to talk about now."

I blew out a breath and crossed my arms. In the last couple of hours, I'd had time to think, and I'd perhaps acted too impulsively. But no. Zephyrus was setting up

Hyacinth's kingdom to fall for his cause. He would have allowed the death of his people solely to help him rise on a foolish quest that would result in nothing but loss and destruction. "Zephyrus is an asshole, Cyn. He planned to use you, and we don't need him."

"No," he said through his teeth. "You knew our standing before the gods and leaders present there was important. You understood the plan and agreed to it." He cracked his fist against the wood, and the chariot trembled with it. "Godsdamnit, Apollo, you understood how much was riding on this." Tears bit at his eyes. "How could you?"

I frowned. "We can't trust Zephyrus, anyway. And now everyone else sees that. He's—"

"He's the fucking god of the west wind," Hyacinth yelled. An icy breeze ruffled the fur around his hood. "He's deeply interconnected with basically every single deity we want on our side, regardless of how they feel about him. Many of which stood in that room and watched that... embarrassment... play out." He growled, his fingers curling into his palms. "And I don't need to tell you this. You knew it walking into this situation. You just let your petty jealousy—"

"You know what," I hissed. "I have been jealous. You're right. Him marching around like he had some hold on you, like you belonged to him. Yes, it burned me up."

"A great fucking analogy since you've burned all of our plans to the fucking ground."

I kicked back against the seat. "We'll go see the other gods again ourselves, and we can—"

"No. No, there's no 'we' in this anymore."

I snapped up again, the ice of my breath catching in my chest. "What do you mean there's no 'we'?"

"You disrespected the hell out of me, Apollo."

"Because—"

"And I could deal with that." He cut me off. "If you swore to me you would not do that again, I could process it and forgive you. But you may have just sacrificed my kingdom by acting on a whim." He pressed his fingers against his chest and wrinkles swept over his forehead. "There has to be at least one person in that room loyal to Zeus. How do you think he might react when he hears about us visiting the wind gods? When he knows we gathered with hundreds of deities and that we're caught up with Zephyrus who has his own fucking ambitions? So much for all the dedications we made at the temples for Zeus. If he finds this out, you might as well have handed my people over to your father yourself."

"I have not." I gasped, reaching for him, but he pulled back. "We can still work this out. Okay, maybe I messed up some, but—"

"You messed up?" he growled. "Apollo, you act like you knocked over a glass of wine. You didn't mess up; you just let your jealousy wreck this entire plan. Something my family has worked on for decades. The fate of millions of people that we've dangled on the complicated strategy of allying with Jupiter to stand against Zeus—a god who could end our country in a heartbeat. This is a plan we have managed to keep fucking quiet up to this point. And you've allowed your pettiness to squander that."

"You know what?" I leaned in closer to him, our knees brushing. "You're right. I can't stand to have someone else flirting with you. And I won't apologize for being petty about it. I'm sorry I screwed things up with Zephyrus and didn't handle that diplomatically. I'm sure there could have been a better approach. But I don't think we've squandered anything. Zephyrus stood in opposition to your aim, and we can still fix this."

Hyacinth's gaze swept out to the icy mountains in the

distance, lingering on the blurring blues of the world. His voice dropped to a whisper that tangled with the snow clattering around. "Are you wanting to fix it because of your error, or for my sake?"

"Your sake."

He shook his head, his lips pinching. "That's the problem. You're choosing me over everyone else."

"Of course I am. I love you."

He turned back towards me, emotions rippling across the hazel color of his eyes. "If you loved me, you'd respect me. And that means you would never," he said through his teeth, "force yourself on me. And godsdamnit we had an agreement. You knew we walked into this situation for me to deal with Zephyrus for the sake of my people. You broke your word to me."

"Cyn, I'm sorry. You're right. I was trying to help you and your kingdom, I swear. But I went about it wrong."

"You think?" He waved my words off. "You say you're trying to help my people, but you're picking me over the rest of the world. Doing that makes you a villain, not a diplomat."

"Then I'm a villain. And I won't apologize for that either because you mean everything to me."

I reached for his arm, but he jerked away from me, his gaze growing distant again. "I don't want to be with a villain." He gritted his teeth. "You don't even see the issue here, and that's the problem."

"I'm sorry, Cyn. Help me see it. I'll do whatever you want."

He stared out ahead of him, his features wrenched with pain, and it ached through me. His next whispered words caught me off guard. "Zephyrus said something to me about you." He turned towards me, his skin's color cool in the ivory light reflecting around us. "He told me that you've vowed to your father to ascend in the spring." His eyebrows pressed together. "Tell me that's a lie."

I stared at him, and my lip trembled. I had no idea how Zephyrus had heard about that though I suppose my father sharing it with others shouldn't surprise me. But this was the worst time for this information to come out. I'd only kept it from him so he could focus. But now, it would look like I'd done so because I wasn't honest with him.

His voice grew into a growl. "Tell me it's not true, Apollo."

I bowed my head, lacing my hands together. "It's true."

He released a sob that clouded into the air. "So... so you've lied to me?"

"No." I raised my face again. "Never, Cyn. But I didn't want to tell you until..."

"Until I'd made a godsdamn fool of myself? Until you acted on your impulses and decided things without consulting me that affect me and my entire fucking king-dom?" He stared at me, his eyes welling with furious tears that he batted away.

"I didn't want you worried about that and upset while trying to navigate everything politically during this trip."

"I don't get the privilege of putting my feelings first. I'm a prince. My people"—he spread his fingers over his chest, his rings glinting in the sun—"must come first before everything. It's my role. I thought you understood that, but you don't care. You just shame me in front of a group of people, put our entire plan at risk, piss off powerful gods, mark me like I'm some damn possession of yours, ruin everything, and act like we aren't making decisions together at all. You aren't thinking past your next fucking step, and you've harmed the citizens of my country with your impetuousness."

I swallowed but couldn't come up with words.

He bowed his head, his robe cutting off his features. "I need time to think."

My heart jumped into my throat. "What do you mean?"

He turned back towards me, and his expression solidified, the decisive edge of a king smoothing over him. "I want us to go separate ways for now. I can't..." His voice broke, tears glistening in his eyes. "I can't do this right now."

"No." A crackling feeling splintered through me, like a star exploding, all of its rippling bits of illumination tearing apart. "Cyn, please. I promise you." I snagged his hand. He didn't draw back, but his fingers draped limp in my grip. "I'll do whatever you ask. We'll fix this."

He nodded. His cheeks glowed scarlet in the wind. "I want us to fix it." He swept his gaze towards me and pulled his hand away. "But not together."

"Hyacinth, I'm begging you." My voice trembled. "Don't do this."

He gave his head a shake. "Maybe you should have considered that before you acted. I want us to split up for now. I need"—he winced—"time to think about things. You and Delon take half the guards and go south towards Ansair. See if you can make alliances there." His words puffed out in clouds in the chill air.

Tears bit at my eyes. I'd wanted to protect him, to save his kingdom, to help. But I'd destroyed his confidence instead. "The guards should stay with you," I whispered. "I can go to Ansair on my own."

He jerked his head in my direction, his expression taking on a glint. "Did you ever consider that I want Delon there to monitor you since I can't trust you to be diplomatic and the guards are for his sake?"

I choked over a breath. We stared at each other. A

gleam of sunlight rippled over one of his eyes, giving the hazel color a honey-touched glow.

The blow of what all I'd done plowed into me, stealing words. I wanted to help. But I had achieved the opposite, and now Hyacinth looked at me like a traitor, a thief, a villain unworthy of a scrap of confidence. "I'll do whatever you wish for," I said, bowing my head.

"Then you'll go to Ansair." His voice rang so cold, it competed with the temperatures for iciness.

I swallowed and nodded as the wind whipped through my coat, a trail of it streaking into my clothing and sending a chill down my spine.

29

Artemis

I ran into the stables, where horses lifted their large noses at me as I tumbled past them. Valerian stood at the end, stacking saddle blankets onto a shelf. "Valerian," I yelled.

He shifted towards me, tension strung over his shoulders. His eyes widened as he took me in—the silver glow around my limbs that rippled along the wood surface of the stalls. "Hey, Temi," he whispered.

"Where's Epiphany?"

The sour expression returned to his face. "She's gone riding."

"Why isn't she with you?" I yelled with more volume than I'd intended. I clenched my teeth to calm myself and huffed out the rest of my words. "She told me she was spending the afternoon with you."

He shifted back towards me, his lips pinching. "She's upset with me."

"What happened?"

He sighed and gave me a tired look. "She stormed out of here on Meadow. Her guards followed behind, but"—

he clicked his tongue—"she's an excellent rider, so it will probably take them some time to catch up with her."

Blood drained from my face. "She's alone?"

The brooding, scowling version of Valerian washed away, and he stepped closer to me, his voice holding a pinch of concern. "Something's wrong."

"Damn it." I kicked a stall. The silver light blurred around my features. Gods, I saw why Apollo insisted on always wearing a veil now. The glow was distracting and annoying. "Epiphany is in serious trouble."

"Why? What happened?"

"Hera is here."

"She's looking for you again?"

Tears stung my eyes, and I couldn't tell if they were more from frustration or fear. "No. Poseidon thinks she intends to harm my companions in order to get to me. We have to find Epiphany... now."

"Oh, gods," Valerian breathed. "I'll saddle our horses."

"I'll let Sappho know what's happening, and I'll return in five minutes."

Valerian didn't answer me. He yanked a rein off a nail, the leather smacking against his hands.

By the time I returned, he had two mares ready, and I jumped onto the back of mine. "Where did she go?"

Valerian growled as we exited the stable. "I'm not sure. Her guards went that way." He jerked his chin towards a path that led toward the mountains.

"Okay." I nudged my heels into my horse, urging her into a gallop. We couldn't waste time.

The wind swept over me, the clattering of our horse's hooves pounding in my ears. Palm trees shivered in a breeze that picked up from the ocean where my father had retreated. I clenched my teeth down hard at that, though. He could help me, but he wouldn't. He never had.

But that was fine.

I didn't need his help.

I'd do it myself.

The path into the forest that curled up the mountain narrowed, and Valerian pulled out ahead of me, jumping in his saddle due to the speed he went and the way his horse weaved through the branches and boulders.

I didn't know what had happened between Valerian and Epiphany, but he had been sulking, and Pip had stormed off. Which meant they'd gotten into a fight. And normally I might have found that annoying, but today it may have pushed Epiphany right into the arms of someone who intended her harm.

And Hera would hurt Pip because of her hatred of me.

It had nothing to do with Epiphany.

And—gods—the irony. I'd wanted her to stay back because I didn't want her involved. But if she had come with me to see Poseidon, she wouldn't be in harm's way now.

Damn it.

That was foolish of me.

I should have kept her sewn to my hip.

Maybe I would once we found her and I gave her a talking to about rushing off on her fucking own.

I knew anger clenched its way around my heart so I could avoid the fear that wished to snarl and swallow through me.

If Hera wanted Epiphany dead, she would probably already be so.

No.

"No," I said again out loud, startling Valerian, who looked over his shoulder. I gave my head a shake, and we continued forward, ducking at low-hanging limbs, our horses clambering along the steep path.

We turned a corner and pulled the reins to slow down as we approached other horses, Epiphany's guards on them.

"Have you found her?" Valerian said, his voice breathy.

Theos narrowed his eyes at Valerian. "No. We've lost her trail. We've gone over this path a dozen times and can't find sight of her."

Panic assailed me again, numbing my fingers, and the wobbly motion of the horse beneath my legs tilted me, my vision spinning with it.

Gods, what if Hera had taken Epiphany? What if we never found her? Damn it, this was all my fault, and I didn't have answers about what to do.

Valerian's expression grew cool and focused, his gaze sweeping over the world. Long-limbed trees tangled together, competing with vines and slender stalks of bamboo that clattered as the wind shook them. Pepperings of gray clouds peaked through the massive boughs of the forest.

"There," he said, pointing to an opening in the branches the size of a large window over a fallen log. Beyond the emerald leaves surrounding it, a drop in the mountain stretched, a hole so deep I couldn't see where it ended. "That's where she'd go."

Theos frowned. "That's quite the jump."

Valerian's eyes tightened as he pulled on his reins and compelled the creature to back up. "Epiphany could make it." He nudged his horse into a run and jumped, ducking his head but still grazing the branches, which shuddered with his motion. His mare made the pass, its feet clicking as it hit the stone on the other side.

Oh, shit.

Valerian and Epiphany had explained how to jump on horseback to me before, but I'd never done it myself.

But I wasn't getting left behind when Epiphany may need our help.

"Yah," I said, urging my horse forward. She picked up into a run and wind rushed over the sweat that had broken out on my skin, my flesh turning to ice. I could do this. The vibration of the horses' gallops echoed through my body, and I leaned in tighter towards her neck, tensing my legs, and then dug my heels into her side.

She reached the end of the path and leapt into the air.

For a moment, we soared.

We transformed into a bird sailing through the brush, limbs scraping my flesh.

And then we stretched out over nothing, the drop hundreds of feet below.

Rocks clattered with the motion, echoing as they tumbled down.

The impact of the horse landing beside Valerian thudded into my bones. But I released a shaky breath. We'd made it.

Valerian nodded at me and then began along the trail again.

The clattering of more horses crossing the gap sounded as some guards fell in behind us.

We turned a corner where a massive tree which had limbs that brushed down to the dirt of the trail. The branches on it jerked and shook, and we slowed.

Meadow pulled at her lead, which was tangled in the branches. Val jumped off his horse, landing with a thump that stirred up dust on the path. "Epiphany," he yelled, walking around Meadow and patting her side. He leaned his head back towards the cliff and screamed again, his voice trembling. "Epiphany!"

"Over here," Theos called.

Valerian and I walked to where he crouched down

beside two other guards, a scrap of pink silk in his hand. Theos looked up at us, his expression haunted. He lifted his fingers, and they glimmered crimson. "Blood," he said.

"No." I swept my face up to take in the world, as if Epiphany stood somewhere within reach and I could will her into appearing.

But I knew what we all were aware of.

Hera had Epiphany.

And she'd hurt her, at the very least.

My heart dropped into my stomach.

30

Apollo

The air warmed as we came down out of the mountains and into a valley gray and dull with the colors of late autumn sweeping into the grasses and painting the trees in the distance. A bird cried, a lonely, haunting sound that overcame the rhythmic clattering of the guard's horses for a moment. I clenched my fists.

The entire day, I had replayed all that had happened.

But my mind kept sticking on Hyacinth.

On how he had looked at me.

As if he finally saw the truth of me.

I had ruined everything. Like I always did. If I had never defied Zeus, he wouldn't have destroyed my mother's village, threatened Temi, sent me to Hyacinth so I could ruin things here as well. Life suddenly felt hopeless and wrung out. I'd carry on with this mission—because Cyn had asked me to. I would keep my word to him even if he didn't think I could do so.

Delon's arm brushed mine as the chariot weaved over the uneven road. The warmth of his limbs against me burned like shame. Hyacinth had sent him with me to monitor me. He didn't believe I meant things for his good; he didn't trust that I would never betray him.

I sighed. I guess I had, in a way.

Godsdamnit. It was the fastest means to shut Zephyrus up, and Hyacinth had been panicking. He wanted him to stop.

Okay, publicly embarrassing Hyacinth in the process wasn't really my intention.

But, Hades' realm, I didn't have time to think.

I just acted.

And now Cyn saw me unveiled. A selfish god who caused destruction of everything he touched. I was a fool to return with him at the end of the summer. As though I could actually help him, instead of just causing more trouble.

It was probably over between us.

Allowing that thought to form, to sit in my mind and take space, hurt. It would never be over for me. Even if he told me that he never wished to see me again. I'd honor his wishes. But I would love him for eternity. Until this world ceased to exist and—gods willing—took me with it.

I ruined everything.

And I was tired of that.

I wanted so desperately to matter, to do good, to love Hyacinth like no person had loved another.

Not just with words, but with my actions.

And I'd already fucked that up in the short time of our relationship.

I had been jealous of Zephyrus. Maybe that was my misstep. Damn it. I kicked the chariot wall, and Delon shifted towards me, dropping the reins onto his lap. "I think we'll make it to Ansair in good timing if we keep up the pace."

I nodded. "What do you know of Niria's connection with Ansair?"

Perhaps this was a test. Hyacinth had said he needed me to focus on his kingdom as much as our relationship. Maybe if I successfully created an alliance with them, Hyacinth would give me another chance.

Gods, all I wanted was to take back every hurt I'd ever caused him.

Starting with the obnoxious way I'd treated him at fifteen, to the headache I'd created for him when I first visited, and scrubbing out the entire morning. The shock on his face. The disbelief in his eyes. What Zephyrus said was true. Why would someone as good as Hyacinth bother with a mess of a god like me?

Delon laughed. "Niria and Ansair's relationship is shit. There's not a maiden's chance in Zeus' bedroom of us making an alliance with them."

That sank into me.

So, this wasn't an actual mission.

Hyacinth had set us up with a task that would fail. The last scrap of hope ripped from me, and I felt as though I stood bare and aching on the icy cliffs of loss. Hyacinth was everything to me. And I'd thrown our relationship away with actions that took a dozen heartbeats.

Delon side-eyed me, his jaw jumping. "Do y'know something interesting about Cyn?"

Discussing Hyacinth with him was at the bottom of things I wished to do, but he'd also gotten stuck with me. "What's that?"

"I love to tease him about his sexual partners." Okay, there was officially something lower on the list of things I didn't want to talk about. And one of them was the fact that Hyacinth was desired by others, that he would likely find another partner, someone better who would actually deserve him. Delon carried on like he didn't notice the change in my mood. "But for all the shit I've given Cyn, I couldn't name a single person he's been with before you."

"He's been with others."

"I know." He clicked his tongue at the horses and urged them back to the center of the road, the sun draping in washes of crisp oranges over the valley ahead of us. "The point I'm making is that I've never heard about any of them. Maybe he told Emrin or Valerian—he was always closest with them—but you're the first partner he's had that he's wanted others to know about."

All the justifications and regrets and anger washed away.

And left me with one thing.

Sadness.

So bitter and bone deep it was like plunging into an icy pond, the grip of it sinking into muscles before I had a proper chance to catch my breath.

I'd ruined everything.

With the only person I'd ever loved. The only person I ever would love… I was sure of it.

And I had destroyed that.

"I'm sure he regrets that now," I said gruffly and leaned farther into the corner of the chariot, away from Delon.

"Do you really think that?"

"Of course." I gestured out to the world. The gold of the sun looped over my hands like my future reached out for me. "He sent us on a worthless mission he knew we couldn't succeed at."

"Yeah, well, he's fucking pissed at you."

"It's deserved."

"That's true." I sighed, and Delon kicked his ankle up on his knee. "I've seen Hyacinth angry a few times. He needs space to blow off steam a bit and think matters through."

"I believe he's already decided." The way he looked at me as he told me to go to Ansair seeped into my bones.

"Maybe take heart that he sent me with you."

"Because he doesn't trust me. He said he wants you to watch and make sure I don't ruin things further."

Delon laughed. "Cyn, you asshole." I frowned at him, but he just gave his head a shake, his eyes twinkling. "He told you that shit to hurt your feelings. Which obviously worked." I cleared my throat hard and crossed my arms. "He sent me with you because he gives a fuck about you. I mean, I am one of his closest childhood friends and a son of a prestigious family from our country. Do you really think he'd risk my life to watch a god... as if that was actually a possibility, anyway?" He shook his head again, his chestnut hair glimmering with highlights of gold in the sunset's light. "No. He needs some space, but he'll come around."

Could that be true? If so, I'd go to Ansair and find some way to get them on our side. I'd do anything to win Hyacinth back. If there was even a glimmer of hope, I'd snag onto it and cling to it like my soul depended on it. I was afraid it did. "I'm not sure. Will he be able to forgive me? I messed everything up."

"Everyone messes up." Delon shrugged. "Even Cyn."

I sighed. There was messing up, and then there was shaming your partner in front of a room full of hundreds of deities and human leaders. The more I thought about it, the more I realized how stupid and impulsive that was. I could have knocked a table of glasses over. I could have punched Zephyrus in his face and see what color his blood ran. That would have been fucking satisfying on a different level. Though it might have actually made people like him more. And Hyacinth was right. I kissed him because I wanted to mark him as mine. I wanted everyone in the room to know he belonged to me. He said I'd disrespected the hell out of him, and it was true.

I hung my head. "It was more than just a small misstep on my part."

"Yeah." Delon raised his eyebrows. "You fucked that one up royally."

I turned towards him. "Is that supposed to be reassuring?"

The horse's hooves clattered along the road, and the sound tangled up with Delon's laugh. "Hades' realm, if I know. If Hyacinth wanted someone who could give you wisdom, he should have sent Len. But he stuck you with me." He shifted his eyes in my direction, a smirk stealing over his expression. "I'm offering the best I've got because I need you to come out of this funk, so I can finagle the rest of your money bag from you during this trip."

I stared at him for a moment, my lips inching up. "I'm a better card player when I'm in a foul mood."

"Noted. I'll work harder on the cheering up aspect, then."

I huffed a laugh but then dragged my fingers back through my hair. Because he was right. I'd royally fucked up.

31

Artemis

"Damn it." I slammed my fist onto the table in the center of the room. The light of sunset poured in, highlighting the texture of the cream-colored walls, brightening shadowy corners.

Sappho looked over her shoulder at me, her eyes holding a touch of irritation, before she shifted back to the shelves in front of her, shuffling through scrolls on them.

Valerian stood against the wall, his arms crossed. Where he had swallowed into himself, I had spent the last half an hour pacing the floor, glaring at Epiphany's guards who milled around the edges of the room and snapping at anyone who spoke. I knew I was being prickly and unhelpful, but it was the only thing holding off sheer terror for me.

We'd found blood.

Which meant...

No, not necessarily. She could be okay. And we'd find her and get her back.

We would.

Valerian shifted, his expression darkening. He had to

feel the same as me, like this was his fault. We probably were both to blame, but thinking that didn't do a damn thing to help.

Sappho unrolled a map and spread it over the table, drumming her fingers against it. "We know a few things. Princess Epiphany was last seen a few hours ago, and while Hera can travel instantly herself, she cannot do so with a mortal." She flowed her ruby-painted nails over the page. "If she wanted her dead—"

"She's not dead," I bit out, and Valerian shuddered.

Sappho sighed. "I agree." She spoke slowly. "Because if that was Hera's intention, she would have left her there for you to find. Which means she has taken her." My body slumped. I needed to calm down and focus. Fury would not help us here. Sappho swept a circular motion around the pale blue color of the ocean on the map. "So, Hera either has her on my island or somewhere she could have gotten to by boat quickly."

"We should be out looking, then. We're wasting time."

"Dionysus' panthers are already searching. And they have far keener senses than you, even in your newly revealed form." Her eyes trailed over the silver glowing along my arms, and I crossed them. "It will take months, possibly years, of dedicated effort before you can ascend to your full power."

Valerian shifted again, his expression turning to one of desperation and hopelessness. I had to turn away from him. I couldn't have him believing Epiphany was doomed. Because I needed to believe that she had a chance.

A panther jumped through the open window, landing on the tile floors with a thump, and glittering before shifting forms. Atara's words rushed together. "We know where she is."

Epiphany's guards, Valerian, and I all jerked our faces towards him.

"On the island?" Sappho said.

"Not this one."

"Which?" She gestured to the map.

He prodded a thick finger to a small dot farther out to sea. "We followed her trail to the beach on the other side. Sea nymphs saw Hera heading in this direction. They believe she wanted them to see her go."

Sappho blew out a breath and shifted her gaze towards the window where the sun set in dramatic layers of light, apricots and burgundies washing over everything. It would be dark soon.

"We go," I said. "Now."

"No," Sappho said. "That's the Island of Sorrow."

Valerian lifted up and stepped forward like he reanimated again. "What is it?"

I growled. "I'm not afraid of an island."

Atara's expression darkened. "The Island of Sorrow is where Zeus punishes gods. It holds the earthly entrance to Tartarus."

Valerian's skin paled. "She plans to lock Epiphany in the abyss of torment?"

"No," Sappho whispered. She paused for a weighted moment and then raised her eyes to meet mine. "She wants to lure Artemis to the island. If she could manage to get her into Tartarus, Artemis would not have access to her powers there, and no one could rescue her. Hera could seal her and her powers and the prophecies that go with those away."

My mouth gaped, but words wouldn't come. This really was my fault. Hera harmed Epiphany solely to punish me. I didn't take her warning. She had asked me if I had known the story of Pandora. What had been in her box? All the hurt and misery of the world. That's what I had unleashed by coming here and chasing answers.

But I had to. This wasn't just about me and what I wanted. I clenched my fingers, and the glowing light blurred. As if I'd sought this. I didn't go out seeking a godly parent, didn't wish for divinity or a powerful prophecy. Fate threw it at me.

I understood now why Apollo thought divinity ruined everything.

I had included Epiphany on this trip, though, pushed her away this afternoon, and encouraged her to share her feelings with Valerian, which sparked whatever caused her to run off.

So, that was on me. And I had to fix it.

"I want to go."

"No," Sappho said so firmly I winced. Her jaw jumped, but she gave her head a shake. "You heard what Hecate told you. Your prophecy affects this entire world."

"If it's my prophecy"—I slammed my hand against the table, causing the map to jump—"then it shouldn't change regardless of my actions, right?"

"If prophecies were that simple, Hera would not goad you. She could change the course, lock you in Tartarus, keep Zeus in authority. Think about that." Sappho leaned in towards me. "There's been a great many of us who have spent our lifetimes trying to remove him from power. Will you throw it all away?"

"What about Epiphany?"

Valerian's nose wrinkled, his eyes flaming as they flipped to Sappho again. His feelings for her had only soured. Sappho nodded. "We'll rescue her, but—"

"But?" I yelled.

"It can't be you. In case anything goes wrong with the mission. It has to be someone else." She skimmed her gaze over the guards. "If we don't wish to bring Hera's wrath onto Niria, it can't be any of her guards that she might recognize."

"The panthers will help as we are able," Atara said, his looming form silhouetted by the bookshelf. "But we are blood vowed not to harm Zeus or Hera. Our lives are forfeit if we do so."

"I'll do it," Valerian said.

Everyone shifted towards him with various looks of incredulity. "Val..." I began.

"I know." His voice firmed. "I'm just a human, and I'm not even a trained guard at that. But that's the thing. Hera is expecting Temi to show up... possibly other gods. She's anticipating a fight, but what if we gave her the opposite?"

"What do you mean?"

He cleared his throat and reached out, brushing his fingers over the dot of an island gently as if it was Epiphany's hand he touched. "We know that a god can transfer their powers to another person so that Zeus' line cannot recognize them. Is there a deity who could veil me? I could go seek Epiphany."

Birds whistled and sang, giving one last performance before settling for the evening. Sappho's jaw shifted. "And if you ran into trouble?"

"I'll go with him," Atara said. "I cannot harm Hera, but I could help with magic, and the panthers could act as a distraction."

I slipped the key Hecate had given me out of my pocket and rubbed my thumb over the back of it. "We have a few deities on our side. I have an idea."

Everyone nodded, and the energy in the room shifted.

The despair of sunset bleeding away as a new moon of hope rose.

32

Hyacinth

The horse I rode twitched his ear, his hooves chuffing up bundles of ivory snow. I shifted in the saddle. It had been a while since I'd ridden, and my muscles ached. Getting off and walking again would be unpleasant.

Len trotted beside me. I had instructed the guards to give us a berth, and their horses marched along at a distance. Grief and anger gnarled their way through me. I didn't want the guards studying me too closely. I'd already noticed some of them giving me looks that veered somewhere between curiosity and sympathy. Neither made me feel comfortable.

I longed to be alone, to stand at the top of a cliff and scream until my voice ran out. To dive into water and let the ice of it embrace me. To lie in my bed and weep the sorrows of my heart until it stopped aching with every beat.

But I was a damn crowned prince heading up a war. I didn't have room for emotions. I didn't have the time to process things.

Len shifted towards me, his voice a golden puff in the air. "Where are we going, Cyn?"

Tears of frustration bit at my eyes. Where could we go that hadn't heard the story of what Apollo had done? Which gods might we seek that wouldn't see me as a fool, or even worse, realize we didn't align with their side and bring the god's wrath or—I shuddered—Zeus' fury onto Niria?

Fuck. This was supposed to buy us time. Not hasten things forward.

I needed to discuss everything with Father.

That had been the plan.

Before Apollo sashayed across the room and destroyed everything.

His name ached through me.

He came to my thoughts in bits and pieces. His eyes, golden and insecure under a star-speckled sky. His hands curving along my body like he touched the sacred. His lips quirking up with mischief.

I still loved him.

Desperately.

But how could he have done that? How could he have used me?

And he hadn't shared something as major as his ascension happening in a few months' time with me. I had to hear it from Zephyrus' mouth, from gossip.

Betrayal.

A bitter reality to embrace.

"Cyn?"

I sighed. Right. Len had asked for me to set the course for the rest of the trip. "I don't honestly know." I gestured a gloved hand out to the lilac forms of mountains we left. Getting away from the Palace of the Four Winds and

Zephyrus was the top priority. "What gods might receive us?"

He nodded. "Should we return home, then? Visit more temples along the way?"

"Would it even matter?" I yelled and then cleared my throat. My emotions felt like a rip current, sluicing through me, capsizing the boat of my resolve. "I think Apollo fucked any chances of Zeus not finding out our plans at this point."

Len tilted his head to the side. "Possibly."

"Do you disagree?"

"What were you anxious about?"

I pulled on the horse's reins, stalling the creature, and Len did the same. "What do you mean?"

"Zephyrus was giving a speech to the crowd, and you were uncomfortable. Why?"

I frowned. The guards had paused and waited for me to carry forward, their forms peachy in early evening light. "I didn't want him to proclaim any kind of connection with Niria. He was manipulating me for his own ends, and I damn well knew it."

Len nodded. "And so did Apollo."

"Apollo acted out of jealousy."

"That too." Len's dark eyes lifted. "But he saw you needed something, and he responded. Perhaps impulsively, but he stalled Zephyrus nonetheless."

I groaned. "He used me to shame Zephyrus in front of a room full of people."

Len combed his gloved fingers down his horse's mane. "And what do you think that will do for Zephyrus' plans that you were not a fan of?"

My breath caught, the ice of the air stinging my lungs. It would likely destroy them. Whatever hopes he had on aligning gods with his goal of coming against Zeus and

Jupiter were probably ruined now alongside his pride. And that… that possibly put Niria in a better position. Could that have been Apollo's aim? Maybe he had a purpose beyond just jealousy that drove his actions. He'd said that Zephyrus' goals didn't align with mine. And he'd explained that he didn't tell me about his ascension because he didn't want to throw off my focus. But, nonetheless…

I clicked my tongue and urged the horse forward again. "I suppose you make a point. But, still… Zeus is likely to hear of this, and then what?"

Len's dark hair fluttered as a gale of wind whirled around us. "Worst-case scenario, we move into a war we already knew we were heading into."

"I guess that's true."

"Who else doesn't like Zephyrus?"

"What?"

"Which other deities were there that you know will definitely not align with Zephyrus?"

I considered that as the horses trundled down into a valley where the snow receded, brown grasses sticking out in low spots. "Flora," I said. "His wife. She can't stand him."

"We could go to her?"

I winced but nodded. "Yes, and she's a part of Jupiter's court as well. Perhaps we could get an impression if anything has changed in our relationship there."

"We head west, then." Len urged his horse into a trot.

I sighed but picked up the pace. Gods, the idea of riding hard for several days on horseback already hurt.

But more than that, the ache of Apollo's actions still rang through me.

Len seemed to imply that it wasn't a betrayal, though. Maybe Apollo was considering my country with his decisions as well. But he'd used me. Publicly. The shame of that burned on my cheeks again, the idea of having to share it with my father sinking into me. I would disappoint him. I would let him down. And the misery of that pooled in my stomach.

I had told Apollo he couldn't just put me first. That my kingdom had to come before us. Is that what he was doing with his actions and keeping things from me? For all my logic and reasoning, I hated the reality of it. Apollo disrespecting me like that—for any purpose—crossed a line. And we couldn't be in a relationship if he kept major things from me.

But maybe he wasn't the only one acting impulsively. I'd sent him away without truly discussing things.

No. It was a good thing for us to have some space. I wasn't even sure I could forgive him yet. If he was here, those feelings would only fester further.

Some small part of me wished I could reverse time, however. Unwind the last week, ignore the wind gods, and hide Apollo in the recesses of my memory, before everything fell apart.

I clenched my teeth and shifted in the saddle as we pressed forward into an uncertain future.

33

Epiphany

I gasped. My eyes ached at the darkness, trying to reach for any scrap of light.

None came.

The world had disappeared.

Dampness permeated the space, a trickling sound of water dripping somewhere in the distance, icy rock pressing against my legs.

A scream echoed in the distance, and hair rose on the back of my neck. I yanked at my arms and rattled chains that held them suspended above my head.

A bolt of pain shot through me like a searing flash of lightning.

For a moment, reality grew fuzzy, and everything blurred as though my mind swept away from my body. I fought against it, gulped in breaths and the clammy taste of the air.

I had done this before. Woken up in this space and moved too quickly, the agony ushering me into passing out.

I eased over, the chains clinking, taking pressure off my shoulder.

Feeling rushed into the muscle there, and I swallowed air with my gasp as another sting of pain coursed through me. Tears hit my cheeks and dripped down my face.

A low growl sounded from somewhere in the distance, and I shivered, tucking back against the uneven surface of the wall. As if cowering would help me. I was chained and injured and sat in the pitch black. Anything could come after me, and I wouldn't see it coming.

I swallowed at the dryness of my throat.

Hera had brought me here. The memory of her dragging me across the stones pierced back into my mind. My legs had scraped over sharp gravel, the pain yanking me into consciousness. I shifted, and the skirt of my dress stuck to my skin. Probably from dried blood.

My entire body ached, and I sobbed again—just once —a hopeless sound that echoed back to me.

Oh, gods. I didn't know how to get out of this.

I was entirely helpless. I hurt so badly I couldn't think straight, and Hera had trapped me in some godsforsaken place.

I would die.

I swallowed again and then coughed at the itchy sensation of it.

This is what Father had meant. *Remember, you're a princess*, he'd said. If I'd done that rather than rushing off on my own, leaving the safety of Sappho's residence, my guards, and Temi, then I would likely still be with them.

Instead, I had let my emotions get the best of me and peeled off into the mountains and right into the hands of Hera.

What did she want with me?

It had to be related to Temi. Did that mean she planned to trade me to her for something? Or threaten me to manipulate her for some purpose?

Gods, I hoped Temi wouldn't capitulate. Whatever consequences would come with it, it would be too much. I didn't wish to die, but I didn't want my life to cost Temi whatever it might.

I whimpered, a note of self-pity that rang through the dark space.

No. I couldn't give into despair. I had no control over what actions Temi might take. Maybe there was something I could do. I leaned my leg out. It ached so much that a rush of pain swept over me. But I ignored it and scraped my foot around until it hit a rock.

I dragged it in my direction. What would I do with a rock, anyway? My hands weren't free. But if someone released me, I could grab it and have some sort of weapon. I shifted it towards me.

A scream echoed from farther back in the space.

I jumped.

My shoulder pulled, and pain seared through me.

My vision blurred.

And the world faded again.

34

Apollo

Flags whipped in the wind from where they hung incrementally through the city of Ansair. Our group ambled through the intricately carved facades of buildings that hunched in towards each other, as if they meant to touch. Hundreds of bodies rambled by, sweet and smoky smells of street food jangling together with the low hum of people speaking.

A breeze swept down my coat, and I tugged it in tighter. Despite moving farther south, Ansair lay in a mountain pass, and it remained cool. I grazed my thumbs along the plain material of the jacket. I wished I'd allowed Hyacinth to choose a more elegant style now. The one I'd chosen looked too common for a god coming as an ambassador of a country. But I had the marks of a high god, and I'd unleashed my veil fully, the light glimmering and drawing attention I longed to hide from. It was all I had to bring to this—my status as a deity—and I didn't want to fail.

Delon had donned a formal outfit in a deep blue color with navy filigree patterns. He kept his shoulders rolled back, his jaw lifted, as if this was a normal thing for him and didn't bother him at all. How nice that must be.

We walked under a massive archway inlaid with gems and designs of ferocious looking winged creatures, and the noise and bustle of the city faded behind us.

A man with sharp, dark eyes stepped before our group and bowed. "Please follow me."

Delon nodded to our guards, and we continued forward through a maze of marble hallways and past several gates before entering a throne room that made Hyacinth's look demure.

Our footsteps echoed over the ivory and gold tiles that reflected light from the seven massive chandeliers hung above. Hundreds of people dressed in richly colored robes and dresses studied us as we strode through the space.

When we reached the throne, our guards bowed, pressing their faces to the ground, and Delon leaned forward, folding his torso towards his knees. I followed his lead and then rose again to find the king studying us, his lips pinched, his dark hair ruffled beneath a crown decorated in hundreds of jewels. "Ambassadors from Niria, I hear?"

"Your Highness." Delon swept into a submissive stance once more. "Thank you for making time to see us. I'm Delon, son of Lord Piers of Niria, and this is Apollo, son of Almighty Zeus."

The king's eyes dashed to me at that, but then he flicked his gaze back to Delon. "It surprises me, Lord Delon, to have visitors from Niria at all. It's been many moons since our countries have even traded together."

Delon grinned, as though this was going in the right direction. "I am privileged to say I have had a rich education, and during it, I've learned a considerable amount about Ansair, including the connections your King Dioson had with our country."

The king scowled and shifted in his seat. "You speak of my great-grandfather and how Niria acted as an ally for him. Your words concern me, Lord Delon."

"Do they?"

"You reference the history of men that are long dead. But you pull up our military ties, which makes me believe you intend to call on them, as though a war fought a century and a half ago would bear decisions I make for my country in the present day."

The muscle at the end of Delon's eyebrow twitched. I'd learned—through more than a few poorly played card games on my part—that was his tell. I cleared my throat. "It's an honor to meet you, Your Highness. I had hoped we could create connections for Ansair that might reach farther than just human nations."

The king shifted to me again, but his expression darkened. "It's interesting as that is not the rumor I've heard carried on the wind."

A chill slipped down my spine.

The wind.

Delon stiffened as well.

So, that bothered him too.

I cleared my throat. "What god does your city patronize, Your Highness?"

The king twisted his mouth up, as though he chewed on words. Eyes of the people in the court sliced in our direction and a nervous energy swept over me. We had only a handful of guards. We had all left our weapons back with our horses and carriage outside of the city—a requirement to have an audience with royalty—and we stood in a deeply protected, walled-in space, where hundreds of people, many armed, stared at us with contempt. Shit.

"Your father," the king said to me, "has long considered our lack of deity-worship to be reprehensible. However, our kingdom considers changing that. Perhaps your party could stay with us this evening." He nodded to a guard next to him, who returned the gesture and shifted dark eyes to us. "And we could discuss more in the morning?"

I hesitated. Everything in me seemed to pull away from the idea, my heart pounding. Something was off. I exchanged a look with Delon, and he smiled. "A gracious offer, Your Highness, but we have already paid for accommodations within the city proper. Let us know whatever time is most convenient for you tomorrow, and we will gladly return at your pleasure."

The king's jaw shifted, and he leaned against his throne. He hesitated for a moment before nodding. "Very well. I'll have a messenger sent for you at sunrise."

"Thank you, Your Highness," Delon said before bowing again and turning to leave the room. Ansair's guards huddled around our group like a dust cloud, intent on consuming us. But Delon kept his eyes forward until we reached the streets of the city. "Let's see if we can find a public dining hall of some sort and get some drinks before we turn in for the night."

My heart sank like a stone into the well of my stomach. That was supposed to be my chance to prove myself to Cyn. And it was a disaster. Something in me already knew that breakfast with the king wouldn't help. In fact... I dropped my voice to a whisper. "I think Zephyrus might have involved himself in this."

Delon looked back over his shoulder where palace staff lingered, their gazes glued on us. "Yeah, I suspected as much myself. We need to stay within the eyes of the court. I feared that if we followed those guards to a bedroom tonight, that may have been our last actions in this life." He grinned at me. "Or mine, at least. I guess Zephyrus couldn't take out a high deity."

I shivered. "Is returning tomorrow a wise idea, then?" Delon, for all his bluster, was just a mortal. And the reminder of how easily an enemy could harm him filled me with panic.

Delon clicked his tongue. "I plan to get many drinks tonight."

A merchant on the side of the street held up silk fabric before us, and we weaved past him. "Getting drunk would help?"

Delon chuckled. "No. But making sure that people in this city know that we're here and intend to visit again tomorrow might."

I nodded, and we pushed ourselves through the crowd and into a bustling dining hall. Delon ordered several drinks and slid one across the table to me. I took a swallow, but then the pit in my stomach grew, like a sinkhole that would slowly consume me. This was my opportunity. And it was already over.

"I'll return in a minute."

Delon frowned but inclined his head to me, and I rose, maneuvering out of the building and walking around the back until I found a ladder that led to the roof. I climbed it and then dropped with a sigh. The city sprawled out, as massive as Niria. The height made my stomach lurch and my vision blur.

It felt good to fear something as stupid as falling.

Because that dulled the actual pain.

Hyacinth.

I'd let him down… in a million ways. I'd embarrassed

him and misread him, and now I had made no difference in shifting Ansair towards becoming an ally for Niria. In fact, I might have done the opposite. The king had sneered at me being related to Zeus. Perhaps Hyacinth's high priest had been right. Maybe I would be most useful if I ascended and had some proper authority and power.

But, no.

I fought my ascension.

Now more than ever.

Because I'd wanted time with Hyacinth.

Which we wouldn't have—once again—because of me.

I'd worried about only having until the spring. Now that time was gone as well. I'd thrown it away with both hands.

I peeled my knapsack off and pulled the leather folio of poetry out. I flipped it open, the thick pages landing with a thump against the cover. On the very last page, Hyacinth's elegant hand had written a poem. Two stanzas. The lettering impeccable in its beauty.

I read the first couple of lines.

It was a love poem.

Of course it was. He'd said to look at it when I needed a reminder of his feelings for me. But I'd ruined that. I pulled the leather cover back, and the pages smacked as it closed.

I bowed my head as tears slipped down my cheeks.

The ladder creaked, and I rubbed my shoulder over the back of my face to wipe the moisture away and shoved the folio into my bag. Delon jumped up onto the roof, landing with a thud, and dropped beside me, offering me a tin mug.

I took it and swallowed some of the alcohol. "How'd you find me?"

"I told a guard to watch where you went."

"What?"

He took a drink from his cup. "The people here don't like us. I don't think getting split up would be wise."

I sighed and set the mug down. Drinking wouldn't help fix anything. "Today was a disaster."

"Yes," Delon said, lifting his face to the pink bleeding over the sky. "We both knew it would be. But I didn't expect how this turned out."

"What do you mean?"

"The king mentioning some sort of alliance with another god and dismissing Niria with such little decorum. Hyacinth was right. Our relationship with Ansair has been neglected. And it may harm us in this war. I had thought they might just be a neutral non-ally, but perhaps they're actually an enemy." He frowned. "Him hinting at Zephyrus has me worried that the wind god might have made some deal with him. Maybe he convinced him to try and capture you in exchange for something?" He gave his head a shake. "We need to be wary of our meeting tomorrow. The king may not have exercised whatever plan he had in front of the eyes of his court, but we'll be alone in the morning."

I studied him, his gold-highlighted hair brushing together in the wind against the shoulders of his formal coat, and I shivered at the meaning of his words. "You picked up on all of that from the meeting?"

He nodded. "That and I had a few guards remove their uniform and talk with some people. It's amazing how much someone will tell you if you purchase them a few drinks."

I clenched my teeth. Even Delon knew how to act strategically and move within a political realm. I didn't know a damn thing about that. As much as I hated to admit it, there was wisdom in my father sending me to mentor under Hyacinth. He had an entire skillset I knew nothing about. And I wasn't anything more than a liability. Gods, it's a wonder Cyn had ever liked me.

"It wouldn't matter, Apollo," Delon said, his eyes on the undulating forms of the buildings that made up the city.

"What wouldn't?"

"Nothing you or I could have done differently would have changed today. And it probably won't help tomorrow either."

"I'd hoped…" But I stopped speaking. It was foolish. Discussing it with Delon even more so.

He tipped his mug back and finished it. "Hoped what?"

I sighed. "That if we got Ansair to align with us, it might show Hyacinth…" I shook my head. "Never mind."

"Hyacinth knew we didn't have a fucking chance to turn them towards us. This was a punishment." Delon grinned. "But we'll try to feel out things more tomorrow and let King Magnes know our impression of what may be happening here in Ansair. So, that will be useful. And there's another perk to this, at least."

"What's that?"

"We can go home sooner than expected." He clapped his hand over my shoulder. "Gods, I long to spend a night sleeping in my bed and have some decent fucking food. Hades' realm, I'm not created for travel."

I smiled, but my body sank at his words again.

Home.

I didn't have one.

Hyacinth had been that to me.

But I'd broken that.

Like every other good thing life had ever offered to me.

So, we'd go to this meeting in the morning and—gods

willing—walk out of it unscathed. And then we would head back to Niria. I'd attempt to mollify Zeus by making offerings along the way. Spring would come—Zephyrus' fucking season—and I'd ascend. I would use my powers and any scraps of authority I could garner to protect Hyacinth and his kingdom.

That all felt so hollow and hopeless.

I'd do it. I'd promised Cyn I would.

But what really mattered to me—Hyacinth—was gone.

Delon studied me, like he could see through my thoughts. "Listen, Apollo…"

"We should go," I cut into his words, "before it gets dark if you want to stop by other public dining houses."

Delon hesitated for another moment before jumping back to his feet. "All right."

I rose alongside him and reached for his mug. "I can return these."

Delon grinned. "If only the proprietor knew a high deity returned his wares, he'd probably give it to you. It could be the first dedication to Apollo, god of the sun." He stretched his arms out, matching the rays of sunset.

I laughed despite myself. "A beaten-up tin mug full of shitty ale. Sounds about right."

"Well, you've got to do something notable if you want to get the good dedications." He knocked his shoulder into mine. "You're working on it."

"Thanks." I sighed, but it felt nice to have his confidence, even if I couldn't find mine. "Let's start our tour of the city, then."

A whistle snaked its way through the cooling air. I grabbed Delon and threw his body onto the roof as an arrow soared just past us.

"Fuck." Delon groaned as gravel jumped with our

tumble. "In the name of Jupiter, who the hell is shooting at us?"

I crawled to the side of the house, my heart pounding with how easy it would be to slip over the side and fall. A group of men in dark clothing whispered to each other, bows on their backs. One pointed in the ladder's direction, and they walked towards it.

I rolled back towards Delon. "Four men, armed."

"Shit." He grabbed my arm and dragged me to standing, pulling me farther from the edge.

"What are we doing?" I looked over my shoulder and then jerked Delon to the left as another arrow slipped past us. "Should we try to reach our guards?"

Delon grimaced, his feet thunking against the roof. "If they are trying to kill us and they discovered our guards, it's unlikely they're still alive. If you want a chance to see Hyacinth and freedom again, you'll stop talking and follow my idea."

"What's your idea?"

The first man made it to the top of the ladder, and Delon sucked in air over his teeth as he weaved around a wood beam. "Run."

35

Valerian

Temi paced along the shore, her fingers clenched. Dark clouds that trailed out like smoke snaked through the atmosphere. Sappho stood speaking with Atara amid a dozen panthers and the guards from Niria.

We waited for Hecate.

I remained on the edges of the group. Where I belonged. Where I should have stayed.

If I'd never touched Epiphany, never given in to the desperate longing I had for her, she wouldn't be in this situation.

But I had, and now I had to rectify my actions.

My heart pounded with worry for Pip. It had always gutted me anytime I'd seen her in minor distress, worrying over her tutors or frustrated with her role. I would have given up my station, anything, to secure her happiness then.

But now a goddess had captured her, harmed her, bled her.

Fury whipped through me. I'd do anything to see her safe.

Temi's brow furrowed, her dark skin glittering in the shine of her newly revealed glow. I needed to do this for her sake too. She felt just as awful as I did, blamed herself as much. But she wasn't the one who had spurred Epiphany into running off. I was. And she desperately wanted to go rescue Pip herself. But Temi was trapped by the circumstances of who she was. A feeling I knew well.

And I needed to do it for Niria's sake, for Hyacinth and King Magnes. They had always been good to me, accepted me, trusted me. Even with one of the most important people in their lives. Epiphany.

And now she was taken and injured.

Possibly killed.

Because of me.

Hopelessness assailed me again.

I drew in a deep breath.

I wouldn't give into that.

I'd follow the plan we had crafted and see Epiphany safe if it was the last action I took on this earth.

The ground trembled, and everyone stopped speaking, heads snapping up. A woman that had to be Hecate from the description Temi had given me stood glowing in a torch's illumination, a snake slithering over her shoulders. I took a step back. I knew I'd been around Apollo and Temi, and they were deities. But this was different. Hecate seeped power, and darkness emanated from her. She looked like the wrathful deities parents told their children about in hushed bedtime stories. Suddenly I felt like a child, extremely mortal and incapable of standing against what all we'd stumbled into.

And Hecate hadn't come alone. Next to her loomed a woman with heavy scarlet lips that reflected the orange of the light and a dark crown perched on her head, the sunset haloing her hair.

Sappho bowed. "Hecate, Persephone. It's an honor."

Persephone.

Queen of the underworld.

Holy shit.

My heart gave a painful lurch, and a tremble stole down me. My brain struggled to come up with words. I stood before two of the most powerful goddesses in the world. I'd never imagined I would meet an ascended god. Much less, Persephone. The only mortals who met with deities were people like Hyacinth and his father—princes and kings. I wondered if he felt the same root of insecurity that I did when he'd been before them. But he'd had time to mentally prepare, at least. I stood here, the only regular mortal on this beach, staring at deities I had scarcely imagined previously.

Hecate kept Sappho's gaze for a moment before shifting to Temi. "You called?"

"We need your help."

Hecate frowned but listened as Temi explained the situation and our plan. She took a deep breath, pressing her fingertips together. "Which mortal would require veiling?"

For a moment I wanted to disappear, to walk back up the beach and into the stables where I belonged. I was no adventurer longing for escapades. In fact, I was the opposite.

But it was Epiphany.

I stepped forward on unsteady legs. "Me."

Hecate and Persephone studied me, their dark eyes and smooth flesh silvery in the moon's light. Persephone grazed her fingers over Hecate's arm, gently. It reminded me of every time I'd touched Epiphany's skin, a brush of fingers, a grazing of arms when interacting with the horses, her hand squeezing mine.

I'd lived for these interactions, like an addict who

sought a hit of something they couldn't afford. Taking small doses that only made the desire grow.

Hecate broke into my thoughts. "Do you fear Hera, mortal?"

The salty breeze whipped over the sweat that had broken out on my forehead, and the ocean's crashing spray thundered between us. "I have never been more afraid. But Epiphany is over there, and I would face anything to save her."

She hesitated for three more heartbeats, looking at me as though she could perceive my soul. "Very well. Persephone?"

I sucked in a breath that ached at my lungs. The queen of the underworld was going to transfer her magic to me? Once again, I felt like I'd tumbled into a folktale. This couldn't be real.

Persephone nodded. "I'll transfer my divinity to you temporarily. The veil will differ from the one Artemis bore." She inclined her head to Temi. "Hera will not perceive you at all."

Hecate's gaze shifted to the panthers. "And I'll use my powers to create more shadows for your shifters to disappear into."

"Do you worry," Temi said, "to get involved with Hera?"

Persephone and Hecate exchanged a look. "No," Persephone answered, her eyes darkening. "Hera thinks herself the most powerful. She's a fool. And she should worry about getting involved with me. Especially as I was dragged"—she side-eyed Hecate who gave her the edge of a smile, their gazes lingering on each other—"from my bed over her nonsense."

Our strange party of magical creatures, goddesses, Temi, and I all boarded a boat and sailed across the dark waters. Hecate drew on the power of the moon—murmuring to Temi as she did so—to use the waves to compel us forward.

As we reached the island, a slash of sharp, mangled ebony shapes that splattered over the navy expanse of the sky, Hecate approached me again. I steeled myself, but a tremble still ran down my arms.

I don't know how the hell I got caught up in gods and wars and prophecies like this. My whole life my greatest hope had been my father's acknowledgement, rising to that station, and—a painful wish I knew would never come to fruition—being worthy of courting Epiphany.

Now I stood surrounded by deities marching onto an island full of monsters in opposition to the queen goddess. But Epiphany was worth it. Finding her and ensuring that she was safe was the only thing that mattered in the world to me.

Hecate uncurled her fingers, a glowing light tied with a leather cord draping over her palm. "Here."

"What is it?" I said as I accepted it and looped it over my head.

"It's a ghost light. I've created it for you, and only you'll see its illumination. It will fade at sunrise."

"Thank you."

Hecate's voice lowered to a whisper, and she leaned in closer to me. Her floral scent, rich with deep plummy notes, filled the air. "I once loved someone enough to take on a mission as foolish as this, as well."

I kept her gaze, the dark intensity of her eyes. "You see me as an idiot."

"No. I admire pure devotion as I see in your heart. And, regardless of the heartbreak, I don't regret experiencing it myself."

I nodded but didn't know what to say in response.

"Time to go," she said.

Persephone walked over to me and pressed her finger-tips against my cheek, her dark eyes locking onto mine. I struggled not to jerk away, and my body trembled. She had to feel it, but her expression didn't change as she released a breath, her glowing diminishing. I lifted my arms, but nothing seemed different. I wasn't sure if it had worked, but Persephone groaned and dropped onto a bench, rubbing her temples with her fingers. Hecate lowered beside her, tucking an arm around her shoulder.

Atara eased up beside me and gestured to a panther. "Stay with Troshon. He'll see you safe."

"Thank you," I said.

We exited the boat. I looked back once. Temi frowned at me from her seat next to Persephone, her shoulders pulling down, the silver glowing along her skin giving her an ethereal appearance, like a spirit. I knew she wished she could be the one going. But the plan was for them to sit back and wait. I shifted and followed the panthers and Atara, who remained in his human form.

Their massive paws crunched against sand. The wind whistled and clattered against ebony rocks that sliced up the side of the island. Something in the distance screeched, a howl that sounded like nothing earthly. I draped my fingers over the only weapon I carried, a blade on my thigh. I wasn't excellent with a knife like Temi, but it would have to do if the time came that I needed it. Not that a weapon would do anything against gods or immortal creatures.

I sighed, and the panther at my side—Troshon— shifted his glowing eyes towards me before pressing forward again.

Atara stopped walking at the mouth of a massive cave

and kneeled, dropping his head to the sand. "Hera, I request an audience with you."

For a moment, only the cool breath of the sea, the growling and screeching sounds of some distant creatures, and the rustling of plants echoed around.

Then a sparkle seared across the sky, and a goddess with thick, golden locks and ivory skin stood before us. She frowned. For a heartbeat I thought she perceived me, but then her bright eyes brushed right past me, as though I didn't exist. My blood ran cold at how close I stood to her, but a spark of hope flickered inside me. Maybe this would work.

Atara stood and straightened his shoulders. "You have disrespected my patroness by harming a guest of hers. We have an agreement."

Hera clicked her tongue. "An informal one. Your patroness"—she spat the word out—"lives at the mercy of the gods. She should be grateful for how little we interfere with her island."

Atara's expression didn't change. "Release the princess to us at once."

"Tell Artemis to have an audience with me, and you may have her."

Fog rolled in over the coast. It might look natural if I hadn't known Hecate created it, the dark wispy vapors sweeping across the shore. The panther beside me nodded towards the cave. I clenched my teeth but stepped in its direction. Troshon turned into a shadow, his footsteps silent, his sleek black body curling into the edges of the cliff. But I felt like a beacon of illumination crunching through the sand, the ghost light sending an eerie blue glow over everything.

As I passed Hera, so close that she could touch me, she jerked her face in my direction. I froze, my heart thundering hard enough to ache my teeth. It hadn't worked. She could see me. But her gaze flowed over me again, though her brow furrowed.

"Return the princess to us, Hera," Atara said more firmly.

"Do your friends truly wish to turn the ire of my husband upon them?"

"Threats aren't necessary. We just want our guest returned to us."

Troshon stepped out of a shadow, his tail flicking. I nodded even though terror coursed through me and eased alongside him into the cave. The volume of the screeching increased, causing the hair on the back of my neck to rise.

The ghost light in the tighter space of the cavern seemed brighter, strange shadows flickering over the crags of the rocks, claw marks scarring the walls, chunks missing in sections like vengeful gods had destroyed portions.

Anything could be in this cave. Just because we suspected Epiphany was here didn't mean that was true. And what if—

We turned around a column, and the eerie light flooded over the form of a woman, her arms suspended above her, her dress tattered and stained, her head lolling.

I ran to her.

It occurred to me later that it could have been a decoy, a god veiled to look like Epiphany, or a trap.

But at that moment, I didn't care. I hit my knees beside her and cradled her cheeks between my hands.

She screamed and jerked away from me, her pupils dilated so large they took over her irises, black pools of terror.

Right. The ghost light didn't work for her.

But she was alive.

She was alive.

"Epiphany," I whispered. "It's me."

"Val?" Her voice trembled, tears streaking down her face and creating tracks over the dust that coated her skin.

"We're going to get you out of here."

Troshon growled, a warning flashing in his eyes. He must sense something. Epiphany shuddered against me, leaning into my shoulder, and I struggled to pull away from her. "Someone's coming, but I'll be right back."

"Don't leave me," she whimpered, so pitifully it tore at my heart.

"I'm not. I promise."

She wept again, her body dropping into itself like she acquiesced.

Oh, gods.

Troshon hissed, and I grazed my hands over her arm once more before following him as he slipped into shadows and between a crevice. Large creatures with the heads of bulls—minotaurs—ambled past us and stopped before Epiphany. One reached out and gave her chains a rattle, causing another whimper to peel from her lips and rent through my soul before shrugging a shoulder and they both returned to the darkness.

Troshon changed forms beside me and whispered, "Her manacles are locked."

"Do you think we could break them?"

He frowned. "I'm going to see if I can find a key. Don't go to her while I'm gone. You won't hear the guards coming."

"But—"

He narrowed his eyes at me, and I swallowed. I wouldn't help Epiphany if I got myself killed. "All right."

He bobbed his head and then transformed and slipped back into the dark.

Sitting there, the ghost light reflected over one side of

Epiphany, highlighting the matts in her hair, the rust-colored stains on her dress from blood—a great deal of blood. She whimpered again, and it tore through me.

Gods, this was torment. Waiting and watching her suffer and not being able to resolve it.

Troshon reappeared, a key in his mouth which he dropped on the ground before shifting forms. "I'll keep watch," he said.

I grasped the key and ran over to Epiphany, rocks scattering with my motion. Epiphany winced away from me, and I whispered into her hair. "It's me, Pip."

"Val." She swallowed, her voice hoarse.

I unlocked the manacles, and Epiphany moaned as her hands dropped by her side. I pulled her into my arms gently as she sucked in air over teeth, and her muscles tensed against me.

"It's okay."

She breathed into my neck, and I brushed my fingers over the gritty texture of her hair, bumping against leaves caught in her curls. "I've hurt my shoulder pretty badly."

"Which one?"

She nodded to her left, and I shifted her, pulling her around, so that the opposite side pressed against me. She shuddered, and I draped my lips against her temple, kissing there. "Just try to stay with me, Pip."

"Okay."

Troshon jumped into his human form and gestured for me to stop walking.

"What is it?" I whispered.

"Something doesn't feel right," he said. "This all seemed a bit too easy."

The ghost light disappeared, and a breath of air whipped over me like a blanket snatched away. A silver glowing swelled into the space, and Hera strode in, crossing her arms. "It did seem easy, didn't it?"

And more of the minotaurs followed behind, Temi and two other unfamiliar women clutched in their hands.

Epiphany leaned in closer to me and then whimpered again, her face contouring with pain. "You shouldn't have come for me."

Hera smirked. "She's right, you know?"

I tightened my grip on Epiphany and took an uneasy step back. But the creatures circled around, clawed fingers reaching out towards us.

36

Hyacinth

Vines climbed the side of Flora's temple, and they bloomed in buttery, apricot tones. The stone of the building crumbled in certain parts, but it lay in the heart of a massive garden, flowers in every color and size and texture growing in bushes, trailing on ivy over the ground, fluttering along thin stems that reached towards the sun.

Mother would have loved to see it.

That thought ached through me.

Her loss seemed to ring brighter alongside my tangled feelings over Apollo.

I could remember her sitting in the gardens that bloomed around her, the silk of her gown draping across a bench. Emrin climbed a tree behind her, and Pip sat, all curved cheeks and chunky legs, on her lap.

I stretched out in the grass beneath her feet, and when she finished reciting a poem, I looked up at her. "I wish I could be a poet instead of a prince."

She cocked her head to the side, her dark curls spilling over her shoulder. "Maybe you can be both."

"No, Mother." I sighed and returned to the scroll I had stretched out in front of me. "I won't have time for both."

"Cyn?" She didn't speak again until I raised my face. "Promise me that if it brings you joy, you won't give it up? Even a king—maybe especially a king—needs an outlet."

"Okay," I grumbled. But I had let my love of poetry fade anyway. Until Mother's death. After that, poetry became a way for me to remember her, the cadence of her bright, happy voice hummed through my mind when I read the poems she'd recited for me. And jotting down a verse or two between all the pressures of my role reminded me of the beauty and goodness in life.

The last poem I'd written was for Apollo.

My heart ached at that, but I gave my head a shake, swallowing memories back, and stepped onto the path to the temple, Len at my side, our guards shadowing us. We made it to the steps when Flora walked out, her curls wildly billowing over her arms, a loose magenta gown draping over her figure and sliding off one of her shoulders. "Hyacinth," she said through a giggle and then a hiccup, which she stifled by shoving her fist into her mouth. "How surprising it is to see you." Then she laughed, so that her eyes wrinkled, and she doubled over.

I hesitated. This wasn't the aloof Flora I'd seen at the Palace of the Four Winds. And she was drunk, wasn't she?

She took another step, stumbling a bit before righting herself. I cleared my throat. "I hope you don't mind us arriving unannounced—"

"Unannounced?" she parroted and then snickered again, sliding her arm through mine. "Oh, I knew you were traveling here, Prince. Forgive me for being—" She waved her free hands around as though that explained everything. "Dionysus is visiting as well. Not that you'll see him. We had a late night, and he won't wake again until at least moonrise." Her nose wrinkled. "You know, it's not our season until the spring." She pulled me forward, and my muscles tensed where she touched me, but I continued walking with her. "Deities get bored. And that causes trouble, don't you think?"

"Well…" A breeze fluttered through the blooms in the meadow, twirling through them as the wind shuddered their petals together. "I've never thought too much idleness served anyone well."

Len shot me a look, and I gave a subtle shake of my head. I had absolutely no idea what was going on. Flora chuckled again, her body vibrating against mine. "No, you aren't one who will face judgment for that sin, are you?"

"Forgive me, Flora. I appreciate the warm welcome but—"

"Oh, right." She straightened and popped her fingers against her forehead. "You must have so many questions. Why am I being pleasant to you? Why did I expect you? That sort of thing?"

I tightened my fingers, and the rings I wore glittered in the sunlight. "If I were to be honest, yes, I am wondering about those things."

"I have another visitor as well. Someone who is eager to see you."

I stopped walking, and Flora stumbled with the motion.

Oh, gods.

Another visitor.

Zephyrus wouldn't have come here too, would he?

And, if so… He had to be furious with me and Apollo. Might he attempt to kill me and my party? Out here in this temple that sat an hour to the nearest small village, no one would know or care if he did. The only protection I had with me were my human guards, and Zephyrus would end them without hesitation. Had I just doomed us all? This was why kings and high lords only met with gods in large groups, surrounded by others who could see their actions. Humans didn't trust deities; they needed them. And there was a big difference between the two. But I hadn't been making the wisest choices since I'd let my heart get involved.

Flora's expression darkened, her scowl reminding me of the one she'd worn at the palace. "No. Not him." She spat the last word out with so much contempt, I winced. "Did you know he tricked me into marrying him?"

"Zephyrus?"

She nodded, her lips pursed, her gaze growing distant. "But I manipulated him as well. So, perhaps it's fair." She shifted towards me as we approached the temple and its shadow stretched out, reaching us, causing Flora's silver glow to brighten. It reminded me of Apollo and being wrapped up in his light. I swallowed back the feelings that crawled through me with that memory. Flora sighed. "I suppose you've heard the rumor that I'm Jupiter's daughter?"

We clipped up the steps, the swishing of our garments echoing off the stone. "I have, yes."

"It's a lie." She smirked. "I created it to get Zephyrus' attention. You know there was a time when I found him charming and"—she giggled but then stifled it again, resting her head on my shoulder for a moment—"handsome. Believe it or not."

"I believe that, actually."

She shifted towards me, a clarity washing over her expression. "Yes, I'm sure you understand. Anyhow, my friend—the one who is here to speak with you—warned me against intertwining myself with him. But I didn't listen to her."

"Why don't you leave him?"

She stopped before a shadowed doorway. Floral scents performed a ballet in the air, sweeping together, the totality of all their distinct notes washing through the space. "I cannot. Marriage between two gods is the highest of blood vows. I cannot harm him, break that commitment, share his secrets, or move against him." She lifted her face to me, her skin so smooth it glimmered like pottery, and she smirked. "Not directly, at least. Now, come, let me introduce you to my friend."

I hesitated for a moment. Len met my gaze, and I gave him a nod. Hera's lot if this wasn't stupid, but something propelled me forward—curiosity perhaps or maybe just confusion. Whatever it was, it overruled the logical part of me that knew stepping into a temple to meet some unnamed being wasn't wise.

Inside, the space became cooler and darker, but the fresh air of the gardens permeated through, golden slips of light falling from windows and sneaking through crumbled portions of the stone where flower-covered vines pushed past the facade and into the building.

The room sat empty save a few pieces of furniture tucked into one corner next to a table where a woman waited. Her gaze slipped up to us though her expression didn't change.

Flora led me to the table, releasing my arm, and dropped into a chaise, her curls splaying out across the cushion like a dark river. "Meet my friend, Prince Hyacinth."

I bowed and took a seat. The woman shifted towards me, her skin smooth, though deeply wrinkled along the edges. Her flesh had a paleness to it but also the glimmering depth of darker tones. Her hair—a wild mass of gray and ivory streaks—flowed over her shoulders like a child's. Everything about her seemed a combination of all attributes that any human could have in one body. It was disconcerting.

"I've not had the pleasure," I said as the guards and Len took seats Flora waved towards.

"Prince Hyacinth," the woman said, her voice rich but somehow as quiet as a whisper at the same time. "I'm certain you've heard the stories of me and my sisters."

Flora sat up, her feet draping over the edge of the couch, satin slippers on them pressing against the stone floor. "Clothos is one of the three Fates, Your Highness."

I sucked in a breath and shifted towards the woman again. The Fates. "I... I didn't know I would have the honor to meet you."

Clothos kept her gaze on me without blinking, her expression giving nothing away, and a shiver ran down my spine. There was no deity above the Fates. They held the story of the world, the future, and the life of every being in it—gods included. "I came here to speak with you."

I nodded but couldn't find words.

"Your future lies before you, and you have a choice to make."

"My future?" As interesting as what was in store for me might be personally, it was my kingdom's destiny I worried about.

"Ah, but,"—Clothos blinked once, so gradually it was like she did the gesture for my sake rather than the need for it—"you have entangled yourself in events that are far greater than you or even your kingdom, mortal prince."

"What would that be?"

She shifted, and her dress rippled slowly, as though the fabric was stiff though it appeared to be silk. "Your attachment to Apollo."

My heart ached again. I still wasn't sure what to do about our relationship. "That has changed some recently."

"Has your devotion to him altered?"

I could feel the eyes of my guards and Len on me. I chewed on that for a long moment, my jaw tightening. Staring at Clothos, at her piercing gaze, I couldn't lie. "No."

"You have a decision to make about that, and it will determine your lifespan. You usher death forward with your choices."

I dragged my thumb under the edge of the table, the gritty texture crackling against my nail. "No disrespect meant to you, but you sit here and tell a mortal I'll die. Forgive me that it doesn't surprise me."

"Do you not wish that you could match your lover's lifespan?"

"That was never a possibility," I said, my voice coming more bitterly than I expected. "Once Apollo ascends, he will live forever. I've always known that."

Clothos studied me for such a long moment that I struggled against squirming in my seat. That look she gave verged on terrifying. Flora twisted her hair around her fingers, and the wind whistled through the open windows. Finally, Clothos bobbed her head. "I can see the path your decision will take you. You will not live to see Apollo's ascension if you remain on it."

I blinked rapidly, like I could brush her words away. Was that because Apollo would stall his ascension, so he could live out life with me? And did I want that if so? Or... did she imply that my death would be soon? After all, he had vowed to his father to ascend by spring, and that season loomed only a few months away. A chill crept along my arms, causing the hair on them to rise. "May I ask you what this has to do with the war?"

Clotho's lips turned down a small amount, not quite a frown, but nearly. "You are wiser than most mortals, yet you still focus on this moment as though it's the only one that matters. This war is irrelevant."

Feelings swept up through me. It certainly wasn't irrelevant to the people in my kingdom, people whose lives and well-being and hope rested on my decisions. "What is relevant, then?"

"Your actions set in place multiple paths, mortal prince. Choose to abandon your relationship with Apollo, and you may avoid your own death." She blinked twice, the motion slow and forced before speaking again. "I do not believe you will make that choice, however. You are not cowardly, and your link to Apollo is not a surface connection."

Her shoulders rose, as if she took a breath, and it was then that I realized she hadn't breathed the entire time we'd spoken so far. "Reconnect with Apollo, and you will die; your story will be a tragedy. But you also lay the foundation for a changing of the gods."

I splayed my fingers out across the table. "Why would you even tell me this?"

Flora clasped her hands together, her mouth growing wide and upturned. "It's a romantic death, though, Prince Hyacinth. Poetic really. You'd like the beauty in it,"—she shrugged—"if you lived to see it, which I supposed you wouldn't. A pity that."

Clothos had shifted towards Flora but turned back to face me. "I am honoring a request by disclosing your future. But do not ask me from whom as I cannot reveal that presently. I've given you a gift, Prince. And a curse. Something no mortal receives. A chance to choose to delay your death if you wish to."

"But I have to give up Apollo for that?" My voice came as a whisper, and that's when it hit me with full force. I would not give him up, even if I stared down my end. I was angry with him, yes. And he could never do what he'd done again. But losing him forever—that was a demise of a different kind.

But how quickly did I usher forward my death if I was with him? And I didn't understand why Clothos would tell me this information. She cocked her head to the side. "You would have to give him up, yes. That is, if he and your companions make it safely out of Ansair. Debatable at the moment."

I sucked in a breath, and the guards behind me shifted, their feet clattering against the stone. "They're in trouble?"

"Some." Clothos spoke slowly, as if she had all the time in the world. I suppose she did. "In nine hundred and eighty-seven out of one thousand paths, they get out of it."

"There's a chance they don't?"

"Ah, Prince." Clothos smiled, an expression that chilled me down to my soul. "There's always a chance of anything. Even you outliving Apollo is a possibility, on some roads."

Terror shook its way through me.

Apollo could only die if the spark holder—his father—killed him. And he was in Mt. Olympus... unless... Oh, gods. Could Zeus have traveled to Ansair? Perhaps Zeus had discovered our deceit and had enough. Apollo felt he rested on the edge of his father's mercy and patience, as it were. If Zeus knew we'd chosen to rise against him, he might act against Apollo rather than risk his ascension. And I had sent him away, pushed him from my embrace, because of embarrassment and anger. It was nearly as bad as Apollo acting out of jealousy.

I jumped to my feet; the chair screeching over the stone. "Forgive me." I bowed hastily to both of the women. "I fear I must go."

Flora stood, but Clothos remained where she sat. She bobbed her head. "Your path solidifies, mortal prince. But you have the strength to see it through."

I kept her gaze for three more heartbeats before bowing and striding out of the temple. Len flanked me, his shoulder grazing mine, wind whipping his jacket out behind him as we reached the outdoors again where night had darkened the sky. "Do we head to Ansair?"

I shook my head. "It would take a week's hard ride to get there." I lowered my voice. "If they are truly in trouble now, it will do them no good by the time we could make it." My heart ached, a helplessness seeping through my bones. And I hated it. Hated not having answers or the ability to do anything about Apollo and Delon or my future. This information didn't help me; it just left me feeling helpless and worried. Which accomplished nothing. I clenched my teeth as I walked over to where we had tied up our horses. "We head home. There's much I must discuss with my father. And, god's willing..." I paused on that vein of thought. I'm not sure gods actually helped at all. "Apollo and Delon will meet us there when we arrive."

Len gave a sharp nod and strode over to his horse.

And our group clattered onto the road again, the wind whipping over long grasses, the darkening silk of the skies belying the storm that lay ahead.

37

Apollo

Delon ran across the rooftop, which glittered in the fading sunlight. The men who wore dark, loose layers lifted their bows as they reached the top of the ladder.

We moved faster. An arrow whizzed past us, and we jerked to dodge it, veering near the edge, and my vision blurred. The ground seemed so small, people walking along the streets like ants streaming through the dirt. We could trip and fall. My stomach lurched into my throat.

Delon pulled up short where the roof ended, and I stopped, my skin clammy. He looked over his shoulder and then around at the world where conversations hummed about us and intertwined with the clattering of the men's feet, the light hazy and bright. "We gotta jump."

I lifted back up. "Absolutely not."

"Here's the thing, Apollo," he said, his speech speeding together and clipping. "These arrows and weapons probably won't kill you, but sadly, I'm mortal. And today isn't the day I wish to meet my end. So, we must jump."

I stared at him for a moment. The men's voices grew close enough that their words became distinct. Oh, shit.

Shit. Shit. I couldn't do this. Delon's jaw worked, his gaze boring into me. I blew out a breath. "Okay."

He nodded and backed up and then dove across the roof to another, scrabbling to gain his balance as rocks tumbled down the side of the building. My blood turned to ice. Oh, fuck. I could not do this.

"Apollo," Delon shouted and gestured for me to come.

I breathed in the spicy scents of the air, stepped back, letting my weight sink into the solidness of the roof. Oh, gods, the roof. We stood above the world, where we could fall. Faintness threatened to overtake me, and I swayed on my feet.

The last time I'd jumped while up at a height, I'd had Hyacinth's hand in mine, the coarseness of his palm steady against my fingers. We'd kissed for the first time that night, and he'd looked at me as though I was worthy of being a god, like I deserved a place in the sky. But during our last interaction, his expression had changed.

I swallowed back at those thoughts.

An arrow shot past me, landing with a thunk into a wood beam on the opposite side.

No. I would do better. I'd prove it to him.

Another arrow swept by, nicking the skin of my arm, and I winced.

Well, the best opportunity to make changes was the present.

I took a deep breath and ran, my feet slapping against the hard surface of the roof. The side grew closer. The world milled about beyond, thousands of people full of their own heartbreaks and fears and worries and loves.

I reached the edge and closed my eyes as I leapt into the air.

I brought Hyacinth to mind.

His fingers brushing over a line of poetry, his irises

turning honey-gold in the sunlight, the v-shaped dimple forming between his brows, the taste of his lips, his hands rough and needing as they dug into the flesh of my shoulders.

Wind whipped over me, cooling the sweat on my brow. I opened my eyes right as I hit the roof with a thump that knocked the breath from me.

Holy shit. I'd just jumped between two roofs.

Delon grabbed my arm. "Come on."

We weaved through laundry fluttering on lines, around chimneys, and past a group of women who gasped at us, jerking back and clutching bundles of clothing in their arms. We reached a ladder and clambered down, landing on a dirt path in an alley.

Delon jerked his chin, and we continued pushing down the road, away from our pursuers. We turned a corner, and half a dozen more men dressed similarly to the ones chasing us stood. One shifted towards us, the blade in his hand catching an apricot glimmer of light. "Hey," he yelled. "Stop."

"Oh, shit." Delon grabbed my tunic in his fist and pulled me in the opposite direction. We slammed back through the alley, weaving through people. The noise of the assassins echoed around us, the rhythmic thumping of their feet, the sharp cries of their yells.

We turned a corner and hit a dead end.

Delon cursed and smacked his hand against the bricks. The men rounded the path as well and unsheathed knives that glittered in the light of the setting sun.

Delon released a breath that whooshed out of him.

But I firmed my stance. We would not die or be captured or thrown in a prison here or whatever the hell these men had in mind. Gods, were these people fearless? I was Zeus' son. And while that wasn't a fact I was proud of, it did normally keep me out of trouble like this. But apparently Ansair lacked fear of my father.

Our pursuers eased towards us. I hadn't replaced the weapons I left off for our audience with the king. I had been so focused on the gnawing disappointment and heartbreak I'd overlooked thinking through things.

But I had one tool—rusty and neglected as it was—that I could use.

I'd spent my entire life avoiding my powers once I realized pushing into them too much would cause my ascension. That magic bubbled up in me all the time, and I had to clamp it down, ignore it.

But what did it matter anymore?

I'd already vowed to ascend by spring and had ruined things with Hyacinth.

If I ascended in order to save Delon and myself, what would it hurt?

I sank into my body, allowing the glittering heat of my powers to rise. It flooded through me in a way I'd never experienced—an ocean hit by a hurricane, a wave rising to destroy.

A golden light formed around me, hot and snaking. Delon stepped away, covering his face with his hands. My muscles shook while attempting to control the magic. It was like trying to hold on to a boulder that tilted in the wrong direction.

I clenched my teeth and willed that power forward. The light exploded, knocking our pursuers over. I snatched Delon's wrist and pulled him with me, running through back alleys and making a dozen turns before stopping and leaning onto my knees, my breath trembling out of me.

I lifted my hands.

Where the red of my mortal blood gave my palms a pinkish hue.

I hadn't ascended.

Damn. Maybe it actually would be hard to do.

Perhaps Temi was right, and I needed to practice.

Delon punched my shoulder. "Yes. That—that right there—is the kind of shit you have to do if you want to receive the good dedications."

I lifted my face. "You nearly died, and you're still thinking about dedications."

"What better time to think about the things that will outlive us?" He chuckled as well and wiped sweat off his brow. "That was a solid move. We need to figure out how to get the fuck out of this city without notice."

I dusted my jacket off. An edge had gotten torn in our flight. It was one of the few items I had that Hyacinth had given me. My thumb lingered on the tear. "I can veil us, so no one recognizes us."

Delon's mouth popped open. "You can magically veil us, and you thought now was the time to bring this up?"

"Well…"

"Forget it, Apollo. You're never getting good dedications."

I laughed, and it felt nice, a reprieve amid everything.

"Come on, then." Delon smiled. "Veil us, and let's see if we can track down any of our guards if they're still alive and get the fuck out of this city before those bastards are after us again. Those assassins wore official seals on their cuffs, meaning they're sanctioned by the king. If he wasn't obvious in his meeting earlier, I'd say that made the message pretty clear. I think it's safe to say we're in enemy territory."

"That or you were right."

"About what?"

"That Zephyrus had made a deal with the king to capture me." I clenched my teeth down at that. I'd endangered Delon if that was the case. He and the guards wouldn't be more than collateral damage to Zephyrus.

Delon scoffed. "Any friend of Zephyrus is an enemy of ours. It's the same thing."

I nodded and pushed the magic out. Veiling was something I could do with ease. It was the only power I'd ever mastered. But maybe it was time to change that.

We worked our way through the crowds and back to the dining house we'd had drinks at—the buzz of the alcohol long burned off with our panic and running—and Delon grumbled. "Having most of the guards remove their uniforms probably saved their asses." He rolled his eyes. "Let's gather them up and get out of here. Hopefully, our horses are unmolested."

Once we gathered everyone and made it out of the city, we found the horses and our carriage next to the rest of our party we'd left with it. Delon sighed and hopped into the seat as I dropped beside him. He looked over his shoulder and spoke to the guards. "We'll travel through the night tonight. I want to get as much distance between us and Ansair as we can."

He clicked his tongue and gave the reins a toss, and the horses clipped out into the amethyst color of twilight, Delon leading them away from the main road.

We remained quiet for several minutes. The trees along the mountainside had darkened into silhouettes draped in fog. There was a peaceful beauty to it. The moon peeked out over the tree line, and I wondered where Temi was and if she was looking at the same sky as me at that moment as well. Gods, I hoped their trip went better than ours.

A whistle broke out over the chuffing sounds of the horses and whispering of the wind. I turned my head towards it. A flame tore across the darkness, soaring at us. "Delon…"

He turned right as the arrow, thick with the acrid smell of burning pine tar, struck the chariot. Dozens more lit the sky, like shooting stars of death. One hit the wheel, and it crackled, the fire jumping onto the wood and licking up it.

"Hades' realm," Delon growled, vaulting down and loosening the leather straps that attached the horses—now startled, the whites of their eyes showing as they tossed their heads. His fingers stumbled over the harnesses. "Can you release the other side?"

I copied his motions as more arrows flew, landing near us. We unhitched the leather, and Delon reached out, smacking the horse's flanks, causing them to panic and rear up, running off into the dark.

"Go ahead," Delon yelled to the guards and gestured to the animals we'd just freed. "See if you can catch them. Me and Apollo will meet you at first light. He has magic that will shield us. But get the horses out of here before these bastards kill them all."

They inclined their heads and galloped in the direction our horses had gone. Delon and I ran away from the carriage where the fire had built, dancing curling patterns of apricot over the mossy boulders that peppered the surroundings. Once we had some distance, we slowed to a walk for an hour into the darkness before stopping at a spot tucked behind fir trees. Delon dropped to the ground. "You'll use a veil again if they come after us? That's not a one-time trick, is it?"

"No, I can do it again."

"Good." He pulled out a bag of shelled almonds and offered some to me. "This will have to do for dinner. We'll see if we can catch up with our party in the morning and find somewhere to buy actual food." He shifted his face in the distance, where a plume of dark smoke whispered into the night sky, and frowned. My stomach growled, and suddenly the dried fruit and bread we'd had on the carriage seemed like a feast.

I accepted some almonds and popped them into my mouth. "You had these on you?"

He shrugged. "Ack, snack for the road. And I knew you wouldn't eat jerky."

I found myself at a loss for words at that kindness and instead took another handful and chewed them before responding. "Thanks." I nodded towards the horizon, which had dipped into the ebony of night. "Do you think they'll find the horses?"

"Yeah, they were frightened, but those two were hand-raised by Valerian. They're loyal and well trained. The guards will get 'em." Delon let out a laugh and brushed his hands together, sweeping away the salt from the snack. "Thank gods we got them free. Valerian would have had my ass if something happened to them."

I pulled my knapsack off and opened it. I considered Hyacinth as a child, best friends with Valerian, spending days horseback riding. That was easy to imagine. Cyn had such a compassionate heart that it wasn't hard to believe he'd get along well with animals. He probably wore those ridiculous robes of his even as a kid. I rolled my eyes but smiled. And for the first time since we'd parted ways, a thought of him didn't hurt. I drew my bedroll out and handed it to Delon.

He frowned. "I can't take this."

"You're mortal as you reminded me multiple times today. The cold is more of a hardship to you. And"—I lifted my arms and allowed the magic to sweep forth—"I have my powers for warmth."

Delon hesitated a moment, but then took the bedroll and folded it out.

And I let the magic soar through me again, the heat of it flooding through my blood.

And my heart raced.

I needed to learn what all I could do, to accept that I was a god. And maybe I could use it for good even. It had saved Delon earlier. It was time to stop fighting it and use what I had to help where I could.

38

Artemis

The minotaur yanked my arm, pushing me forward farther into the cave. My flesh ached where his fingers dug in, and I longed to jerk away from him. I could take him down. But, no. I had agreed to this and seeing Epiphany alive—if seriously hurt—firmed my resolve.

It had shocked me when Hecate had suggested we let ourselves get caught. She had stared out over the mist of the ocean while we sat in the boat as the waves bobbed us, the moon round and bright in the sky as though it rolled over the dark silk of night, its reflection tumbling in broken undulations of ivory over the sea. Hecate gasped and turned towards Persephone. "Hera has realized our ruse."

Persephone jumped up, her arms trembling from the loss of her magic. It made my stomach sink, knowing another goddess had given up her powers for decades for my sake. How much had Amara suffered for me? Persephone bit her lip. "There's a chance they might still get out."

Hecate's eyes glazed over, the silver glowing around her brightening, and then she shook her head. "Unlikely."

"We have a second option."

Hecate frowned. "He'll be furious."

"I'll make it up to him," Persephone said with a smirk.

Hecate sighed but nodded and turned towards me, explaining the plan. So, I fought against providing retribution to the bull-headed creature that continued digging his claw-like fingers into my flesh and kept my gaze focused on Epiphany instead. Hera had hurt her. Badly.

But she was alive.

And this idea would work.

Persephone and Hecate had both veiled themselves to appear as mortals. They'd obviously had more practice with the magic than Apollo ever had. Where his veil often shifted or shimmered—his true nature shining through—theirs remained swallowed down.

Hera tapped her finger against her chin. "I told you, Artemis, to abandon this foolishness. But you chose not to."

I hadn't forgotten that she had killed my mother, and even if Mother had accepted her fate, it changed nothing for me. Venom laced into my words. "You're a snake, Hera. And one day soon you'll fall. That's my prophecy, to undo you and your legacy… but it's your own fault. Your actions are what's leading to it."

Hera gave me an annoyed look but tossed hair over her shoulder. "You have nothing to fall from. So, you can't understand."

Epiphany shuddered, and Valerian pulled her in tighter, his eyes bouncing between all the creatures in the room.

"I never want to be like you," I said. "I would never hurt and murder others for the sake of my renown."

Hera's jaw shifted. "You're right about that, at least.

You won't get the opportunity." She nodded to the mino-taurs holding us. "Throw them all in the pit."

Valerian released a breath that caused his lips to quiver, and Epiphany whimpered. The creatures walked back farther into the cave, rolling a massive stone aside. The screams and cries that had screeched in the background magnified in volume. Epiphany trembled, but a smirk stole its way over Persephone's mouth and magic sparkled over her. From the other side of the cave a sweet and tangy scent filled the air. A rumble echoed through the rocks, plum-colored smoke pouring into the cavern, and every torch wisped away as if the sigh of a ghost had snuffed them out.

In the murkiness, his dark form silhouetted by moon-light, his ebony robes draping against the stone, stood Hades. "Hera," he said, his voice low and sinister. "You have crossed me and mine."

Hera hissed and pushed forth her powers, lighting the cave in her glow, shadows slipping over everyone and casting their eyes like dark hollows, their features dimpled and sharply defined. "You have no business here, Hades."

Persephone removed her veil, her silver light sweeping into the space and adding another layer of illumination amid the dark. Hades met her gaze for a lingering moment and then turned towards Hera, menace flooding his expression. "You've broken your vow and threatened my wife."

Hera gaped and gestured towards Persephone. "She... she tricked me. I... I didn't know."

"She tricked you?" Hades said dryly.

Hera swiped her tongue along her teeth as though she checked to make sure of their sharpness before proceeding. "It's not valid."

Hades' frown deepened. "Would you like me to call forth the vow to test its validity?"

"No," Hera gasped the word out. She gave her head a shake and then trailed her eyes over everyone in the room before turning back to Hades, her words coming as a growl. "Name your price. What must I do to appease you?"

Hades' jaw ticked, and he took a deep breath as though this was all a tremendous bother. But his eyes slipped to me as he spoke the words Persephone had asked him to say before we allowed ourselves to get caught. "Vow to Artemis that you shall not harm her nor stand against her now or in the future, or reveal who she is to other gods, including Zeus, and your debt is paid."

Hera's mouth gaped, and then her nose wrinkled before she stomped over to me. She yanked my arm and pulled a knife free from her waist and sliced it through my skin. I jerked back at the sting, but she clenched her nails into my flesh, drawing blood that dripped down along my wrist.

She cut herself and pressed the wounds together, her eyes boring into mine. "I vow it." She hissed as the magic burned through me, but then a cruel smile crept up on her face. "But, to you only." She turned, throwing the knife.

I stretched my hands out like I might stop it.

But the blade hit its target.

Striking Valerian in the neck.

Hera disappeared, the floral scent mingling richly alongside the dampness of the cave.

Val stumbled, blood pouring forth from the wound.

Epiphany screamed.

Valerian fell to his knees right as Persephone reached him, taking Epiphany from his arms.

"Valerian," I yelled. Epiphany tumbled from Persephone's grasp and dropped to the floor with a thud, her tattered dress sopping up mud. Her fingers hovered above Val, and then her face lifted towards me, terror a tattoo in her expression.

She wanted me to fix it. But… I couldn't heal. Or… if I could, I didn't know how. Val touched the knife, and then his hand dropped again. Epiphany cried as Persephone and Hecate lingered near both of them.

I turned towards Hades. "Please…" He remained stoic, his dark eyes glinting in the low light. "I understand that you have no relationship with me, but please help him."

Hades tilted his head. "I fear I cannot."

"But… but, he'll die."

"He's a mortal, Artemis," Hades said gently. "Mortals die." His voice dropped to a whisper that barely rose over Epiphany's weeping. "The underworld is not as fearful of a place as many make it out to be, especially for those with good hearts like your friend. He will be at peace."

"No." I looked over my shoulder, where Epiphany brushed Valerian's hair back. "Please. I'm begging you."

Hades studied me for another moment, his lips pressed together. "I do not have healing powers, I'm afraid."

Fear and hopelessness crawled over my flesh. I'd struck enough animals to know the wound Valerian had was a death blow. He had minutes if we were lucky, and there wasn't a damned thing we could do to restore him. But I couldn't just let him die. What was the use of being a goddess if I didn't have the ability to fix anything? I turned back towards Hades. "Can Poseidon heal?"

Hades paused for a moment, his imposing form unnaturally still. "He can, yes."

I gasped and ran out of the cave, hitting the sand of the coast and dropping to my knees, whipping incense out of my bag and lighting it faster than I'd ever managed before. "Poseidon," I prayed, bowing my head. "Lord of the seas. Father." I bit the word. "Please hear me and come to me."

For a minute, nothing happened.

The sea crashed against the beach.

My arms stung where it bled, dripping down my elbow, punctuating the sand.

Epiphany's cries and Valerian's gasping breaths echoed out of the cave.

A hopelessness washed through me, like it would drown me. I had no control over this situation and could only hope my father would answer my call.

Then the water parted, and Poseidon rode onto the shore, his stallion giving its head a shake and salt spray trembling from its mane. Poseidon jumped down from his horse and met me. "Yes?"

For a moment, words wouldn't form. He'd come for me. I was still angry and hurt, but a twinge of gratitude pinched at me. "My friend is dying."

"I told you that was likely to happen."

I breathed through my teeth. "I want you to heal him."

"No. I do not interfere with mortals anymore."

"I want you to heal him for my sake." Tears broke loose and fell down my cheeks. "You owe me."

Poseidon's expression turned curious, his dark skin highlighted silver by the moon. "How so?"

"You created me. And whether you intended to be involved with me"—tears came earnestly, grazing along my collarbone—"that was still a choice you made. I deserve more from a father. So, I say you owe me, and I want you to heal my friend... quickly... before it's too late."

"Losing mortals to death is a reality of what we are,

Artemis. Better for you to learn to deal with it and focus on your fate."

"I can't concentrate on it if I caused his death. And you can fix it. So, if you wish for me to focus, do so."

Poseidon's expression didn't change. Five heartbeats passed, and he inclined his head. "Very well."

I followed him into the cave where everyone stood around Valerian, his color ivory, his eyes closed. A chill swept down my spine. He looked dead. Epiphany had grown quiet, her puffed cheeks shadows beneath her red-rimmed eyes. Her fingers trembled as she brushed over his jaw.

Poseidon walked over, nodding towards Hades before pressing a hand over Valerian's heart and using the other to dislodge the knife. An ivory shimmer, like sea foam under sunlight, swept over Val's skin and he sputtered and sucked in a breath, his color flooding back into his flesh again.

Epiphany clapped her hands over her mouth and then dropped against his chest, wrapping her arms around him even as she winced from the motion. "Oh, Val."

Poseidon sighed and laid his palm on Epiphany, the same magic coursing its way over her, melting away the scratches and bruises.

Valerian pulled Epiphany closer. "It's okay, Pip."

"Oh, gods." She wept again and pressed her nose into his shoulder. Valerian dropped his head against the ground and rubbed his fingers down her back. Relief flooded through me. I didn't know if that would actually work, and suddenly the fear I had shoved down in favor of action fizzed through me, leaving me shaky.

Poseidon walked over to me. "Do you feel I have paid the debt owed you, then, Artemis?"

I frowned. "No. But I thank you, anyway."

"Very well."

He turned to leave, giving another nod to Hades and Persephone who stood speaking quietly together. But I followed him to the gaping mouth of the cave. "There's one more thing I ask from you, and then I promise to not call you again."

"What is that?"

The stallion knickered on the beach, chuffing its tremendous hooves into the sand. "I want your horse."

Poseidon's composure dropped, and he crossed his arms. "That's my best creature."

I could punch him since the animal clearly had more value to him than I did, but he had just saved Valerian's life. I cleared my throat. "It feels like an appropriate gift for a daughter, then. I've taken a liking to horses recently, and I think one befitting a goddess would be ideal."

Poseidon's jaw jumped, and he stared at me for another long stretch before nodding. "Very well. You may have him." He clicked his tongue, and the stallion galloped up. Poseidon pressed his nose to the horse's snout and whispered to him, scratching behind his ear before turning back to me. "He's deeply intelligent and immortal, but headstrong. Don't attempt to saddle him; it would prove fruitless. His name is Arion."

"Hello, Arion," I said. The horse shifted towards me, his bright, perceptive eyes studying me. "I think we're going to get along well."

Arion whickered, and Poseidon sighed but offered him another pat before receding back to the ocean. I trailed my fingers down Arion's fur, the velvety texture of it softer than any other animal's hide I'd touched. Arion gave his body a shake, energy vibrating through his muscles.

Hecate stepped up beside me, lifting her face to the stars wreathed in a scarf of gray clouds. She crossed her arms as her eyes skimmed over the stallion. "Did your father leave you something?"

I smiled, brushing a finger along his long nose. "He did."

She nodded. "An immortal horse born of the sea seems a fitting companion for Artemis, high goddess of the moon."

My heart raced, but then I lifted my face to the sky as well.

And I thought perhaps she had a point.

39

Epiphany

Every moment from the time we left the cave, as we crossed the sea, when we made our way back to Sappho's residence, and when I finally separated into my private chambers, seemed fuzzy and like a dream. I kept expecting myself to wake up at home, my blankets tangled around my legs from an unsettled night.

Attendants drew a hot bath, and once they left, I peeled off my filthy clothes, easing into it. Poseidon had healed me, but phantom aches racked through my body, my shoulder throbbing. I sank beneath the water, coughing as the soap I'd generously poured into the tub burned my sinuses.

I scrubbed at the blood, and it dripped off of me in dark tides. But the dried, caked blood under my fingernails would not come out. I picked at them, peeling flakes that fluttered towards the bath like crimson snowflakes. Gods, most of that was likely Valerian's.

Because he had almost died.

A tree clattered against the frosted window in the room, and I untangled my hair, starting at the ends. It would probably take hours to get all the debris and knots loose.

I swallowed.

The entire night flashed through my mind.

The surprise of Hera finding me, the terror of being chained in that horrific cave, the relief when Valerian had arrived, and then the panic as I watched blood pour out of him, gushing with each swallow he took.

He should have died.

If it hadn't been for Temi's connections, he would have.

But he never would have been in that position in the first place if it wasn't for his relationship with me.

Every time he had pushed back with me about us coming together, he had worried about my future. He'd never mentioned what had now become painfully obvious to me.

He risked everything for my sake.

Yes, I could ruin my reputation. But my family loved me, and they were powerful. In the worst-case scenario for me, I had to deal with rumors and some shame... nothing new, really. But Valerian could lose all of his respect, his ability to work with other attendants and stablemen. While I didn't believe Father would turn him out, if the others he worked with grew to distrust or dislike him, he could lose his career.

I had put his reputation on the line without thinking about it. No wonder his mother hated me. I winced as my finger found the sharp edge of a pebble in my curls. Water dripped onto the tile floor as I dislodged it and set it on a small table by the tub.

My thoughtlessness wasn't because I didn't care for Valerian, but that I had believed love would conquer all.

But I was a princess.

Him being entangled with me could cost him everything.

I flinched as I pulled another knot loose and my hair drip, drip, dripped into the water.

I had to let him go.

For his sake.

I never wanted him harmed because of me again.

I understood what he'd meant now, about having to look me in the eye when I suffered and knowing he was the cause.

Because I had experienced that. His emerald eyes had met mine as his life poured out onto the stone, and I knew it was my fault. I knew his death was on my hands.

So, I had to release him.

I sank down into the water as that settled on me.

It weighed on me as we packed the next day, made our goodbyes to Sappho, and loaded the boat. Once the ship pulled away from the shore, I leaned against the rail. The ocean stretched around like blue silk. Niria—and our future—lay ahead somewhere in the distance.

Valerian eased down beside me. "It's a relief to leave the island."

"Yeah, it is," I whispered and pushed up to standing. "I'm going to go below deck. I'm tired."

He frowned, his lips pursing, the healthy color of his cheeks deepened by the wind. "Of course."

And I walked across the floor and clomped down the stairs, my heart sinking to my toes.

But it was for the best to end us.

Even if my soul ached at the idea.

40

Hyacinth

Returning home right as the crisp winds of winter reached Niria was like slipping into a favorite robe, tasting a bite of a food I hadn't had since childhood, holding the hand of someone I trusted without hesitation.

It was comforting amid the chaos we had endured.

After thanking each of the guards who'd traveled with us and saying my farewells to Len, I ambled through the hallways of the palace and sighed, my body bone-weary, exhaustion crashing into me. I straightened as I approached the throne room, inclining my head to the attendants.

They opened the jewel-inlaid doors, and one spoke, his voice echoing around the chamber and drawing the attention of the advisors and high lords that stood near Father where he sat on his throne. "His Royal Highness, Prince Hyacinth."

I strode down the carpeted walk, water trickling in the pools alongside the walls as the eyes of the room pinned on me. And, gods, it was too much. My resolve felt like it might break. I reached the front and bowed. "Father."

Father studied me for two heartbeats and then stood, his robe draping against the stone at his feet. "Everyone out," he said, his voice booming through the space. "At once."

The crowd scuttled from the chamber, the room emptying, the running water a hushing melody broken by the occasional fish jumping out of their pools. When the door closed with a thud, Father turned towards me and squeezed my shoulder. "What is it, son?"

"I…" Words flooded through my mind. Things I needed to tell him about Zephyrus, Flora, the gods, the war, and… Apollo. But they wouldn't form. They stuck like honey candy, clinging to my brain, and I gave my head a shake as the hopelessness of the last weeks pierced through me again. "Father, it's…"

"Cyn," he whispered and then clutched his arms around me. I sighed and leaned against him, letting him hold me up for a moment. "It's fine. Take your time. But take a seat, and tell me what's the matter?"

And so, I lowered into the throne beside of his, cleared my throat, and started at the beginning. Father kept his gaze steady on me, not interrupting other than nodding or occasionally humming a response, his eyebrows cinching together. When I finished, I swept my hands out as if I could make sense of it all, repair my mistakes, undo the issues.

Father sighed and removed his crown, dropping it onto his lap. "Well, your trip was successful, then."

I gasped. "How can you say that?"

"You traveled intending to find information on who may align with us or not. And you've produced that. Perhaps it's not all that we hoped for, but we know where we stand now."

"Aren't you"—I ground my teeth together—"disappointed in me?"

His expression washed away, and he leaned in closer to me, squeezing my arm. "Of course I'm not."

"But I failed you. Apollo and I ruined this mission."

"Why do you believe that?"

I clenched my fingers, and my rings bit into my flesh. "We publicly made a mess of everything."

Father's jaw worked, his gray streaked hair glimmering in the silvery light that flowed in from windows. "I can see Apollo's actions have hurt you. But what I understand from your account is that you both sussed out information about Zephyrus and avoided a disastrous alignment of our country with him. I agree with your take that he likely wished for the attachment for his benefit at our expense. And if he means to stand against Jupiter"—Father gave his head a toss—"we couldn't go along with that. I don't intend to anger two high-gods at once. Inciting Zeus is foolish enough on its own."

His forehead wrinkled, and it hit me how old he looked. His lines had deepened in the last years, his shoulders hunching. He sighed and clapped my shoulder. "No. The trip was a success, and it puts us in a better if more immediate position. A guard from Apollo's party arrived this morning. They suspect Ansair stands against us as well."

I knew I should respond to the political implications, but words spilled out of my mouth before I could stop them. "They're back?"

"They should be in a day or two. They ran into some issues but made it out, unfortunately with unfavorable news. But, once again, at least we know where we stand."

I nodded, but my mind shifted to Apollo. I trembled as

if all the fear I'd felt for him in the last week of travel had knotted its way into my muscles and suddenly loosened.

"Hyacinth?" Father said.

I raised my face. "Yes?"

"It's okay to forgive him."

A peacock strutted by an open window, shaking long feathers out, its cry shrieking through the space. "He shamed me… publicly."

Father sighed. "Yes. But"—he waited until I lifted my gaze to meet his—"you're still in love with him."

I smoothed my hand down my lapel. "I'm an idiot. Relationships have to be built on respect."

"True. But no one's perfect. Not even gods." Father chuckled. "Maybe especially gods. From what I understand, however, you believe Apollo was attempting to help you. He's followed through with the mission you sent him on, and the guard tells me he saved Delon and the other's lives. That does not sound like a man who feels no remorse."

"How do we move forward, though? How do I look at him knowing what he did?"

Father smiled, a gentleness permeating his features that he reserved for Emrin and Epiphany and me. And for Mother. They had loved each other like no other couple I'd ever seen. "You start with a conversation, Cyn. Love isn't just founded on respect, but also on realizing your partner is a flawed person." He laughed. "Or god, however it may be. If I could list off all the stupid, thoughtless things I did to your mother over the course of our marriage…" He scratched his forehead. "Well, we'd be here a long while. We didn't have a perfect relationship, but we worked to make it a good one."

I nodded, but I needed time to think. I wished to share

with him what Clothos had said. If I reconnected with Apollo, I ushered forth my death.

But I knew if I told him that, it would give him pause.

And something in me didn't want that.

I wanted his approval of our relationship.

Because what he said was true, regardless of everything, I was still in love with Apollo. Something in him sparked some deep, secret place within myself. Like he held a piece of my soul and had gifted me a portion of his. There was no other person on earth I'd met that I felt that connection with. And being away from him had me emotionally wrung out. I wanted nothing more than to find a way forward together. But was I willing to pay the cost that may come with that? I swallowed. Hard.

Father clapped my shoulder. "You look like you need an opportunity to rest."

I huffed a breath but nodded. "Perhaps you're right." I hugged him again, felt the steadiness of his presence, and then retreated from the room, the weight of my thoughts heavier than the crown I wore.

41

Valerian

My horse flicked her ear and stomped hard enough to stir dust up in the road, and I reached out and scratched her mane. An overcast sky brought a touch of a cool breeze that ruffled everyone's hair around.

"It's good weather for traveling," I said to Epiphany, who trotted alongside me. "Should make our return trip home easy."

She met my gaze for a heartbeat before nodding. "I hope that's so." And then she clicked her tongue and guided Meadow up farther ahead in the group.

Theos cut his eyes to me and frowned. I forced my expression to remain neutral. The guards' disapproval of whatever they perceived going on between Epiphany and me—what had spurred her to leave the stables angry after speaking with me alone and right into Hera's hands—hung thick as molasses in the air between us all.

Epiphany reached Temi, who sat atop Arion. His coat reflected aqua under the sun that peeked out behind gray clouds. Gods, would I love to see how fast he could go at full speed. I wondered if Temi would allow him to sire and if he would be compatible with our mares. I wasn't even sure the creatures could birth whatever would result. Perhaps it wasn't worth the risk.

Temi said something to Epiphany, and she laughed.

Arion provided a pleasant distraction from the fact that Pip was—once again—avoiding me. I bit the inside of my cheek as a breeze whipped through the evergreen trees, rustling their needles together.

When that knife had struck me, it was Epiphany that came to mind first—worry that I might drop her, fear for her life rather than my own—and then the pain took over, the struggle to breathe. But when Poseidon's magic had swept through me, bringing the world into clarity, Epiphany was the foremost thought for me once again.

I had believed that I could stand back and watch her marry someone else. Perhaps, after she'd left, I would find someone that fit my station.

But as my blood had flooded the stone of that cave and my soul seeped its way out, my greatest regret was standing back.

And I didn't care anymore. Nothing brought me joy like seeing her smile; nothing improved my day like a few minutes spent with her. And if I had used my life to spare hers, I would have done so gladly. We'd both nearly died. We could have lost everything. I might have lost her. And all the conventions, the expectations, the cultural beliefs didn't matter to me anymore. I loved her down to my marrow. Maybe that was enough. Maybe that mattered more than my station in life. Epiphany told me a person's worth should be judged based on their actions. And, without pausing to consider it, I was willing to forfeit my life if it meant her safety. Perhaps that made me worthy after all.

Marriage was an impossibility between us.

For now, anyway.

With the country already facing political upheaval.

But maybe…

Maybe in the future—if things went well for Niria and the public had more room for grace for an unusual situation—perhaps then we could.

I would try at least.

But that came back to the issue at hand. Epiphany had scarcely made eye contact with me since we'd left Lesbos. Her answers to my questions were one or two words and spoken quickly before she moved away from me.

And with the godsdamn guards hovering around her and watching me like I was a prisoner that they transported rather than a trusted part of the group, I couldn't find out why.

And it was about to burn down my resolve. When Temi fell back some, I urged my horse alongside hers. "Temi."

"Valerian."

"I need to speak with Epiphany alone."

She shifted towards me, the silver light around her glowing against her dark skin. "I can ask her."

I swallowed down a sigh of frustration. "You didn't ask me before you arranged for her to slip the guards to speak with me."

"Yes, well…" She pinched her lips together. "I expected that conversation to go better. Perhaps I'm learning from my mistakes."

The wind picked up, ruffling through Arion's dark mane. "I need to talk to her."

"Are you going to upset her again? We have more travel ahead of us, and there's no cake to be had currently."

289

I readjusted on my saddle. "What does cake have to do with anything?"

She snorted a laugh. "You have so much to learn." She slid her long fingers down Arion's enormous neck and then sat back up, her shoulders dropping. "I'll ask her if she wants to speak with you"—she raised an eyebrow—"and if she does, I'll make a way this evening. That's the best I offer."

"Thank you."

She nodded and pulled away from me, and I returned to traveling in quiet, the guards occasionally frowning in my direction.

As night descended, and the moon that had lost a slice of its fullness stretched out over the sky, I stood in a clearing on the other side of the wood line, bare trees stretching out in silhouette against the stars.

I had waited for what felt like forever, crickets chirping as my breath misted out into the air. My heart sank. She wasn't coming. Perhaps she'd moved on herself. Maybe this was as foolish as I thought it was.

A crackling of sticks caused me to lift my face, and then Epiphany stood there, her skin paled by the moon-light, her dark curls tangling in the wind. She crossed her arms, strands of hair striking across the soft curve of her cheek.

She was so beautiful it hurt.

"You wanted to speak with me?"

I took a step closer to her and longed to reach out for her hand, to feel the warmth of her against me. I kept my hands to myself. "Why are you avoiding me?"

She released a breath that clouded the air, her shoulders dropping. Her eyes misted. "Are you serious?"

"Yes."

"You almost died."

I chuckled. "I'm aware. It was unpleasant enough to make it memorable."

She stared at me and then blinked fiercely, her dark lashes batting against her cheeks. "You almost died," she said again, her voice breaking. "I... I held you in my arms and watched the blood pour out of you." Her nose flared. "You should be gone right now because you came after me... because... because you're willing to die for me, but" —she flung her hands out, her dress rippling with the motion—"but... we can't be together... because of our circumstances... And... and I can't..." Her words cut off with another sob.

I stepped in and drew her into my arms. "It's all right now."

She clenched her fingers into my shoulders, her body shaking. "It terrified me, Val. I thought... I thought I would lose you forever."

"I know." I brushed my hand over her curls.

She breathed against me for a moment but then pulled back. "I just... I can't keep doing this." She paused, midnight-blue wrapping her up like a cloak. "You were right. We'll harm each other." Her voice dropped. "I'll cause you hardship."

I cupped my fingers against her cheek, the velvet texture of her skin gliding against my rough hands as I lifted her face. "I've changed my mind about what I said."

She sucked in a breath. "What do you mean?"

"If you spoke with your father"—I shuddered as much at the idea of the king knowing about our relationship as from the cool evening air—"then I'm willing to do what-ever I can to make this work between us. It's worth the cost for me."

Her eyes glistened. "I don't want to hurt you."

"You avoiding me"—I swallowed—"is hurting me.

And I've focused too much on stressing over what might take place. But, gods, Epiphany. A goddess stole you and locked you in the entrance of Tartarus, and we both nearly died. And maybe I'm realizing that worrying didn't prevent any of that. I've been pushing away both of us enjoying what we have today out of fear of what could happen, and I'm done with that now..." I chuckled breathily, and it puffed out as a cloud in the air. "You asked me to face the future with you, and I'm willing to do that."

She didn't speak for a moment, the warmth between us hovering like a pocket tucked against the wind. "You want to be with me?"

"In whatever manner I'm able to, yes."

She shivered and dropped against my shoulder, and I looped my arms around her, pulling her in as if I could shelter her there. "Okay," she whispered.

I was terrified.

Of risking everything, of what the king may think, of what my friends—high lords and palace attendants alike— would say. But I'd risk anything for her, and the weight of her body, warm and trusting against my chest, smothered any lingering doubts.

I kissed the top of her curls and tucked my chin on her shoulder.

"We'll face it together, then," she whispered.

"I mean, we've already dealt with vindictive gods, bodily injury, and near death. What's the worst that can happen, right?"

She chuckled and leaned back, grazing her fingers through my hair. "Right," she said and then kissed me, the lushness of her lips parting against mine.

And, at that moment, I believed it.

Maybe we'd find a way.

42

Artemis

My feet pattered across the tiled-floors of the palace of Niria. It was a relief to be back, to have taken a luxuriously hot bath and slept well for the first time in months. Epiphany remained asleep, but the sun peeked over the mountains outside the windows, throwing a hazy peach over the world, and I had received news. So, I strode through the hallways, away from Epiphany's room, where I had spent the night.

Guards in their navy uniforms lifted their faces as I passed, their eyes widening, the occasional one gripping his fingers tighter around his weapon. Damn the marks of a high deity. My whole life I'd slipped past people's notice, whispered through the woods, tucked behind marketplaces.

I'd have to get Apollo to teach me how to veil as soon as possible.

I reached the door to mine and Apollo's suite and opened it. Sunlight flooded into the space, and I blinked away from the brightness. Apollo stood by an open window, his tunic still holding the dust of travels, the silver glowing fully unleashed and sparkling alongside the morning light.

My heart jumped. I couldn't remember the last time I'd seen him unveiled without purpose.

"Apollo."

He turned, and the look in his eyes gutted me.

His face transformed as he took me in, the markings of a high-god coursing over me.

I didn't realize until that moment that I cared deeply what he thought about it. And if he saw my divinity as something disgusting, it might break me.

I hadn't had time to process it for myself yet.

And I suddenly felt like a child, looking up to her older brother, longing for his approval.

"Temi," he whispered. I swallowed, and it didn't shift the knot in my throat at all. Apollo walked over towards me and pulled his arms around me tight. "It's so good to see you."

I melted into his grip, and all the tangled up, anxious feelings within me left with a sigh. "I've missed you, too."

We remained standing like that, a cool breeze sweeping in from the window Apollo had kept ajar, mauve clouds lazily swimming across a brightening sky. When Apollo pulled back, he grasped my hand and drew me over to a settee where we both sat. "Tell me everything."

So, I did. He stayed quiet until I told him about Hera and our mother. Then he hissed, his expression tightening. At the end of the story, Apollo dropped against his knees, a muscle in his jaw jumping. "Poseidon, that bastard. Fuck all the gods. I think you may be the only good one. If the other deities want to come for us, let them try." He smiled at me. "My odds are on you, Temi."

I chuckled, dropping my head to his shoulder. "It

sounds like our prophecy is me and you against the world, so that's probably a positive thing."

He made a sound in the back of his throat but squeezed his arm around me. "If I had to be stuck with another deity to face that with, you'd be the only one for consideration."

"Thank you, Apollo." I leaned up. "Now, tell me what's wrong?"

He dropped his gaze to the patterned rug at the ground where sunlight dimpling through a tree's limbs glittered in waltzing patterns. "My trip didn't go as expected either."

"Your turn to share."

His lips tightened, grief flooding into his expression, but then he explained their time at the Palace of the Four Winds, the issues with Zephyrus, his mistakes. I cringed but squeezed his fingers. When he finished, he tossed his head, batting away tears. "I've ruined everything."

"Have you spoken with Hyacinth yet?"

His voice dropped to a hush of a sound. "I wouldn't know what to say... even if he wished to see me."

"Perhaps—"

A knock cut us off, and we both stood. "Come in," I said.

The door opened, and Hyacinth stepped in, a gold-threaded robe on, his crown glimmering in the sunshine. His eyes lingered on Apollo for a long moment before darting to me, his eyebrows raising. "Temi." He bowed.

I inclined my head. But his attention had already shifted back to Apollo. "I heard you had returned."

Apollo tensed beside me, his gaze holding so much longing and desire and pain it ached at me. He nodded.

Hyacinth fluttered his fingers together. "I'm glad you made it safely."

"You too," Apollo whispered, his eyes shimmering.

Hyacinth cleared his throat and bowed to both of us again before sweeping out of the room, his robe tumbling through the air as he pulled the door shut behind him.

Apollo slumped as the latch clicked in place. Tears broke free, trailing down his cheeks, and he sucked in a shaky breath. "You see."

"Oh, Apollo." I drew him in against me and held him as he wept, wishing I had magic that could fix a broken heart.

When he stopped crying, he leaned back. "I've destroyed it all."

"Would you take my advice if I gave you some?"

He brushed his shoulder over his cheeks. "I would."

"See if you can find him alone and talk to him. He obviously still cares about you if he's eschewing his schedule to come visit you first thing. Share with him what you shared with me."

Apollo studied me for several heartbeats and then tucked my braids back. "All right, Temi. I'll try." He offered me a gentle smile. "I'm guessing you want to learn how to veil."

I huffed but nodded. "That might be helpful."

43

Epiphany

Father sat at the head of the table, ripping a piece of his bread, honey dripping onto his thumb with the motion. Silk fabric that suspended across the ceilings tangled together in a splash of colors as Hyacinth discussed political alignments—or the lack of them—with Emrin. But I remained silent, staring at my plate, not eating.

Everything tumbled through my mind, Valerian's near-death, Temi's prophecy, the war my brothers talked about as if they conversed about the weather, Val's lips against mine.

"Epiphany," Father said, drawing me out of my thoughts. "How was your trip?"

Color flooded my cheeks as Emrin and Hyacinth both shifted to face me as though they just realized another person sat at the table with them. "It was fine."

Emrin grinned. "Lord Galeson has sent half-a-dozen letters a week in your absence. I believe he must write to you daily."

I grabbed my goblet and took a swallow of wine. "How considerate of him."

Father's gaze bore into me, not in the normal, endearing way, but as if he tried to piece me out. "Could we speak alone after breakfast, Pip?"

I lifted my face and met that gaze.

He knew.

A guard in our group must have said something to him.

Anger sluiced its way through me like lava. Damn ever having a moment of privacy, a chance to steady my own words and make my own appointment to discuss things with Father. No, as normal, my life was on display. I raised my chin. "If you're wishing to talk about what I think, let's do it now. I'm over all the secrets."

Father looked towards the attendants lining the walls. "Perhaps a better conversation to have privately?"

My eyes darted around the room but then landed back on him. "Dismiss the attendants if you're tired of gossip about me, but Hyacinth and Emrin might as well hear it."

He cleared his throat and turned, flicking his ring-adorned hand toward the attendants. They exited the hall, closing doors behind them. Hyacinth's eyebrows had drawn together, dimpling his forehead, and Emrin frowned. But Father sighed. "One of your guards spoke with me about... a delicate issue on your trip."

His voice wasn't unkind but held a wariness.

"Valerian," I said.

Father nodded. "I don't put full stock into what an anxious guard suspects after a long, hard journey. I wished to hear your take, Epiphany."

All three of them stared at me. But I didn't care anymore. I was tired of living under a glass case. I had minded propriety, kept my distance from Val on the trip back, didn't speak in hearing of palace workers who could gossip about it in front of his mother. But this was my family. And they would either have to accept me as I was or not. "What you heard is likely true. Valerian and I are together."

Father's shoulders dropped, but Hyacinth's lips snapped apart, color draining from his skin. "Together?"

"Yes," I said, turning to face him. "We're a couple."

He stared at me for a moment where the room stretched so quietly, I felt like I could hear all of our hearts beating. Then he jumped out of his seat, storming in the door's direction. I stood as well. "Hyacinth."

I started walking away from the table, but Father spoke. "Let him go, Epiphany."

"But…" I gestured towards him. "He's going to…"

"Valerian is his friend. They will have to work this out between the two of them. You and I still need to talk."

I dropped into my seat but kept my posture upright. "I'm in love with him. And I won't back down from that."

Emrin stared at me, horrified, but Father pressed his fingers together and tapped them against his chin. "Did he use this trip to approach you?"

I gasped. "Of course he didn't. He never would have. I was the one to approach him."

Father's gaze grew distant for a moment, but then he nodded. "You're a princess, Epiphany, to a country that's about to face a war. I don't believe our people could tolerate a scandal, and we can't hinder our relationship with Segion by offending Lord Galeson and his family. But"—Emrin and I both shot our faces towards him— "here is what I can allow. You may be with him if you are discreet."

I gasped, but Emrin jumped from his seat. "Father, you cannot be serious."

"Emrin—"

"No," he growled, smacking his napkin against the table. "Hyacinth just gallivants off and causes a hundred issues because he's involved with a god, and now you're going to let Epiphany—what?—sleep with a stableman?"

"Ermin," I said, shock and hurt coursing down me.

Father stood as well and fixed him with a look. "Son, I understand that you're upset, but—"

"I'm upset?" he said through his teeth. "I'm the only one of your children following the rules, and yet I'm the one about to get a lecture. This is bullshit."

"Emrin," Father said in a voice I rarely heard him use, stern and imposing.

"No." Emrin's nose wrinkled into a sneer, and he turned, striding out of the room, his footsteps clipping against the floor.

Father sighed as the door slammed, and he scratched his forehead. I shifted back towards him and blinked, words not coming. "I'm sorry," I finally said.

"I'll speak with your brother. We're all under a tremendous amount of stress at the moment, and it's bringing out our worst, I fear." He blew out another breath but then brushed his thumb over my cheek. "Do you agree?"

"With?"

"Your and Valerian's relationship. It must remain quiet."

I clenched my teeth but nodded. Being a princess wasn't something I could run from. I'd learned that, if anything, on our trip. And us keeping things private might spare Val the worst of any gossip or issues. "Of course."

"Valerian's a decent young man." Father bowed his head. "I always wished his father would claim him... now more than ever. But our family is who the entire country looks to during uncertain times. You understand that, don't you?"

"I do, yes."

I truly did, for perhaps the first time in my life. I had

caused a huge issue on our trip by behaving impulsively. If Valerian would risk everything for my sake, then I wouldn't deny our relationship, but I also didn't want to harm our families or the kingdom either.

"And"—Father took a deep breath but brushed his fingers over my curls—"I believe it would be wise for you to keep up your connection with Lord Galeson for now."

"But—"

"Epiphany." His tone stalled my words. "Our country is diving into a war with very limited allies. We cannot risk cutting off those we have. You needn't make him any promises or act on false pretense, but if you could continue the relationship, it would help our kingdom... possibly tremendously."

I didn't like that. It felt like a betrayal to not only Valerian, but Gale as well. Galeson was kind and didn't deserve for me to string him along. But a war meant hundreds of thousands of lives, and I was committed to doing my part. I bit my lip. "Okay."

He leaned in and kissed my forehead. Well, it could be worse. I had feared Father forbidding me or feeling angry with Valerian.

Him allowing us to be together was a good outcome.

But then I remembered that Hyacinth had rushed out in search of Valerian.

44

Hyacinth

I stormed into the stables, the sweet scent of hay whirling through the air, birds cooing in the rafters. Valerian stood facing a stall, running his fingers down a horse's muzzle.

"Valerian," I growled.

He whirled around, his eyebrows drawing together. "Cyn."

I reached close enough to him I could punch him, and my fingers curled up. "What the hell were you thinking?"

He ducked his head. "So, Pip told you?"

"How could you?" My voice came out louder than I intended, and the horse startled, pawing at the ground and nickering. "Have you slept with her?"

Val's lips parted, the color draining from his face. "I'm not answering that."

I jumped a step in closer to him, my breath trembling against his cheek. "Like hell you aren't. You'll answer me now."

His voice took on a hard edge. "Oh, is that my future king speaking to me?"

"It is." I bared my teeth, clenching them down to keep from snarling.

The color came back to his cheeks. "Did you know your sister approached me at the beginning of our trip, and I turned her down? Made for a hell of an awkward time after that, too."

I studied him for a moment, blood hot and coursing through my body. The horses' breathing filled the space between the pounding rhythm of my heart. "And so, what happened?"

"She told me she was in love with me." His voice raised and his eyes shimmered. "And, damn it, I've been in love with her for years."

"So, you just acted on your feelings and forgot yourself. Forgot who the fuck she was."

His nose flared, and he shoved me. I stumbled back a step, surprise blooming through me, as he growled out his words. "Never once in my godsdamn life have I forgotten myself for even a fucking moment. I've never been given a chance to."

I parted my lips to speak, but Valerian swiped his hand out, stalling me. "You know what, Cyn? What your sister said to me is true." He slammed his fist down on the stall. "I have a right to be judged based on my character and actions. And I've not done one thing to Epiphany that I regret or that was ill intended. I would die for her—which I have proved. I've always held her with the highest respect. You think some high lord with his head up his ass like you would treat her as well?" He scuffed his boot across the floor, hay gliding away to reveal murky dirt. "I deserve a chance. And fuck you for not seeing that."

"Val," I whispered.

"No," he snapped, his eyes darkening. "Don't." He turned on his heel and stormed out of the stable.

I stood staring at the doorway he'd passed through for several minutes, a cooling breeze trailing through the open windows that caused goosebumps to rise over my flesh. Oh, gods. I'd messed up. I clenched my fingers into my palms until they grazed the metal of my rings.

A heaviness swept over me.

I shouldn't have reacted like that.

I had assumed the worst of Valerian and acted like it was my place to protect my sister. As if she was helpless and Val was a villain. And neither was true. Godsdamnit, I had just headed up the law to allow widows to have more control over their own destiny, and yet here I was making an ass of myself and acting out of antiquated beliefs that I didn't even buy into. What the hell was I even doing?

Gods, emotions swirled their way out of me lately.

Ever since Apollo…

I gave my head a shake, shoving that thought back, and turned, walking out of the stables, across the gardens, over the fence, until I reached the path I'd beaten down as a teenager. At the end of the trail, I climbed to the top of the cliff, the air biting as it whipped over my skin and walked over to where the waterfall roared its way down the falls, mist peppering out and causing me to shiver as I sat on the cool stone.

I swallowed and clutched my arms around my knees, resting my chin on them. The sun sank in the sky like my mood, being consumed behind dark clouds. Footsteps echoed across the precipice, and I didn't need to look to know who they belonged to. He walked with so much grace for someone with such a big personality, his steps quiet but sure. I kept my gaze ahead at the sweeping colors of the horizon as Apollo sat beside me, crossing his legs. "I saw you head this way."

I shrugged, leaning farther against my knees. The

ebony stone, slick with water, reflected the bruised color of the sky.

Apollo picked up a pebble, tossing it between his hands. "I wanted to come see if you were okay."

"Yeah, well, I'm not." I paused for several heartbeats. "Our kingdom is not in a good position for this war, I've returned from this damn trip only to find out my closest friend is"—I made a sound in the back of my throat—"with my sister, and then I screw up things with him mostly because I'm pissed with you."

Apollo chewed his lip, his gaze on the darkening sky. "That's understandable."

"Seriously?" I turned towards him. "That's all you're going to say?"

He blinked twice, his golden eyes growing large. I wondered why he wasn't wearing his veil anymore, but I didn't know how to have this conversation with him, much less ask about that. "Yes," he said. "I acted like an ass. I hurt you. It's reasonable that you might lash out at others."

I sighed, resting my hands behind me, my fingers dipping into a puddle of cool water. "You know, out of everything—the gods we've angered, the war looming, my family..." I turned to face him. "It's you that scares me the most."

"Why?" he whispered.

"Because..." I drew my hand back and wiped it on my pants. "I'm so in love with you, even despite you acting like an utter idiot, that it makes me sick with it."

Apollo sucked in a breath, his lip trembling. He bowed his head, his curls rippling in the breeze.

I breathed in the mist and let the great, swelling feelings rise within me. "I'm still so mad at you that there's a part of me that wants to push you off this cliff."

Apollo laughed, his shoulders dropping, and he tossed

the pebble over the falls. "I'd find that unpleasant, but it would be fair."

"It would be." Wind fluttered our clothes around, and I shivered. "But, right now I'm sitting here realizing what it's like to act out of emotions and utterly fuck up a relationship"—his eyes lifted—"and it's making me realize that maybe I've been unfair as well."

His eyebrows cinched. "You haven't been. Everything you've felt and said is true. I messed up terribly." His voice dropped to a whisper. "I ruin everything I touch. And I'm so sorry for it."

I sighed. "And I worry too much about always fitting the mold and having the right appearance. Maybe we're both too hard on ourselves." I paused, taking a deep breath. "It hurt me that you didn't tell me about your ascension."

His chin dropped. "I know."

"I understand now what you were trying to do. And I'm aware that I said my kingdom and my duty to it had to come before everything. But I think I was wrong about that." I weighed that out in my mind. But I knew I believed the words I spoke. He meant well, and now he beat himself up over his choices. We couldn't always be perfect.

And, even more than that, I wanted him. Desperately. Enough to pay the highest cost for it. "You're the only person who truly gets to see me. Our relationship has been... more... to me."

"I feel the same," he whispered.

I met his gaze, the sadness and hope in the look he gave me ripping through my heart. I snaked my hand out, finding his. He froze, his muscles tensing, and I slipped my fingers into his, our flesh melding like flowers blooming between grasses together, stems twining alongside the other. "There's something I want to do almost as much as shoving you into this lake, though."

"What's that?" he whispered.

"Kiss you."

A muscle in his jaw tensed. "I would like that."

I leaned in, the grassy-sweet smell of him hitting me. His form wrapped around mine, and our mouths met. The taste of him, the sturdiness of him beside me, felt like an eclipse fading, the sun coming back out, the world illuminating again.

Our lips parted, and I bowed my head against his. "I love you, Apollo. It's stupid and confusing and difficult, and I'm convinced it's going to be tragic for me. But being apart from you has been like trading a flower for the thorn. I don't want to be separated anymore."

"I don't either. I promise, Hyacinth, I will never do anything like that again. And I won't keep any more secrets from you. I swear it." He swallowed, his eyelashes fluttering against my cheek. "You're everything good in the world to me. I shall never love another as I do you." His hands coursed along my arm like he carved me into stone, like he could capture me forever with his touch. "I don't think I'll ever love anyone again. You've ruined me."

"That sounds like a long eternity for you."

He breathed a laugh. "If you allow me to spend your mortal life with you, then every moment of missing you in that eternity will have been worth it."

I pulled away and trailed my thumb over his cheek. "Can we try again?"

"Yes." He nodded. "Yes, please."

I grazed down his neck and kissed the edge of his collarbone. And then I stood, the wind pushing me back a step. "There are some apologies I need to make, but first, I want to blow off some steam."

Apollo rose alongside me, and he cocked up an eyebrow.

I laughed. "Not like that. Though…" I slipped my fingers between his again. "Tonight, yes. I've missed that as well."

His face still shone red, but a chuckle bubbled from his lips, his eyes twinkling. "Have you just been using me for my body?"

"Yeah, that and your amazing connections."

His laughter filled me like wind rippling into sails, soaring me back onto the course I'd lost. He walked us over the shimmering rocks and down the trail. "I had actually promised Delon a game of discus. He says I owe him."

"Didn't you save his life?"

Apollo smiled, touching my hand gently, as if he grazed the tender petals of a new bloom. "That's complicated."

I took in the radiant sunshine of him. His hand linked with mine, our future stretching ahead. "I actually think that sounds perfect, golden boy."

He rolled his eyes at the nickname, but his fingers tightened around mine. A hopefulness flooded through me that I hadn't felt in a long time. I had been such an idiot. Did I seriously believe I could end things between us? I trailed him like the sun he was, golden and radiant. And I would follow him anywhere, right into the maw of death, if necessary.

Damn that prophecy and Clothos as well.

Of all the mistakes I'd made, the regrets I had, the actions I wished I could undo, splitting from Apollo topped the list. I wanted him in my life, and I'd risk anything for it.

He looked back over his shoulder once, as if to make sure I existed, that I still stood there. I offered him a smile, and he turned, leading us towards the discus field.

45

Artemis

Epiphany fumed, her breath coming like a hiss. "How could he?"

I pulled in closer to her. The gardens had shifted in the time we'd been gone. All the lush greens of late summer were long since tucked away and overtaken by muted grays and browns, flowers cut back for the season, trees empty of leaves. "I'm sure he just overreacted at the moment."

"Cyn knows," she said through her teeth and clenched her fingers tighter, "that Valerian cares a great deal about what he thinks, but he went and acted like an ass."

I sighed. "We all have those moments. He'll apologize."

"Will they be able to move past it, though?"

I considered that as a single remaining leaf twisted on a limb and twirled its way to the ground. "I think so. Relationships have bumps. It's part of it. They respect and care about each other too much to let one argument ruin everything."

Epiphany swallowed, her curls tangling in the breeze. "I don't know." She kicked her head back. "Sorry. I'm focusing only on my own problems. How is Apollo?"

I leaned against my hands as they scraped over the wood of the bench. "Having his own issues."

"Brothers are exhausting."

I smiled.

But it was good to see Apollo. He had hesitated for a heartbeat when he saw the marks of the high deity on me, but then he'd pulled me in as though we were just Apollo and Temi, brother and sister. As though nothing had changed.

It was in his embrace that everything had solidified for me. It didn't matter about our prophecy or our destinies. Our actions defined who we became.

There were wicked gods and compassionate ones.

We didn't get to choose divinity.

But we could choose what we did with it.

An idea had formed in my mind of who I wanted to be. It wasn't anything new, actually. It would just be me leaning into who I already was. Artemis, goddess of the moon and the hunt. Protector of women. Known for her bow and knife skills. I smiled. Yeah, if I had to be a goddess, that's what I would become.

A gale swept through trembling tree branches, clattering them together. The few remaining leaves crackled like a cruel fist smashed them.

I shifted towards the stretching expanse of the mountains beyond the palace walls, where the wind thundered its way across the valley.

"Oh, gods," I gasped.

"What?" Epiphany said.

"The wind. It's moving from the West."

Epiphany frowned. "Is that unusual?"

"Yes." I grabbed her hand and pulled her up. "It only does that in the spring. Oh, shit. Zephyrus must be here. Epiphany, we have to warn our brothers."

Color slipped away from her face, but she nodded, and we ran across the gardens, the grass squishing under our feet.

46

Apollo

Delon threw the discus at me, and I jumped, the brass of it banging my fingers. My feet hit the ground with a chuff.

I slung the disc farther down the field, its form spiraling and blurring. Hyacinth and Len ran towards it, Delon ahead of them. Watching Hyacinth run—his gaze ignoring the discus and lingering on me instead—caused my heart to flutter about in my chest.

He'd forgiven me.

I'd never ask for anything again. I'd love him for each moment, every breath I could manage. My looming ascension still posed issues, but I refused to feel hopeless about it. We'd make it work.

"Apollo!" Temi screamed.

I turned towards her.

I wonder, now, if I hadn't done that.

Might I have noticed the way the breeze shuddered?

Might I have had time to intercept?

But I did turn.

The whites of Temi's eyes glimmered. "Zephyrus is here."

I gasped and shifted around again.

But too late.

The wind jerked back like a rope, the discus caught in the eddy of its wake.

"Cyn," I screamed, running towards him.

But the disc reached him first.

It cracked against Hyacinth's temple, and his neck snapped as though it had unhinged. The sound of it seared itself into my mind, sank down into my bones, ached into my heart, so that I would hold it forever, so that it became a part of me.

Zephyrus' laughter trailed on a breeze right as my knees struck the turf hard enough to rip up skin and grass. Hyacinth lulled against the ground as he hit it.

"No," I roared, grasping his shoulders and pulling his head onto my lap.

Temi and Epiphany jogged up at the same time that Len and Delon arrived.

"Cyn," Delon gasped.

Epiphany fell beside us and reached her trembling fingers out towards him before popping them over her mouth. "Oh, Hyacinth."

"No," I screamed again.

And I tapped into my powers.

I could heal.

Maybe if I tried hard enough.

If I pushed enough.

My entire life I'd practiced reservation with my divine nature, never letting those powers more than tingle into my blood.

At that moment, I released those boundaries like clouds sweeping from the sky, allowing the sun to beat down.

And the magic surged through me as if it consumed

me, burning nerves, peeling away skin, glowing like the stars had fallen and caught the world on fire.

The group covered their eyes, backing away.

But I didn't stop.

I forced the magic even harder.

Heal, godsdamnit. Please heal.

The powers glimmered and sparkled; they sizzled through me. My flesh ached like it ripped off and replaced itself, my heart stopped pounding and then roared forward again, as if every inch of me transformed into something different.

Something not of the human world.

I froze, shifting Hyacinth's face towards me. "Cyn?"

His head slumped.

His body remained still.

"No," I howled. "Please." I leaned in closer to him, brushing my nose over his skin, breathing in his jasmine scent. "Please, Cyn. Don't leave me. I didn't have time to" —I choked over my words, tears tracing down my cheeks —"tell you everything. I didn't even get to say I love you." My thumb traced over the contour of his jaw, scraping along the rough flesh there. "Hyacinth, I'm begging you."

Nothing happened.

But my body had taken on a new awareness. The sun sweeping across the sky called to me. The magic washed through me like it never had before.

But it didn't matter.

I lifted Hyacinth's hand and kissed his fingers, the cool metal of his rings scraping my lips.

The magic didn't fucking matter because in the end, when I needed it most, it hadn't helped.

I rested his hand down, gently, against his chest.

He didn't have one of his ridiculous robes on. I sobbed again over that thought. He'd died unadorned.

My powers glowed like a spotlight, leaving us—for a moment—alone in the world.

"Hyacinth," I said again. "Cyn…" I traced my finger over the coarse edge of his hair, down the noble line of his nose, over his lips. But words wouldn't come. What could I say to the love of my life as he lay still and broken in my arms?

A silvery essence swept over his flesh, trembling along his form.

I brushed my hand over it but felt nothing but air.

As the light drifted from him, his skin grayed, his features darkening.

I gasped.

It was his spirit leaving him.

It had to be.

I didn't know how I could see it.

But I could not allow it—would not allow it.

I poured myself back into my powers and pushed a veil out that wrapped around us like a shell, flooding the air in golden layers of my magic, thickening the surrounding shield until it consumed us, until the sun darkened and there was only Hyacinth and me, cocooned together.

My body trembled.

But I would not let him go.

Hours compounded onto themselves.

I remained still other than my fingers tracing over Hyacinth's features. My muscles shivered from the exertion of holding us there like that, from attempting to heal him. But what else could I do?

Plum-colored smoke filled the surrounding space and caused me to lift my face. Hades stood, his arms crossed, his mahogany curls resting on his shoulders. "What are you doing, Apollo?"

I leaned over Hyacinth, placing an arm across him. "You cannot take him."

Hades raised an eyebrow. "What is your plan? Do you intend to stay here with his corpse for the rest of eternity? That's dark, even for a god."

I growled. "Do not call him a corpse."

Hades' expression softened, and he bent down beside me, resting his arms on his knees. "He's dead."

"No," I yelled. And tears started again. I licked one off of my lip, and salt filled my mouth. "Please." I looked up at him. "Tell me there's something you can do."

Hades studied me for a long time. "You knew he was mortal."

"Please."

Hades sighed. "You need to release his spirit, so he isn't caught in the in-between, and let his body go, so that his family can lay him to rest. Now that you've ascended, your father will look for you."

I'd ascended.

I'd known it, hadn't I?

That's what had happened.

I'd forced so much magic, I'd finally taken my divine form.

And it didn't help at all.

A shaky breath tumbled out of me. I had forgotten entirely about his siblings and father, about Temi, the world, everything except Hyacinth. "I can't let him go."

"I'll make you a deal."

I snapped my face up. "Yes, anything."

Hades cocked his head to the side. "You haven't even heard the trade yet."

"Tell me what it is." The golden glow of my magic hovered around us. "I'll do whatever you ask."

"If you promise to spare Persephone in the future,

should that moment arise…" I nodded. "I'll create a new flower in his honor… a Hyacinth flower."

I gaped, my mouth bobbing open and closed several times before I could produce words. "What kind of fucking deal is that?"

Hades gripped my arm. "It's a good one. A way to commemorate his memory. You know he would appreciate it."

I shifted back to Hyacinth.

The beauty of his form, even in death, nearly broke me again, and my powers surged forth.

I remembered how they did that with his touch, the hazel of his eyes turning to honey in the sun, his laughter vibrating through my body, the taste of his lips on mine, the tickle of him whispering into my shoulder, the v-shaped dimple forming on his brow, the way he studied every detail with such carefulness.

How he'd called me 'golden boy' as though it was an endearment.

I shuddered.

Hades was right. Hyacinth would want to be well-remembered and honored. And he deserved it. I let more tears fall and they trailed down my neck as I lifted his hand and kissed the tips of each of his fingers, and then traced my palm down his cheek once more.

I turned to Hades and nodded once.

I dropped the shield, the magic flooding back into me.

It was night.

The moon illuminated as a bright crescent against the navy of the sky.

And sitting cross-legged under its light, Temi raised her face, her golden eyes glowing against the dark. Others huddled nearby, but I could only focus on her before shifting back to Cyn.

The silvery essence swirled up and up and up.

Away from Hyacinth.

And then gone.

I bowed into myself as if the weight of my broken heart would pull me crashing into the earth, and Hades gripped my shoulder. "I'll keep my bargain, Apollo. Will you keep yours?"

"Do you want me to vow it?"

"No. I believe you."

I swallowed and inclined my head.

And he disappeared.

Temi rose and walked towards me, her movement slow and uncertain. When she reached me, I stood and draped against her, and she clutched my shoulders as though she could hold me up.

"I'm sorry."

"Don't," she said. "I understand."

I shuddered and then swayed, pressing my fingers to my temples. My head ached and my stomach lurched. For the first time in my life, I felt truly unwell. Like I couldn't walk. I tried pulling the sensation away with my magic, but it didn't help.

Temi frowned at me. "Earth sickness must be setting in."

"Oh."

Earth sickness.

Because I had ascended.

I shivered and patted her hand. Her breath whispered against my skin as she spoke. "I'm going to go tell his family that it's safe to come over. It is, isn't it?"

I hesitated for a moment. If I could do anything to bring him back—tearing the entire world apart included—I would. But he was gone. "Yes."

She kissed my cheek and turned towards the shadowy outline of people in the distance.

And I dropped beside Hyacinth once more. A hundred things pierced through my mind. I wanted to apologize for all the stupidity, for falling in love with him, for staying, for embarrassing him, for causing his death.

I sniffled as lights moved on the field, glowing balls of orange that bobbed.

Lanterns.

With people.

I could not bear to encounter.

I swept into that magic of the sun, of fire and light and energy.

And gold dappled the grass.

As I disappeared into the heavens.

47

Epiphany

"I can't face today," I whispered.

Valerian shifted, his skin gliding along the bare flesh of my back as he pulled me in tighter. The coarse sheets of his bed grazed my cheek, and my eyes pricked. But tears wouldn't come. They hadn't yet though I desperately wanted them to. But it was like my body froze in disbelief. This was just another nightmare. And I'd wake up from it soon.

Ashen light filtered in through a small window. Valerian's apartment was a compact room with a bed barely big enough for the two of us to lay side-by-side, a stack of bows placed neatly against a wall, and three pairs of boots lined against a closet.

It was, perhaps, one of the favorite places I'd ever been.

I had spent much of the midnight hours of the last week there.

Valerian grazed his fingers through my hair. When he spoke, his voice came gruffly. "I wish I could have been there yesterday."

I swallowed. "I wish you could have too."

As the matriarch of the family, it fell to me to stand next to Hyacinth's body as priests offered prayers for his soul the previous day. I shivered. It was still surreal that he was gone. That the last interaction we'd had was filled with anger and grief. That I would never get to talk to him, to apologize, to wrap myself in his jasmine-scented hug again.

Valerian turned away from me, like his thoughts followed the same path as mine, and he had to pull back from it. I shifted towards him, trailing my fingers over the hair on his chest. "He loved you, Val."

Valerian closed his eyes, his dark lashes brushing his cheeks as tears slipped down his face, along his jaw. I wished I could join him in crying, but my body seemed unwilling to relent. I leaned up and kissed his temple, breathing against his skin.

But I didn't know what to say.

Grief and regret wrapped us both up.

Valerian ran his calloused hand over my shoulder. "Who is making the offerings today?"

"I am."

His fingers stilled. "You?"

I released a breath and tucked in closer to him, like I could hide from the day ahead. "Who else could? He wasn't married, and I'm his closest female relative. It probably should be Apollo, but…"

Birds started their morning raucousness, trill notes sent out mournfully on crisp air. "Temi still hasn't heard from him?"

"No." I rose, my feet dropping to the cool wood of the floor. I'd have to leave before the palace woke and could catch me slipping out of the apartments. "She's worried about him, has summoned him multiple times to no avail.

But how do you find a god who doesn't want to be reached?"

Valerian sat up as I snagged my dress off of a hook and pulled it on, tying the ribbons back in place. He stood and drew me into his arms. "I wish I could stand at your side today, be there to support you."

I sighed and kissed him. "I wish you could do that as well."

The air seemed to thicken around us, making it hard to breathe. We had gained so much in each other and lost just as much with the next heartbeat. It felt like all the sorrows of the world would drown us. I grabbed my slippers and pulled them on. "I have to go."

Valerian bowed his head. "Epiphany?"

"Yeah?"

"I'm sorry."

I tucked my arm around his waist, my fingers pressing into the gentle give of his flesh. "Why do you say that?"

His eyes glimmered in the low light. "Your last moments with Hyacinth were tainted because of me and—"

"That's not true." I clenched my grip tighter. "And Cyn wouldn't want either of us to feel guilty like we both do. We should try to honor him by focusing on the good memories we have."

Those hit me like a wave. Hyacinth's brow furrowing as he glanced at me with concern. The older brother who had taught me to climb trees and—alongside Valerian—ride horses. The sibling who let me sleep in his bed when I'd had nightmares and scoffed at my tutors with me when I complained. And the person who—I hadn't realized until he was gone—held our family together. He was who Father relied on, who Emrin looked up to, who I trusted with my vulnerabilities.

His loss left an aching gap between all of us. Publicly, we managed, accepted the gifts of condolences from the high lords, attended the ceremonies, followed through on the rituals.

But privately, we fell apart. And we didn't have our cornerstone—Hyacinth—to lean on.

Hopelessness poured around so heavily it might drown us all.

Valerian drew me into his arms, and I leaned into his steadiness for a moment before kissing him and drawing on a hooded cloak as I exited his room, pulling the door slowly, letting the latch whisper into place and studying the dark halls for any flicker of movement before easing my way through them.

The offerings would begin at sunrise. I had little time.

Once I'd rushed through dressing and made it back out with Father and Emrin to a high hill in the far corner of the palace grounds, the sun just peeked over the hills, casting the horizon in rippling washes of rose. The weather had been strange over the past week, heavy hours of rain alternating with sunshine, the air cooling and then warming again, the sun not rising reliably. But on that day —on the morning we lay Hyacinth's body to rest—the sun eased up as it should, raising its face to a lavender and periwinkle sky scarcely marred with thin clouds.

Our family stood next to the funeral monument where workers had erected it. It was a wonder they'd finished it so quickly. The carving on it depicted Hyacinth, his chin raised, flowers at his feet, a crown on his head.

Gods, was he young.

And beautiful.

And wasted.

I wish we had words to commemorate him.

But Hyacinth was the poet. Not any of us.

Father leaned down to the sarcophagus—intricately carved on the side with a man sitting in a meadow looking at the sun in the distance. Whether it was rising or setting, I couldn't say. Father kissed the top of it and spread his fingers out over it, his rings glinting and reflecting over the cool surface of the stone.

I blinked hard and shifted towards the crowd. Thousands gathered, but I only let my gaze drift to familiar faces. Valerian stood next to Temi, where she had clasped an arm around him. His expression was hard, but his eyes shimmered. Delon and Len flanked them, heads bowed.

The high priest raised his voice, his words indecipherable as my thoughts overwhelmed me. It wasn't until everyone stared in my direction I realized he talked to me. His bushy brows pushed together as he spoke again. "Who presents the offerings?"

I moved a step forward, my hands clenching the bundle I held.

The gold, for his passage to the underworld.

The soaps and wines and dedications for him.

The jasmine scent of the oil he loved to wear.

I took a shaky breath as I advanced another step.

Light flashed through the sky, golden and burning. The crowd covered their faces with their hands, many crying out.

Gold dappled the grass.

The radiance of it dimmed, shrunk into itself until it became an oval form of silver just beyond the mass of bodies. People shuffled away, and it moved towards us. Our guards raised bows and drew swords, but Father lifted his hand. "Wait."

The guards hesitated, their weapons lingering aloft.

The clicking of them blended together with the clattering of tree limbs.

My arms trembled, but Father didn't break his gaze from the light.

When it stopped moving, the glow softened further.

And Apollo stood wreathed in it.

But he appeared unlike I'd ever seen him before.

He looked like a god.

His entire body emanated heat, his silver glare illuminating the crowd, his irises as bright and piercing as the midday summer sun, his arms holding thousands of flowers. He bowed deeply to Father. "If you'd allow it," he whispered, "I would like to make the offerings."

A sheen spread over Father's eyes, but he nodded. "You may."

Apollo inclined his head again and then turned to the sarcophagus. He draped the flowers over the top. Their floral scent blossomed into the air, making the entire grove sickly sweet. I didn't know how he found so many blooms in so many colors and shades during the winter. And it seemed his hold was endless, the blossoms draping along the surface, piled a foot high over its form.

Apollo kneeled, removing his knapsack and pulled out a bag of gold, oils, jars of honey, and other bundles, and then he removed a scrap of paper, tucking it under a jug before rising, reaching his hand out and letting his fingers graze the edge of the stone right where the rays of sunlight reached the carving of my brother's face.

He turned, dipping towards us again, and then pushed back through the crowd. Temi disentangled herself from Valerian and strode after him.

But I stood under that tree.

As the people cleared out.

And the sun rose.

And the world kept moving forward.

Father squeezed my arm, and Emrin hugged me before they both left.

Valerian walked up once the grounds stretched nearly empty again. "Are you okay, Pip?"

I gave my head a shake and stepped over to the offerings, pulling the paper out and letting it unfurl over my hands.

The edge rippled as though someone had torn it from a folio, and the paper dimpled in spots, like tears had landed on it and then dried.

Writing—Hyacinth's writing—decorated the page.

It was a poem.

My hand trembled as wind swept over the parchment, making the words harder to read as the letters bobbed about, but I pushed through.

A NEW DAY *dawns*
Where I sit beneath the rays of your light
I raise my face
A heavy task
When I wear a crown
Laced with hopes and sorrows
But then you flood my senses

SUNSHINE
And gold
And laughter brighter than starlight
And I know
Like a flower, I'm ephemeral
I will not be here forever
But my love for you
Will last

Until the sun burns out

BENEATH IT, the writing changed. Large looping letters written by another hand formed four words.

AND MINE FOR YOU.

I TRACED my fingertips over the page and sobbed, tears finally coming.

48

Apollo

Months passed.

And my life changed.

Temi had centered me as she often had. She crafted my new reality—a cottage in the heavens, far from my father —where I could watch Hyacinth's kingdom.

She'd convinced me to visit Zeus' court, to play the game for Hyacinth's country's sake, to stop fighting the sun and guide it across the sky. Amazingly enough, Zeus had yet to catch onto our dissension, either because the gods present at the Palace of the Four Winds were too afraid to tell him, or because he assumed the actions that occurred there were primarily about my personal relationship with Cyn.

But—I leaned back in my chair, and the clouds by my feet scattered as I lifted my ankle up to my knee—Zeus was becoming more demanding. Twice he'd asked me to channel the sun's power to harm those he stood against. So, my dissension against him would soon be obvious. But that worry would have to keep for now.

Other than fretting about that, I had nothing else to do

for the day. I sat on my throne and watched as spring flowers made their slow stretch up, leaves unwinding, petals unfurling.

I didn't watch all the blossoms, however.

There was one in particular I waited for.

A new flower.

The green leaves of it had already fanned out.

Perhaps this was the day the blooms would show.

I edged forward on the seat, resting my chin on my hand.

My stomach dropped with the nearness of the edge, the world far below.

But if I closed my eyes, I could feel Hyacinth's rough fingers in mine.

The wind whipping around us.

I swallowed back at the tangle of different emotions that assailed me.

A breeze shook its way through long grasses, and birds whistled and chirped.

A crack of thunder resounded, tearing through the peacefulness, darkening the clouds that wisped through the heavens. A sour feeling swelled within me like a wave rising to crash. I didn't break my gaze from the world below as I spoke. "Hello, Zeus."

He stepped out until he crossed my path, the thick muscles of his legs swirling up the mist. He frowned. "Will you not even rise to greet me?"

I dropped back into the chair and tapped my fingers against the armrest. "Forgive me. I'm tired today."

He glowered. Another boom of thunder sounded, the world growing dark. "Are you attempting to raise my ire?"

"No, I'm not."

"I called for you yesterday."

I slipped my gaze up to him with a sigh. He wanted me

to manipulate my powers as a weapon against innocents. And I wouldn't stand for it. "I received the invitation but didn't desire to attend."

He took two steps closer to me, his eyes ebony dark. The clouds burst with his movement, rain sweeping over the valley. "It was not an invitation. Let me make this clear to you. When I call for you, you will answer. When I tell you to do something, you will follow through. Do you understand me?"

A mean, hard-hearted smile curled up on my face. The kind that a starving wolf might don as he stumbled over an injured creature. I stood, rolling my shoulders back, and stepped in close enough that the crackling electricity of him zipped along my skin.

I dropped my voice to a low whisper. "No, let me make this clear to you." He growled, but I raised my hand to stall him. "You did everything within your power to force my ascension to become the god of the sun."

"Yes, and you'll—"

"I'm not finished," I snarled. "You have achieved your ends, and now, I'll inform you of your just rewards." I swiped my palm up, and the sun's heat grew intense, piercing through the rain clouds, causing sweat to trickle over both of us. "I control the sun. And if you fuck with me"—his eyes flared, but I continued—"if you so much as look at me the wrong way again, I will keep the sun from rising on any city that has a temple in your name. The people will die in numbers this world has never seen before, and they'll blame you. You will lose all of your tributes, all of your power. And the mortals will finally see you as the monster that you are."

His nose wrinkled. "I should kill you now for speaking to me in this manner."

I huffed a laugh and dropped back into the seat. "You

won't do that, though, will you? It would open my role for one of Jupiter's children to take, which would endanger you even more than me. So, that's a baseless threat as far as I can see."

And I wouldn't care if he did, anyway.

He growled, his fingers curling into fists. Lightning slashed across the sky. "What are you wanting, Apollo?"

"Nothing." I lifted an ankle to my knee, clouds whirling around with the motion. "I want you to leave me alone. Don't call on me and don't bother me. And, in exchange, I'll play my role with the sun." The meadow below gleamed in fresh raindrops. "Oh, and I want Hyacinth's kingdom. No other gods can touch it. It's mine."

He yanked a bolt of lightning from the sky, the white-hot light of it casting dark shadows that undulated over his face. "I could wipe out his kingdom right this minute."

I took a deep breath. "Do so if you wish to make my entire existence's purpose to destroy you," I hissed the words, like a blade slicing into the air. "I swear to every god that has ever had the misfortune of walking this atrocious world, I will."

The glow hovering around me increased, competing with the lightning for luminance. Zeus swept the bolt out across the sky, and a heartbeat passed before a boom thundered, rattling my chair. "This is what would become of you," he whispered. "You fell for a fucking mortal, and now you'll spend your existence pouting in this hovel." He gestured to the cottage. "You're as weak and useless as you ever were."

I drew a spark of sunlight to myself and curled it between my fingers. "What you say has truth. I did fall in love with a mortal. And I lost him." I snapped my gaze up to meet his. "Which is why I can claim without hesitation, I have nothing holding me back." I dropped my voice to a hiss of a sound. "Ending myself to destroy you would make me fucking giddy."

He frowned and turned, speaking over his shoulder. "Don't forget yourself, Apollo. You're more disposable than you believe." Another thundering roar sounded, and he disappeared.

That was a lie. The war was only heating up, Jupiter becoming more openly aggressive. Zeus needed me in my place.

I blew out a breath and leaned forward in my chair.

The flowers had bloomed.

Asshole. He made me miss it.

Their lilac and lavender and blush petals peeled apart like kisses.

Hyacinth.

A showy damn flower.

He'd love them.

I smiled even as tears bit at my eyes.

I didn't fight them.

I let them flow over my cheeks, slide down my neck, pool along my tunic.

"What are you crying about, golden boy?"

I froze.

My heart stuttered.

A breeze ruffled through my hair.

I turned and there stood Hyacinth, his hazel irises sparkling in the sunlight, his eyebrows drawing together, forming that v-shaped dimple over the tan of his skin. He wore a robe in burgundy silk that swept around him, edged with detailed embroidery of flowers.

"Hyacinth," I whispered.

He walked over towards me, cocking his head to the side. "You know, I would have expected more of a response than this."

I blinked and rubbed my eyes. "I've seen you hundreds of times since your death. You're not real."

He kneeled beside me, and the breeze fluttered through his short hair. He reached out and clasped his hand around mine. His touch came warm and firm, his long fingers draping over my flesh. I gasped. "You just touched me."

He smiled. "Do you think I'm real now?"

"Cyn?" I blinked more tears away and traced my knuckles along his jaw, curling my palm against his ear, trailing down the length of his neck. I sniffled. "You can't be real."

He slipped his hands over my cheeks, the smell of jasmine filling the air, and he pressed his lips to mine. I closed my eyes and leaned in towards him. Perhaps I'd finally cracked. But at that moment, I didn't care. I drew him onto my lap and kissed him back.

That kiss was like a million flowers blooming at once, a thousand sunsets over rippling waves, a hundred poems so pure they broke your heart. I parted his lips and tasted him, my fingers gripping into his robe, my thumbs grazing the notches of his spine.

He pulled away from me and brushed his nose over my cheek.

I opened my eyes.

He still sat there, beautiful and perfect and him, him, him. "Cyn, how are you here?"

He grinned, his teeth sparkling. "You made a deal with Hades, remember?"

"A fucking terrible deal. He created a flower in your name."

Hyacinth laughed, the vibration of it echoing into me. "It's a lovely flower."

"It's pretentious, like you."

333

He scoffed and kissed my cheek. "My spirit is bound to that pretentious flower, thank you."

I sucked in a breath. "Wait. Do you mean…"

"Yes. Whenever the Hyacinth blossoms, I can be with you."

Tears choked me, and I swallowed hard. "Then I will plant Hyacinth all over the world and make sure the sun always shines on it. There will never go a day where it doesn't bloom."

Sunlight sparkled over the threading on his robe, and he whispered, "Then I shall spend eternity by your side."

I kissed him again, this one harder, pulling his lip between my teeth. He groaned into my mouth, and I snagged my fingers into the back of his neck. By the time I pulled away, we both breathed heavily. "What are you?"

He shrugged. "I guess I'm a nature deity, like a nymph?"

"A nymph?"

He smirked. "Is that acceptable for you, Apollo, high god of the sun? Are you willing to be involved with a low deity?"

"Yes," I choked the word out. Emotions sparkled through me like the sun above us still dappling through clouds. Moments of bright sunshine alternated with the looming storm welling up in my chest. "Cyn…" I swallowed "I'm so sorry. It's my fault you died."

He lifted my hand and placed a kiss over my knuckles. "What's done is done, Apollo. Let it go." His expression tightened. "Did you mean what you said to your father?"

"My father?" I shifted back against the chair, and Cyn eased up, sitting on the arm of the throne. "You heard our conversation?" He nodded, and I clenched my teeth. "What part?"

"Would you really kill humans in order to bring him down?"

I blew out a breath and swept my gaze around the clouds as though Zeus might still stand there. I side-eyed Hyacinth. "No. But he believed it, didn't he?"

"I think so."

"Good."

He fixed me with a strange look. "Do you know why I always called you 'golden boy'?"

I could nearly feel the glowing of my eyes, the ways I reflected my father. I bowed my head. "My coloring? My connection to Zeus?"

He snagged my chin and lifted it, not speaking until I met his gaze. "No, that's not it."

"Why then?"

He placed his hand on my chest, and a smile slipped up on his face. "It's because you have a golden heart."

I released a puff of a breath. "I've fucked up a tremendous amount of your life for you to believe that."

He tangled his fingers with mine, and my heartbeat thundered through me as he shook his head. "Everyone makes mistakes, Apollo." He paused for a heartbeat, kissing the tip of each of my fingers like I had done to him when he laid broken and lifeless in my arms. I shivered, and he whispered his next words into my neck. "Your worst moment doesn't define you."

For several long minutes, we curled up together, breathing the other in, hands scrambling over flesh as if we could anchor ourselves in place. Hyacinth broke the silence, his expression taking on a serious glint. "We still have work to do."

"I know."

He leaned back, his eyes growing thoughtful. The Hyacinth flowers in the world below us fluttered, their petals tangling together. "You told your father you just wished to be left alone here? I assumed you'd given up on the cause."

"I already said that I lied to him."

"I thought you didn't like to lie?"

"I'm trying new things."

He smiled. "So, you're still going to help people stand up to him?"

I drew him against me again and kissed the hollow between his collarbones. "Cyn, I've been meeting with your father and Temi regularly. I'm there with them for as long as I can tolerate staying in the human world until the earth sickness pushes me back." His touch pulsed through me, and I draped against him. "I promised you, no matter what happened to us, I'd see this through."

His voice hummed with laughter. "I thought you were trying out lying?"

I chuckled alongside him but drew back and brushed my thumb along the sharp edge of his jaw. "Never to you, though."

He pressed his mouth to mine, and a hunger came with it, my skin burning with desire for him. He drifted away from me and peeled his robe off, dropping it to the stone path.

"Hey"—I snatched it up and draped it over the arm of the chair—"aren't you worried about wrinkles or whatever?"

He laughed. "I thought you found my robes to be pretentious?"

"Well, maybe they suit you."

He grinned, his mouth on mine again, soft and open and heaven, heaven, heaven. He sighed, a joyous sound that bubbled against my lips. "We have a lot cut out for us."

"Yeah."

"And I have much I need to do. Reparations I must make. Few mortals get a second chance. I'm not sure where I belong in all of this anymore, but I plan to use my time wisely."

I bobbed my head.

"We can spare an hour or two first, though, right?"

"You can spare however long you want, Cyn. No one even knows you're here yet." I cleared my throat, unsure of where to take the conversation. "Would you like to see my house?"

He cocked an eyebrow up as though I was suggesting more than a tour, and my cheeks warmed, but he only smiled. "Definitely."

I rose, clasping his hand with mine, and gestured to the cottage. "It's small and boring. You're bound to hate it."

"Thankfully, a god with a big personality lives in it. Might make up for it."

I paused walking and grazed my fingers against his neck, gently, like I touched a flower that could fall apart if I moved too quickly. "I didn't get to tell you... before... everything. But I love you. So much."

He smirked. "Of course you do. You aren't even making fun of my robe, which, by the way, I bargained with Hades for."

"You did what?"

He laughed heartily at that and tugged my hand. "Come on. Show me this awful house you live in."

I followed him.

The clouds of war swelled across our future.

And I had decided to mechanically go through the motions. To honor the promise I'd made to Hyacinth.

But now—I tightened my grip against his—I had something to live for.

337

Something to fight for.

I looked back over my shoulder, where fog peppered over the view of the city of Niria, where rain swept over valleys in the distance, where lilac mountains stretched into the heavens.

So much was about to happen.

Hyacinth grinned at me, his eyes turning honey gold in a splash of sunlight.

It could wait for a few hours.

But then... then we'd have to face the future that roared its way towards us.

Bonus Content

Bonus content for this series can be found at www. authornicolebailey.com/FATEbonus

Acknowledgments

To my husband who shuffled his schedule around so I could write, brought more than a few dinners home when I was under a deadline for this series, and regularly does a hundred little, wonderful things that probably explain why the romances in my series are so sappy… I love you.

Thank you to my mom, who has believed in me every step of the way and also lets me brainstorm with zero context regularly. Conversations with you brought so much nuance to King Magnes in this book and I so appreciate it!

To Natalie, my writing bestie, who sends me green scrunchies and fake Hyacinths that cannot die, who writes with me at five in the morning and eleven 'o'clock at night (often on the same day) because we have the same priorities. (Note, they might be questionable.) And who roots for me and pushes me to be better and brings a lot of joy to this exhausting career. I love and appreciate you!

To Debbie, a wonderful writing friend from the very beginning. I've loved watching how our journeys have evolved and am so grateful for someone as compassionate, encouraging, and lovely as you! Thank you for cheering on this series the way you have!

To Milly, my developmental editor, you helped craft this book to be even more emotionally devastating than I had initially crafted. Ha! This series is better for the shaping and thoughtfulness you brought to it! I can't say how much I appreciate your love for this story! It keeps me excited even when I'm on my fiftieth read through.

To my line editor, Amy, thank you for polishing this book and helping it shine!

To Stefanie Saw, I didn't think the cover design for this book could top the first one, but you proved me wrong. I appreciate you lending your vision and talent to this series for a second book!

To my early reader, Stefanie, thank you for suggesting Arion for the name of Temi's horse! As soon as I read it, the name seemed obvious, but it evaded me before your suggestion.

To my ARC early readers, thank you for your support and love for this series. I appreciate each of you!

To every one of my readers, you reading these books allows me to continue publishing them. I cannot say how thankful I am! Apologies for tears shed and sleep lost. But I hope you enjoyed this story as much as I did crafting it!

Printed in Great Britain
by Amazon